ROBERT MUCHAMORE

ROCK
WAR

h
Hodder
Children's
Books

HODDER CHILDREN'S BOOKS

First published in Great Britain in 2014 by Hodder Children's Books
This edition published in 2016 by Hodder and Stoughton

9 10 8

A CIP catalogue record for this book is available from the British Library.

ISBN 978 1 444 91454 2

Typeset in Goudy by Avon DataSet Ltd, Bidford-on-Avon, Warwickshire

Printed and bound in Great Britain by Clays Ltd, St Ives plc

The paper and board used in this book are from wood from responsible sources.

Hodder Children's Books
An imprint of Hachette Children's Group
Part of Hodder and Stoughton
Carmelite House
50 Victoria Embankment
London EC4Y 0DZ

An Hachette UK Company
www.hachette.co.uk

www.hachettechildrens.co.uk

Robert Muchamore worked as a private investigator before starting to write a story for his nephew, who couldn't find anything to read. Since then, millions of copies of his CHERUB and Henderson's Boys books have been sold worldwide.

Robert lives in London, supports Arsenal football club and loves modern art and watching people fall down holes.

Praise for Robert's writing:
'These are the best books ever!' Jack, 12

'So good I forced my friends to read it, and they're glad I did!' Helen, 14

'The CHERUB books are so cool, they have everything I ever wanted!' Josh, 13

'Never get tired of recommending CHERUB/*Henderson's Boys* to reluctant readers, because it never fails!' Cat, children's librarian

'My son could never see the point of reading a book until he read *The Recruit*. I want to thank you from the bottom of my heart for igniting the fire.' Donna

'Pacy writing, punchy dialogue and a gripping plot, it's got it all.' *Daily Express*

'Crackling tension and high-octane drama.' *Daily Mail*

'Punchy, exciting, glamorous and, what's more, you'll completely wish it was true.' *Sunday Express*

BY ROBERT MUCHAMORE

The Rock War series:
Rock War
Boot Camp
Gone Wild

and coming soon . . .

Crash Landing

The CHERUB series:
Start reading with *The Recruit*

The Henderson's Boys series:
Start reading with *The Escape*

Prologue

The stage is a vast altar, glowing under Texas moonlight. Video walls the size of apartment blocks advertise Rage Cola. Close to the stadium's fifty-yard line, a long-legged thirteen-year-old is precariously balanced on her big brother's shoulders. She's way too excited.

'JAY!' she screams, as her body sways. 'JAAAAAAAY I LOVE YOU!'

Nobody hears, because seventy thousand people are at it. It's noise so loud your ears tickle inside. Boys and girls, teens, students. There's a ripple of anticipation as a silhouette comes on stage, but it's a roadie with a cymbal stand. He bows grandly before stepping off.

'JET!' they chant. 'JET . . . JET . . . JET.'

Backstage the sound is muffled, like waves crashing against a sea wall. The only light is a green glow from emergency exit signs.

Jay is holding his queasy stomach. He's slim and easy on the eye. He wears Converse All Stars, ripped jeans and a dash of black eyeliner.

An immense roar comes out of the crowd as the video walls begin a thirty-second countdown film, sponsored by a cellphone maker. As Jay's eyes adjust to the light, he can see a twenty-metre-tall version of himself skateboarding downhill, chased by screaming Korean schoolgirls.

'THIRTEEN,' the crowd scream, as their feet stamp down the seconds. 'TWELVE, ELEVEN . . .'

On screen, the girls knock Jay off his skateboard. As he tumbles a smartphone flies out of his pocket and when the girls see it they lose all interest in Jay and stand in a semicircle admiring the phone instead.

'THREE . . . TWO . . . ONE . . .'

The four members of Jet emerge on stage, punching the air to screams and camera flashes.

Somehow, the cheering crowd always kills Jay's nerves. Thousands of bodies sway in the moonlight. Cheers and shouts blend into a low roar. He places his fingers on the fret board and loves the knowledge that moving one finger will send half a million watts of power out of speaker stacks the size of trucks.

And the crowd goes wild as the biggest band in the world starts to play.

1. Cheesy Crumbs

Camden, North London

There's that weird moment when you first wake up. The uneasy quarter second where a dream ends and you're not sure where you are. All being well, you work out you're in bed and you get to snuggle up and sleep another hour.

But Jay Thomas wasn't in bed. The thirteen-year-old had woken on a plastic chair in a school hall that reeked of burgers and hot dogs. There were chairs set out in rows, but bums in less than a quarter of them. A grumpy dinner lady squirted pink cleaning fluid on a metal serving counter at the side of the room, while a banner hung over the stage up front:

**Camden Schools Contemporary Music
Competition 2014**

Debris pelted the floor the instant Jay moved: puffed wheat snacks, speckled with cheesy orange flavouring. Crumbs fell off his clothes when he stood and another half bag had been crushed up and sprinkled in his spiky brown hair.

Jay played lead guitar in a group named Brontobyte. His three band mates cracked up as he flicked orange dust out of his hair, then bent over to de-crumb a Ramones T-shirt and ripped black jeans.

'You guys are *so* immature.'

But Jay didn't really mind. These guys had been his mates since forever and he'd have joined the fun if one of them had dozed off.

'Sweet dreams?' Brontobyte's chubby-cheeked vocalist, Salman, asked.

Jay yawned and picked orange gunk out of his earhole as he replied. 'I barely slept last night. Kai had his Xbox on until about one, and when I *finally* got to sleep the little knob head climbed up to my bunk and farted in my face.'

Salman took pity, but Tristan and Alfie both laughed.

Tristan was Brontobyte's drummer, and a big lad who fancied himself a bit of a stud. Tristan's younger brother Alfie wouldn't turn twelve for another three months. He was Brontobyte's bass player and the band's most talented musician, but the other three gave him a hard time because his voice was unbroken and there were no signs of puberty kicking in.

'I can't believe Jay gets owned by his younger brother,' Tristan snorted.

'Kai's the hardest kid in my year,' Alfie agreed. 'But Jay's, like, Mr Twig Arms, or something.'

Jay tutted and sounded stressed. 'Can we *please* change the subject?'

Tristan ignored the request. 'How many kids has your mum got now anyway, Jay?' he asked. 'It's about forty-seven, isn't it?'

Salman and Alfie laughed, but stifled their grins when they saw Jay looking upset.

'Tristan, cut it out,' Salman said.

'We all take the piss out of each other,' Tristan said. 'Jay's acting like a baby.'

'No, Tristan, *you* never know when to stop,' Salman said angrily.

Alfie tried to break the tension. 'I'm going for a drink,' he said. 'Anyone else want one?'

'Scotch on the rocks,' Salman said.

Jay sounded more cheerful as he joined the joke. 'Bottle of Bud and some heroin.'

'I'll see what I can do,' Alfie said, before heading off towards a table with jugs of orange squash and platters of cheapo biscuits.

The next act was taking the stage. In front of them three judges sat at school desks. There was a baldy with a mysterious scab on his head, a long-limbed Nigerian in a gele headdress and a man with a wispy grey beard and leather trousers. He sat with his legs astride the back of his chair to show that he was down with the kids.

By the time Alfie came back with four beakers of orange

squash and jam rings tucked into his cheeks there were five boys lining up on stage. They were all fifteen or sixteen. Nice-looking lads, four black, one Asian, and all dressed in stripy T-shirts, chinos and slip-on shoes.

Salman was smirking. 'It's like they walked into Gap and bought *everything*.'

Jay snorted. 'Losers.'

'Yo, people!' a big lad in the middle of the line-up yelled. He was trying to act cool, but his eyes betrayed nerves. 'We're contestant seven. We're from George Orwell Academy and we're called Womb 101.'

There were a few claps from members of the audience, followed by a few awkward seconds as a fat-assed music teacher bent over fiddling with the CD player that had their backing track on it.

'You might know this song,' the big lad said. 'The original's by One Direction. It's called "What Makes You Beautiful".'

The four members of Brontobyte all looked at each other and groaned. Alfie summed up the mood.

'Frankly, I'd rather be kicked in the balls.'

As the backing track kicked in, Womb 101 sprang into an athletic dance routine, with four members moving back, and the big guy in the middle stepping up to a microphone. The dancing looked sharp, but everyone in the room really snapped to attention when a powerful lead vocal started.

The voice was higher than you'd expect from a big black guy, but he really nailed the sense of longing for the girl he was singing about. When the rest of Womb 101 joined in for the chorus the sound swamped the backing track, but they were all decent singers and their routine was tight.

As Womb 101 hit their stride, Jay's music teacher Mr Currie approached Brontobyte from behind. He'd only been teaching for a couple of years. Half the girls at Carleton Road School had a thing for his square jaw and gym-pumped bod.

He tapped in time as the singing and finger clicking continued. 'They're really uplifting, aren't they?'

The four boys looked back at their teacher with distaste.

'Boy bands should be machine-gunned,' Alfie said. 'They're singing to a backing track. How's that even music?'

'I bet they win as well,' Tristan said contemptuously. 'I saw their teacher nattering to the judges all through lunch.'

Mr Currie spoke firmly. 'Tristan, if Womb 101 win it will be because they're really talented. Have you any idea how much practice it takes to sing and dance like that?'

Up on stage, Womb 101 were doing the *nana-nana* chorus at the end of 'What Makes You Beautiful'. As the song closed, the lead singer moved to the back of the stage and did a full somersault, climaxing with his arms spread wide and two band mates kneeling on either side.

'Thank you,' the big guy shouted, as the stage lights caught beads of sweat trickling down his forehead.

There weren't enough people in the hall to call it an eruption, but there was loads of clapping and a bunch of parents stood up and cheered.

'Nice footwork, Andre!' a woman shouted.

Alfie and Tristan made retching sounds as Mr Currie walked off.

'Currie's got a point though,' Jay said. 'Boy bands are dreck, but they've all got good voices and they must have rehearsed that dance routine for weeks.'

Tristan shook his head and tutted. 'Jay, you *always* agree with what Mr Currie says. I know half the girls in our class fancy him, but I'm starting to think you do as well.'

Alfie stood up and shouted as Womb 101 jumped off the stage and began walking towards the back of the room to grab drinks. 'You suck!'

Jay backed up as two of Womb 101's backing singers steamed over, knocking empty plastic chairs out of the way. They didn't look hard on stage, prancing around singing about how great some girl's hair was, but the physical reality was two burly sixteen-year-olds from one of London's toughest schools.

The one who stared down Alfie was the Asian guy with a tear-you-in-half torso.

'What you say?' he demanded, as his chest muscles swelled. 'If I see *any* of you boys on my manor, you'd better run!'

The boy slammed his fist into his palm as the other one pointed at Alfie before drawing the finger across his throat and stepping backwards. Alfie looked like he'd filled his BHS briefs and didn't breathe until the big dudes were well clear.

'Are you mental?' Tristan hissed, as he gave Alfie a hard shoulder punch. 'Those guys are from Melon Lane estate. Everyone's psycho up there.'

Mr Currie had missed Alfie shouting *You suck*, but did see Tristan hitting his brother as he got back holding a polystyrene coffee cup.

'Hitting is *not* cool,' Mr Currie said. 'And I'm tired of the negativity from you guys. You're playing after this next lot, so you'd better go backstage and get your gear ready.'

The next group was an all-girl trio. They dressed punk, but managed to murder a Paramore track by making it sound like bad Madonna. Setting up Tristan's drum kit on stage took ages and the woman judge made Jay even more nervous when she looked at her watch and shook her elaborately hatted head.

After wasting another minute faffing around with a broken strap on Alfie's bass guitar the four members of Brontobyte nodded to each other, ready to play. When the boys rehearsed, Salman usually sang and played, but Alfie was a better musician, so for the competition he was on bass and Salman would just do vocals.

'Hi, everyone,' Salman said. 'We're contestant nine, from Carleton Road School. Our group is called Brontobyte and this is a song we wrote ourselves. It's called "Christine".'

A song I wrote, Jay thought, as he took a deep breath and positioned his fingers on the guitar.

They'd been in the school hall since ten that morning. Now it all came down to the next three minutes.

2. Hot Scruff

Dudley, West Midlands

Summer Smith was almost fourteen. She had plastic clips keeping blonde hair off her face, a white school polo shirt stained with charcoal from art class and black no-brand pumps with her little toe peeking through a split in the side.

Most year nines thought Summer was hot, despite being a scruff, but all the boys got turned down. She'd always find the remotest spot in a classroom and barely spoke to anyone. She did homework in the library at morning break and went home most lunch-times to make sure that her nan was OK.

There was an empty chair between Summer and Michelle Wei. Michelle's black Prada trainers and soft leather schoolbag hinted that her parents were loaded, and a photograph might give the impression of a girl who spilled tears if she dropped to a B, but as soon as Michelle moved you knew different.

Michelle was twitchy. Her eyes were hypnotic, dragging

you into a mind where crazy and brilliant battled for the upper hand. As Summer copied notes on Tudor England into her folder, Michelle chewed Bubblicious, tilted her chair and wound hair round her fingertips.

Mr Wilson pretended not to see, because you'd never get Michelle to work. A teacher's best hope was that she didn't disturb the rest of her class.

Summer glanced across as Michelle snatched a rugby ball off the next desk top. It belonged to a lump called Kevin, who watched dumbly as Michelle stuffed the elliptical ball up her white shirt.

'Mr Wilson!' Michelle shouted, as she shot up. 'I need the bathroom.'

She didn't really say Wilson, she made it sound ridiculous. More like *weeeel-shawn.*

The balding teacher was three years from retirement. He'd been here before and didn't even look up.

'Sit *down*, Michelle. Nobody's playing your games today.'

Michelle thrust out her rugby ball stomach and staggered between desks towards the classroom door with her feet wide apart.

'I'm having my baby,' she yelled, as she rubbed her back. 'The head's poking out of my vagina!'

Vagina made a few kids laugh, but Michelle got on most of her classmates' nerves. Mr Wilson hopped up from his chair and blocked the door.

'Back to your seat and stop being silly.'

Michelle wasn't strong enough to push the elderly teacher

aside, so she screwed up her face and attacked verbally.

'You dirty old man,' she yelled, as she pointed at Wilson and turned to face the class. 'You're the father. You can't keep denying it.'

'Sit down!' Wilson demanded. 'Nobody is interested in your performance.'

'Oh my god!' Michelle yelled. 'The baby, it's coming!'

She squatted down and slowly pushed the rugby ball out of her shirt.

'It's a boy!' she gasped, as she held the muddy ball up high. 'I'm going to call him Eggy-Wegg.'

Turning on Mr Wilson had raised the class's enthusiasm for Michelle's craziness. There was more laughter and a few kids even applauded the miracle of birth. The noise level was rising and Mr Wilson had to act swiftly before everyone went nuts. He picked a metal dustbin off the floor and banged it hard on his desk top.

'QUIET,' he shouted. 'If you don't settle there *will* be full class detention.'

Most kids piped down, apart from a few giggles. Michelle was now tiptoeing at the back of the classroom, with a finger over her lips, making *shush*ing sounds.

'Naughty, naughty,' she whispered. 'We don't want detention, do we?'

Mr Wilson knew Michelle wouldn't settle down without a fight, so he reached for a small green pad on his desk and wrote her name on it. Being *green slipped* meant you had to sit in a special classroom in silence until the bell went for the next lesson. Three green slips in one term earned a letter home to your parents.

'There you are,' Mr Wilson said, as he rattled the slip in the air. 'If you do need the toilet you can go on your way to the referral classroom.'

Michelle kissed the rugby ball before putting it back on Kevin's desk and skipping towards the door.

'I can prove that he seduced me,' Michelle announced, pointing at Mr Wilson as she stood in the doorway. 'His private parts are freakishly mutated. Full details will be revealed in tomorrow's newspapers.'

Mr Wilson shut the classroom door and spoke authoritatively. 'Show's over, get back to work.'

But Summer kept giggling after everyone else had settled down. Half the class looked her way as she tried desperately to stop. It was a real surprise because she was usually so quiet.

'Shut your gob,' a boy sitting at the desk in front hissed. 'You'll get us all detention.'

Mr Wilson looked flustered as he came towards Summer, but he spoke gently.

'Summer, I happen to find that kind of personal attack very offensive. Perhaps you could tell me what *you* find so funny about it?'

The idea of a baby named Eggy-Wegg had tickled Summer, but what really set her off were the contortions of Mr Wilson's face. He was trying to keep calm, but his cheeks, eyebrows and upper lip kept twitching and for some inexplicable reason these involuntary movements seemed funny.

Summer could hardly tell Mr Wilson that she found his face funny, so she shrugged and took a deep breath before talking.

'I'm sorry, sir,' she said, holding a hand in front of glowing red cheeks. 'I can't help it. I've just got the giggles.'

Mr Wilson drummed a finger on Summer's exercise book. 'Concentrate.'

'Yes, sir,' she agreed, but as Mr Wilson turned away his lower jaw twitched and his right eyebrow shot up, making his eyeball bulge.

Summer wrapped a hand over her mouth, but before Wilson took three steps she was laughing again. Instead of turning back, the teacher stormed to his desk and tore off another green slip.

'Enough!' he shouted, finally losing his temper as he held the slip aloft. 'Pack up your things, Summer. You can join Michelle in the referral classroom.'

3. Not Being Mean

The drums exploded, the bass line thumped and Jay plucked the first riff on lead guitar. Salman grabbed the microphone and spat words like bullets:

Christine, Christine, I'm not being mean,
Your body's not the best that I've ever seen,
But I'm a desperate guy, never catch a girl's eye,
And I can't deny, that you've got nice thighs,
Christine, Christine, I wanna have you.

Christine, Christine, you've got bad zits,
Your hair's like wire and you've got no tits,
But a girl like you is the best that I can have,
You're the only girl I'm able to nab,
Christine, Christine, I wanna have you.

> *In a pub,*
> *In a tub,*
> *Or behind the youth club,*
> *Christine, Christine,*
> *I wanna have you,*
> *I wanna have you.*

> Christine, Christine, you gave me lice,
> Your dad's a drunk and your mum's not nice,
> But your body's warm on a frosty night,
> When the lights go off I pretend you're all right,
> Christine, Christine, I wanna have you.

After this came a riff from Jay, then a repeat of the first verse and chorus. Salman wasn't about to land a gig as an opera singer, but he had a decent tone and his Pakistani twang gave Jay's lyrics a slightly exotic feel. The two guitar players knew their stuff, but every rock band is anchored by the drums and Tristan was all over the place.

Jay was so close to the drums that he couldn't hear Salman's singing. Mr Currie had taught them the golden rule: a band has to keep playing no matter how bad it gets. But by the end of the song three members of Brontobyte were playing different parts, while Tristan pounded on relentlessly, unaware that anything was up.

'Thank you, everyone!' Salman shouted, when the din finally stopped.

Alfie and Tristan's mum, Mrs Jopling, sat with Salman's

grown-up brother in the audience, but they kept quiet and the only noise was a few jeers and ironic *bravos*. Womb 101 made wanking gestures.

Mr Currie jumped up to help clear the stage ready for the final group. Jay unplugged his guitar and stormed across towards Tristan.

'What the hell were you playing?'

Tristan brandished his drumstick. 'Sounded bloody great to me.'

Jay gasped. 'Are you insane? You were all over the place.'

Tristan knocked his snare-drum flying as he charged forwards. In his anger, Jay hadn't properly considered the consequences of winding up his drummer, who was bigger than him and did judo.

'You wanna take this outside?' Tristan roared. 'Any time, any place, stick boy!'

Mr Currie forced himself between the two lads. 'Hey, hey! It's all good experience. We'll come back from this.'

'He'll still be a shite drummer,' Jay said, emboldened now that there was an adult protecting him.

Jay got a withering look from the judges as he jumped off the front of the stage in a huff, leaving the others to carry the drums out to the van. He glimpsed one judge's marking sheet: *Drummer poor, guitar vocals OK, 4/10.*

Jay still had his guitar around his neck as he stormed up the back to grab a drink.

'We heard you were supposed to be good,' a guy from Womb 101 said.

'Epic,' someone snorted. 'Epp-ick.'

Jay ignored sly comments from the rest of Womb 101 as he grabbed a beaker of orange and tipped it down in two gulps.

'Sorry about earlier,' Jay told them. 'Alfie's only eleven, you know? He says dumb stuff.'

A guy with a gold tooth gave a deep laugh. 'Sucking up now won't stop you getting mangled.'

'Right,' one of his singing partners agreed, as he cracked his knuckles. 'See you up Melon Lane, boy, and you'll stagger home to Mummy in *baaaaaaaad* shape!'

'I'd rather you didn't stab me,' Jay said, trying to turn the threats into a joke. 'Red clashes with my pale complexion.'

'What the hell is Brontobyte, anyway?' one guy asked.

'Computers,' Jay explained. 'You know like megabytes, gigabytes? A Brontobyte is like millions and millions of gigabytes, or something. It was our drummer's idea.'

A few guys shook their heads and Gold Tooth summed it up. 'Geeky name. I thought us being named after something out of a book was bad.'

As Jay grabbed a custard cream, the fat music teacher from George Orwell Academy called her pupils down to the front. The final band was taking to the stage as Salman and Alfie grabbed drinks and walked up to Jay.

'Thanks for helping with the drums, *mate*,' Salman said angrily.

'I just lost it,' Jay said, shrugging. 'Tristan has no clue. I can drum better than him. Alfie, you're *ten* times better.'

'Leave me out of this,' Alfie said. 'You two can piss off to your own houses. I'm the one who cops it when Tristan's in a mood.'

'We're never gonna be any good unless we get a drummer who can keep time,' Jay said.

Jay didn't get a response because Tristan and Alfie's mum was coming their way.

'You were all bloody great,' Mrs Jopling said.

She was quite sexy and had a footballer's wife thing going on: fake tan, false nails, designer sunglasses resting up in her hair and UGG boots. She embarrassed Alfie with a kiss on the cheek before scowling at Jay. 'Why'd you get up in my Tristan's face?'

'Nothing,' Jay said, with a shrug.

'I thought you were mates,' she added.

Jay didn't reply. He'd get nowhere telling Mrs Jopling that her darling boy was a crap drummer.

As Salman jogged off to tell Mr Currie that he was leaving with his big brother, the last band stopped playing. The tall woman in the gele walked up on stage, taking the microphone as gear got dragged off stage behind her. She put her lips too close and a shriek of feedback ripped through the PA system.

'We've had quite a few delays and we're running late,' she said, sounding all upbeat like someone presenting TV for five-year-olds. 'The standard was high, but sadly there can only be one winner. It is with *great* pleasure I announce that the two hundred and fifty-pound musical equipment voucher and the place in the final of the Camden Schools

Contemporary Music Competition goes to . . . Womb 101!'

Salman and his brother had headed out of the door as
Womb 101 and their fans jumped around down by the
stage. Tristan had joined his band mates after packing his
drums in the school van, and carefully stayed far enough
from his mum not to get kissed. Mr Currie was a few rows
behind, holding a Post-it on to which he'd carefully jotted
the judges' scores.

The judges had given marks out of ten for musicianship,
presentation and overall performance, plus up to five
bonus marks for any band that performed an original
composition.

'At least they liked my song,' Jay said, as he peered over
Mr Currie's shoulder and saw that they'd averaged four out
of five in the composition box.

'Where were we overall?' Alfie asked.

'Fourth out of nine,' Jay answered, resisting the temptation
to point out that they'd have dropped to seventh without
the composition marks.

'I came here thinking we could win,' Alfie said dejectedly.
'We were *immense* in rehearsals last week.'

'Bands are like football teams playing away from home,'
Mr Currie explained, as he tapped a finger against his
temple. 'Jamming with your mates is one thing. Nailing it
in front of an audience is completely different.'

But Mrs Jopling had her own theory, which she expressed
with folded arms and an indignant tap of her furry boot.

'You lads could have outplayed Jimi Hendrix and still lost

with them judges,' she said. 'It was all fixed.'

So that's where Tristan gets it, Mr Currie thought.

'You can't deny Womb 101 were better than us though,' Jay said.

Mrs Jopling gave Jay a dirty look before turning towards Mr Currie. 'So, is it OK to take my lads home?'

Mr Currie nodded. 'Of course. Thank you for coming out to support us. I'll take Jay back to the school in the van. He can help me unpack the equipment before I drop him home.'

Tristan nodded in agreement. 'Seems fair, seeing as he threw a hissy fit and didn't help us pack up.'

Jay finally lost it. 'Up yours, mummy's boy,' he snapped.

'At least my mum can go five seconds without spurting out more babies,' Tristan shot back, as his mother gave a sly smile of approval.

Mr Currie interrupted. '*Everyone* calm down, it's been a long and tiring day.'

'So what do you want for tea?' Mrs Jopling asked, as she led her sons out of the hall. 'Mickey Ds or KFC?'

4. New Fish

Summer felt dazed as she hit the corridor. She'd never had a green slip before and wasn't comfortable being in trouble, even though it was no biggie unless you got three in one term. She looked left and right as it dawned that she had no clue where the referral classroom was.

She was about to go back and ask Mr Wilson when she heard a voice. Michelle stood ten metres away, leaning over a metal stair rail, gabbing into a nifty Samsung.

'You in class . . . ? No way . . . ! Oh sweet . . . Yeah, fah sure! I'll meet you over there.'

As Michelle pocketed the phone she noticed Summer behind and barked, 'What?'

Summer backed off instinctively, not knowing if Michelle was going to kiss, claw, or try to punch her lights out. When nothing happened, Summer waggled her green slip.

'How'd you get that?' Michelle asked incredulously. 'Been

in your class near three years and never heard two sentences out of you.'

Summer shrugged. 'I speak when there's something worth saying.'

Michelle's eyes became slits and she spoke accusingly. 'You saying I talk crap?'

'I didn't mean anything about *you* at all,' Summer replied anxiously.

Summer was taller and stockier, but had no taste for rolling around the corridor fighting the class loony.

'You're right, actually,' Michelle smiled. 'Some of the boys in our class: yabber, yabber, yabber. All they do is talk crap.'

'Only *some* of 'em?' Summer asked, before smiling slightly.

'Boys in our class . . .' Michelle said, tutting with contempt as she started down the stairs. 'Clammy scum.'

'I don't know where the referral classroom is,' Summer explained, as she followed.

'A new fish!' Michelle said. 'I'll tell the guards to go easy on you.'

Four flights took them to the ground floor, with the school reception on the left and a long corridor of science and home economics to their right.

They turned towards the classrooms, with a fusion of cookery and chemicals in the air. Michelle stopped at the first door. Summer knew it wasn't the referral classroom because they'd had year eight science in there.

Michelle pounded on the classroom door, then ran off howling, 'Moose! Moose!' at the top of her voice.

Summer would cop the blame if she didn't leg it. As she started running, Michelle flung another door open down the hall and shouted, 'Science is dead. Long live Jesus!'

At the end of the corridor was a set of doors with an *Emergency Only* sign on them.

'What you waiting for?' Michelle asked, as Summer felt a stitch burning down her side.

Michelle crashed through the fire doors and sped down into the school basement. Summer was in uncharted territory, but Michelle jumped the bottom half of a staircase and cut expertly through a graffiti-strewn door into a boys' changing room.

The air was all piss, shower steam and BO. Michelle straddled bags and shoes as she headed towards the exit on to the playing fields at the far side.

The outdoor air was crisp, the damp pavement covered in mud clumps where boys had scraped off football boots. Twenty metres away, dirty-legged year eights chased footballs around a soggy pitch.

Summer rubbed cold arms and shuddered nervously as they headed past the school library, towards the recently opened music and drama block. Michelle looked as though nothing had happened as she swung her leather bag from side to side.

Up above, a dark-skinned science teacher shouted from

the window of his classroom. 'Michelle Wei, you are in *major* trouble!'

As Summer tried hiding her identity by walking close to the bushes, Michelle spun around and gave the teacher a two-fingered salute.

'Your wife is a moose, Mr Gubta!' she shouted.

Summer jogged ahead, rounded a corner and crashed breathlessly against the wall at the entrance to the music block.

'Are you insane?' she shouted furiously.

Michelle laughed. 'Obviously!'

'We'll get in so much trouble,' Summer blurted, as she put her hands on her head. 'What was the point of that?'

'It gave me a buzz,' Michelle said, then made a sound like a bee and circled her finger through the air. It ended with her painted nail landing on the tip of Summer's nose. 'A tiny edge to drag me through another dreary day.'

'My life's complicated enough,' Summer complained. 'The referral classroom isn't out here, is it?'

'Deductive powers worthy of Sherlock Holmes himself,' Michelle replied, before grabbing Summer's arm. 'Get moving. I've got plans for you.'

They cut into the main entrance of the music and drama block. The big theatre space off to one side was empty, but twangs and toots came from a row of music practice rooms. Michelle threw open the door of practice room five, where two year eleven girls were hanging out.

'Wass-up, deputy dawgs?' Michelle said, flicking her wrist

and putting on a deliberately naff home boy act. 'How's my girlz hangin'?'

The room was about a third the size of a classroom. It was pristine, with a polished wood floor, white walls and lots of electrical sockets for plugging in equipment. There was a table and a whiteboard scored with lines for musical notation and a battered upright piano.

Summer stood by the door in silence as Michelle made introductions.

'My big sister Lucy,' Michelle explained, as she pointed towards an Asian girl sitting behind a drum kit, then turned on a skinny black girl with a huge afro, perched atop the piano. 'That's Coco, our bass player.'

Lucy pointed an accusing drumstick at Summer. 'Why is this object standing in *my* rehearsal room looking like someone forgot to take the hanger out of its shirt?'

'Her name's Summer,' Michelle explained. 'But you might remember her as Evita, from my spectacular year seven musical.'

Summer reached for the door handle. 'Listen,' she said anxiously. 'It's nice meeting you guys, but I can't get into any more trouble today. No offence, OK . . . ? I'm just gonna head back to the main building and find the referral classroom.'

Summer twisted the handle, but Michelle's shoulder hit the door, banging it shut.

'What are you doing?' Summer shouted, as Michelle grinned manically.

'You have a great voice, Summer,' Lucy said in a much friendlier tone. 'Best thing in that musical by miles.'

'You're forgetting my sleek moves with the maracas,' Michelle said. 'And this had to be fate. Summer *never* gets kicked out of class. She makes Miss Goody Two-Shoes look like a grave robbing crack addict. But just as I got off the phone to say I'm gonna come over here and jam with you gals, guess which little princess got kicked out of class right behind me?'

Lucy climbed from behind her drum kit and stepped towards Summer. She was sixteen, with a stockier build than her sister and dark sweat patches on a grey boys' PE shirt where she'd been hammering the drums. Summer felt a little sick.

'Just let me out,' she said, shaking her fists with frustration. 'I don't want to sing.'

Lucy was now right in her face. 'We've been auditioning singers for our band,' she told Summer softly. 'But they all suck. Can't you at least give us one song?'

Summer thought about bundling Michelle out of the doorway, or screaming for help. But Lucy would surely side with her sister and the music room was soundproofed. Resigned to singing, she stepped out towards the drum kit and cleared her throat.

For some reason the song that came to mind was 'Wichita Lineman', a Glen Campbell country number that she remembered one of her mum's blokes singing when she was a toddler. Summer's unaccompanied voice lacked enthusiasm, but it had a depth and richness that had no business coming from a thirteen-year-old girl.

'You've got some pipes on you!' Lucy said enthusiastically. 'Keep going.'

Summer felt her cheeks burn as she shuffled her dirty plimsolls and looked at the floor. 'I only know the first verse.'

'Join our band,' Lucy begged. 'You've got a great voice, why not use it?'

Summer shook her head. 'I've got a lot on my plate.'

While Lucy pleaded, her younger sister turned angry.

'What's on your plate?' Michelle shouted accusingly. 'You never talk to anyone. You never do anything. You might as well be dead.'

A wounded look flashed over Summer's face. Lucy thought Summer was about to cry and she pushed Michelle away.

'How you gonna persuade her like that?' Lucy said angrily. 'Her voice is awesome, but you can't force someone into the band.'

'You *never* back me up!' Michelle shouted, as she smashed the side of her fist against the whiteboard. 'Oww!'

'I don't back you up because you never think,' Lucy shouted, as she grabbed the door to let Summer out of the room.

Summer smiled, but her relief didn't last. Along the hallway Mr Gubta was speaking furiously to a music teacher.

'A-ha!' Mr Gubta said triumphantly. 'Is your partner in crime there as well?'

Summer felt like a ten-ton weight had landed on her back as Michelle stepped out behind with *couldn't give a damn* written all over her face.

'How's your fat, ugly, skank, cow, pig, moose of a wife?' Michelle shouted, as she waved to Mr Gubta. Then, with no trace of remorse, she whispered softly in Summer's ear. 'He's had it in for me ever since I wedged his highlighter pen in my butt crack and mooned him.'

5. Kitchen Sink Drama

Mr Gubta lectured Summer in the music block, then Mr Obernackle made her sit in his cramped head of year's office and *expressed his disappointment*.

She was a *good girl*, a *clever girl* and the *last person he expected to see sitting in this office after school*. Michelle was a *toxic influence*, and he was disappointed that Summer had shown such *poor judgement* by associating with her. Normally a first offender would get a warning. But this was a *very serious incident*. They were considering *a talk with Summer's parents*. Obernackle wanted this behaviour *nipped in the bud*.

Summer felt blank as she sat there looking down at Obernackle's shiny suit trousers, wondering why his office smelled like sour milk. She nodded and said *yes sir* when she thought she was supposed to, and didn't bother trying to explain how it all happened. Teachers always thought they were smarter than you and the implausible story behind her innocence would only drag things out.

Her bus home stopped by a row of shops a few hundred metres from the Carr Road estate where she lived. Summer had a stress headache and aching feet after standing for the ten-minute ride. She wanted to go straight home, but there was nothing in her flat for dinner, so she cut through the automatic doors of the Spar supermarket.

It was all ready meals by the entrance. She fancied microwave Chicken Korma or Crispy Tacos, but a pack for her and her nan would be six quid. So she got the £1.29 *big value* macaroni cheese, a bag of tangerines, a large tin of baked beans and a white loaf. She counted out coins as she waited behind a man buying lotto cards, and had just enough to treat herself to a small bag of chocolate Minstrels, which she crunched as she strolled aimlessly towards home.

Kevin, from Summer's class, stood astride his BMX in front of an off-licence. He broke away from a couple of younger lads and rolled slowly alongside her. He was tall, with broad shoulders. Summer had experienced a moment of attraction on sports day, when Kevin had lain at the edge of the playing field in shorts and trainers, eating a cheese roll while sweat drizzled down his muscular chest. But Kevin wasn't the brightest and his high-pitched voice was a shocker.

'Ow's it going then?' he chirped. 'Ya get in trouble with old Obernackle?'

Summer raised one eyebrow. 'He pinned a rosette on me,' she said. 'What do you think?'

'What's a rosette?' Kevin asked, completely missing the sarcasm. 'Want some help with the shopping?'

It was hard to tell whether Kevin was being nice, or planning to impress his pals with some hilarious scheme that involved making Summer chase around the estate after a Spar bag. So she didn't answer. She just sighed and then felt a bit bad as Kevin turned his bike in a lazy circle and freewheeled back to his friends.

'See you then, Summer.'

'I suppose I'll have to,' she sighed, once Kevin was out of earshot.

The slope up to her flats was uneven, with grass tufts growing out of cracks in the tarmac. The sun had made a late breakthrough and a rough crowd of boys kicked a ball around. Good parents didn't let their lads out amidst the smashed bottles and dog turds.

A man with a toddler in a buggy held the gate open for Summer. She stepped through and only noticed the *out of order* sign on the lift after jabbing the up button. Her feet were dying and if the concrete stairs hadn't been so rank she'd have taken her plimsolls off before heading up.

After eight flights breathing mildew, carrying the shopping and her schoolbag, she felt down as she walked along a gloomy hallway and unlocked the steel-barred gate over the door of flat twenty-three.

'Heya, Nan,' Summer said, faking cheerfulness as she dumped the bags and ripped off her pumps.

Her swollen feet glistened with sweat and her little toe

bore the white circle of a popped blister.

'You're late, love,' Summer's nan said, as her granddaughter joined her in the living room. 'I dropped the bleedin' remote down the side and missed my show.'

The room was cosy, if a bit shabby. The wallpaper was peeling up near the ceiling. There were pictures of family members and long-dead cats, but a statue of Jesus on the cross took pride of place over the flickering gas fire.

Eileen Smith was only fifty-eight, but she had severe asthma and a spinal injury after being knocked down by a hit-and-run driver. Even twelve steps to the bathroom exhausted her.

Summer reached down between armchair and wall and fished the remote from a bed of sweet wrappers and moulding peanuts.

'Is it ITV you want?'

Eileen nodded. 'God bless you. The oxygen man hasn't turned up. I don't suppose he will now, either.'

Summer backed away with a sigh. She checked the gauge on the oxygen bottle beside her nan's chair.

'You've got a quarter of a bottle,' Summer said. 'That's enough for tonight and tomorrow.'

Summer wanted to sit in her room and get her head straight, but Eileen needed to breathe pure oxygen two or three times a day, so she walked back to the passage, took her mobile from her coat pocket and dialled the number printed on the empty cylinder by the front door.

It cut straight to a recorded message when she dialled.

'Welcome to NHS West Midlands oxygen supply service. Please have your patient number ready to assist with your enquiry.'

The phone rang thrice more before another voice cut in. 'Nobody is currently available to take your call. Our opening times are 9 a.m. to 4:30 p.m. Monday to Friday and 9 a.m. to 12:30 p.m. on Saturdays. Please call again during these hours. Goodbye.'

Then it went dead and Summer cursed as she pressed the *end call* button.

'Something up, love?' Eileen asked.

Any kind of stress made her nan's asthma worse, so Summer adopted a breezy tone. 'Just forgot the time,' she said. 'I'll have to call tomorrow morning and ask why they didn't turn up.'

'I'll need a delivery tomorrow, Summer. I told you to call them last week, when we still had a bottle and a half.'

'I forgot,' Summer growled, then moderated her tone as she went back through to the living room. 'I need a shower, then I'll make our tea. There's macaroni, or I can do beans on toast.'

Eileen locked her fingers together and smiled. 'Whatever you want, love. Beans on toast is nice and warm.'

'I was going to get some mince and cook a proper spag bol,' Summer said apologetically. 'But it's late and my head's throbbing. You don't mind if I shower first, do you?'

'Of course not,' Eileen said. 'And your feet are rubbed raw! How many times have I told you to wear socks?'

'I hate how they stop the air getting between your toes,' Summer said, before diving into her little bedroom and grabbing the bath towel hooked on the back of the door. In the hallway she unzipped her bag and took out a wodge of tissue she'd stolen from the school toilets. Eileen's incapacity benefit didn't go far and this trick saved a pound or two every week.

Summer left the bathroom door open in case her nan called out. She dropped her skirt, unbuttoned her polo shirt and tugged it over her head before holding it up to the light to inspect the charcoal stain. Worried that the black powder would affect something else in the washing-machine, she took it to the kitchen across the hallway, plugged the sink and rinsed the stain under hot water and a sprinkle of laundry detergent.

As the shirt squelched under her hands, Summer glanced down at her sore feet on the cracked lino. Her knickers came from the market and were past their best and her bra was cutting into her sides. Her hair hadn't been cut properly for ages and one of the clips had fallen out, leaving a tangle in front of her eyes.

Summer wasn't fourteen yet, but she felt haggard, like one of the young mums you saw around the estate. And at least they had cute babies to look after, instead of a middle-aged nan who got cranky and depressed because she couldn't leave the house.

She felt rotten thinking like that about her nan. Eileen had brought Summer up from age six. She was the only person who'd ever really loved her and it wasn't like she'd got sick deliberately. But that didn't stop Summer from feeling trapped.

A tear welled as she remembered Michelle in the rehearsal room: *You never talk to anyone. You never do anything. You might as well be dead.*

Maybe Michelle was nuts, but she'd summed up Summer's life. Tears streamed down as she rested her forehead against the cupboard over the sink and let the hot tap scald her wrists.

6. Jay's Odd Conception

It was gone five by the time Jay and Mr Currie had carried the drums and equipment from the school van and locked them away in the music rooms. Jay sat up front with the young teacher for the ten-minute ride home.

'You've got to admit, Tristan's not a very good drummer,' Jay said, as the van took a slow turn out of the school car park.

It was starting to get dark. The traffic was at a rush-hour crawl and Mr Currie had glazed eyes. He was as disappointed as any of the kids. A win would have got Brontobyte's picture in the local paper, boosting his music department. And the two hundred and fifty-quid voucher would have replaced the tambourines and maracas that got wrecked when a supply teacher let the year tens riot.

'Sir?' Jay enquired, after a long silence. 'Anyone home?'

'I'll support and advise pupils who form their own groups,' Mr Currie answered diplomatically. 'But I don't get involved in band politics. And you moan about Tristan, but your little display at the end of the performance was *totally* unprofessional.'

Jay looked out of the side window. 'I acted like a dick,' he admitted, as a cyclist nearly clipped the van's side mirror. 'But come on, sir. You've got a degree in music. Tristan is holding back the rest of our band. Alfie's awesome, Salman plays well and has a really cool voice.'

'It's not my job to tell students that they're no good, Jay. In fact, if I did that and Mrs Jopling complained, I'd probably lose my job.'

Jay understood that the young teacher was in a difficult position, so he tried a different tack.

'Supposing I talked everyone around and agreed to look for a different drummer. Are there any kids you'd recommend?'

Mr Currie considered for a few moments before answering. 'We've got a couple of decent drummers in the sixth form, but I doubt they'd want to hang out with year eights. There is one guy though. A year nine called Babatunde Okuma. He might just be the best drummer in the school.'

'Why haven't I met him?' Jay asked. 'I mean, if anyone's decent you usually see them around in the practice rooms.'

'Babatunde's only been at Carleton Road since half-term. He doesn't have anywhere he can play at home, so he comes down and bangs the hell out of a kit after school. I usually have to kick him out of the rehearsal rooms when I lock up.'

Jay smiled. 'And he's not in a band or anything?'

'Not as far as I know,' Mr Currie said. 'His family moved down from Nottingham a couple of months back.'

'Maybe I'll try catching up with him,' Jay said. 'Does he seem like a nice guy?'

'I'd say so,' Mr Currie nodded. 'But you've got to approach this carefully, Jay. Just listening to another drummer is going to cause friction. I've seen bands tear themselves apart over less. And you can't keep getting yourself up in Tristan's face like you did earlier. There won't always be an adult who can step in and if it gets physical it's not gonna be Tristan who gets a bloody nose, is it?'

'I know,' Jay agreed, as the van parked across the end of an alleyway. 'Although you'd be surprised how fast I can run when there's some big guy trying to batter me.'

'Don't mind if I drop you back here, do you?' Mr Currie asked. 'I'd rather not get mixed in the jam out on the main road.'

'No worries, sir,' Jay said, cheering up as he opened the door of the battered Transit. 'Thanks for taking us out today. I'm sorry we didn't play better.'

Mr Currie gave a slight smile. 'You'll probably learn more from today's experience than you would have done if you'd won.'

'Night, sir,' Jay shouted, after he'd grabbed his guitar and schoolbag out of the back.

The slim thirteen-year-old only had a T-shirt on and he shivered as the van's rear lights disappeared. The narrow alleyway stank of the giant metal bins from the council block on his right, while the opposite side was a graffitied metal fence with a bus depot beyond. Teenagers played on a paved courtyard overlooking the alley and Jay moved swiftly, because they'd spit or throw stuff if they spotted you.

Jay's family owned the two brick buildings at the end of the alleyway, looking out on to a busy main road. They'd been part of a Victorian terrace, the rest of which had made way for the flats.

The ground floors were commercial. Thomas' Fish Bar was a takeaway run by Jay's mum, Heather. Jay lived over the shop, sharing cramped quarters with Mum, stepdad, two half-sisters and all but the oldest of his five half-brothers. The White Horse pub next door was owned and run by Jay's auntie Rachel, who lived above with four kids, plus her eldest's boyfriend and two grandkids.

An automatic security lamp came on as Jay approached the cobbled yard behind the fish and chip shop. It lit up three shamefully tatty cars and a yellow Transit van with *BIG LEN* stencilled on the side.

Big Len was Jay's stepdad. He'd once been a top session musician, filling in for less talented celebrities on some of the biggest-selling records of the nineties. Now he played a Yamaha keyboard in old folks' homes and scraped a living from bingo games hosted afterwards.

Len had built a practice room in the cellar under the chip shop and spent hundreds of hours down there giving Jay and his family music lessons. Presently, the softly spoken giant sat on a ledge at the rear of his van, with a cigarette illuminating the gold rings on his bulky hands.

'All right, boy?' Len asked, with a heavy Irish lilt. 'How goes it?'

'Fourth outta nine,' Jay said dejectedly, as he put his guitar down on the cobbles. 'I thought you were coming down to cheer us on and meet Mr Currie.'

Len pointed towards the back of the chip shop. 'Had a day and a half here. Electricity blew out this morning and they've only just turned up to fix it. Shop's lost a whole day's trade and it'd be more than my life's worth to leave your ma.'

Jay noticed a face pressed against the van's side window. Six-year-old Hank was Heather and Len's son. Jay was fond of his youngest brother. He blew a raspberry and got a poked-out tongue in return.

'Tristan did us in,' Jay explained, as he looked back at Len. 'He's crap.'

Big Len nodded as Hank wrapped arms around his dad's shoulders and nuzzled the grey hairs on his neck.

'You won't get far without good drums,' Len agreed. 'Now get inside with that T-shirt. I'm cold just looking at you.'

The back door was only locked late at night, so Jay went straight inside. Usually, he would have seen clear through the small back room into glass cabinets and crackling deep fryers. But today he was confronted by four candlelit women.

They were his mum Heather, his auntie Rachel from the

pub next door, chip shop assistant Shamim and a woman he didn't know. Jay mumbled a quick hello before putting his foot on the staircase.

'Get your butt over here,' Jay's mum shouted. 'Did you win?'

Jay rested his guitar against the wall and walked reluctantly through flickering light towards the women.

'You look like a coven of witches,' he joked.

'I'll have you straight in the cauldron for that,' Heather laughed, as she pointed at the stranger. 'This here is Mags. You've heard me and Auntie Rachel telling stories about Mags. Ibiza with the girls, before you were born?'

Jay's family had run the chippy and pub for three generations, so it wasn't unusual for old faces to drop by. He vaguely remembered Mags from a couple of stories about his mum's schooldays and now he was annoyed that he had to stand here pretending to be interested.

'Good to finally meet you,' he said brightly.

Mags was hard to make out in the candlelight. All Jay could see was white skin and stretched lips that reminded him of the Joker.

'So is he one of your boys with Chainsaw Richardson?' Mags asked. 'He looks different from the other two I saw.'

'Bag o' bones you mean,' Heather laughed, as she grabbed Jay, pulled him close and ran her hand up his torso before giving him a big kiss on the cheek. 'You could play that ribcage like a xylophone.'

'Mum,' Jay protested, as he tried to pull away. 'God!'

But Heather ignored his obvious embarrassment. 'You're like a block of ice. Did you go to school with just that T-shirt on?'

'Blazer's balled up in me bag. I did the band thing, didn't I?'

'You still should have put it on to come home,' Heather said.

Jay smiled. 'Of course, I'd have been warmer if I had the leather jacket you said you'd get me.'

Heather laughed. 'Give us a break, kid, you're not on about *that* again.' Then she looked at Mags. 'Jay here is the odd one out. My three oldest boys and Kai, my fifth, were with Chainsaw Richardson before he went on the run. Jay's dad is a copper.'

Mags' jaw dropped, as Jay tugged free of his mum's grasp.

'*You* went out with a copper!' Mags howled, before shrieking in mock horror.

'Not exactly,' Auntie Rachel laughed. 'Tell Mags how it happened. I guarantee you'll wet yourself when you hear this.'

'Does everyone have to know my life story?' Jay complained, as he cringed with embarrassment. 'I get enough stick for being one of eight kids without *that* story getting around.'

But Heather waved off her son's protest. 'Oh, stop being a princess! It wasn't long after I married Chainsaw. He reckoned the police was following him, so he gets me to go to one of his lock-ups in a van and load it up with all these stolen laptops. What the sod didn't tell me was that the bloody van was nicked as well.

'So I'm coming round the back of Hampstead. Early Sunday morning, nobody about. Suddenly this copper pulls me over. He had me bang to rights: stolen van with no tread on the front tyre, stolen laptops in the back and me with a prior conviction for handling stolen goods. I had three boys under five and I couldn't risk having 'em all put in care.

'As this copper's about to put the cuffs on me, I look at him and I see he's younger than me. Barely twenty and a virgin if you ever saw one. So I turned on my feminine wiles and asked what I could do to make all my problems go away.'

'Oh my days!' Mags shrieked. 'That's outrageous.'

Jay was glad it was candlelight because nobody could see his cheeks burn.

Heather laughed as she finished her story. 'So I shagged this copper and nine months later, out pops little Jay.'

'Ta-da!' Auntie Rachel added.

'What did Chainsaw say?' Mags gasped.

'I was straight up with him,' Heather said. 'He weren't happy, but it was his own sodding fault for putting me in a nicked van. Call me a slut if you like, but it was that or lose my kids.'

Chip shop assistant Shamim hadn't heard this story before and covered her face as her body shook with laughter.

'Do you ever see your dad?' Mags asked Jay.

Jay answered reluctantly. 'One weekend a month,' he admitted. 'And sometimes he takes me away in the school holidays. Usually fishing, or something else boring.'

'He's always been really good about paying maintenance,' Heather said. 'And Jay's our little brainbox.'

'Well, I can read and write,' Jay explained. 'Which is smart compared to *certain* members of this family.'

'Meow!' Shamim laughed.

'So can I go upstairs now?' Jay asked. 'Or have you just thought of some other way to embarrass me? Maybe the time I peed myself when you tried to take my photo alongside the guy dressed as a Cadbury's Creme Egg?'

'You can go now, sugar plum,' Heather teased. 'Unless you want another kiss from Mummy.'

Jay thought of his stomach before heading off. 'What's for tea?'

'Candle wax unless that electrician gets a bloody move on,' Heather said, before giving a serious answer. 'I don't really know, mate. We'll probably end up getting takeaway or something.'

Jay grabbed his guitar and schoolbag and took it up the dark staircase to the second-floor room he shared with twelve-year-old half-brother, Kai. The room overlooked the main road, and with no electric the walls glowed blue from streetlamps and the petrol station across the street.

After sliding his guitar under the lower bunk, Jay moved towards the window and grabbed the curtains to bring in more light. As he reached up, Kai jumped out from behind the door. Before Jay knew it he was on the ground with muscly arms crushing his chest.

Kai had been born several months after his dad Vinny 'Chainsaw' Richardson got sentenced to eighteen years for his part in a brutal security van robbery. As a toddler, Kai had worked out that he was tougher than Jay and he'd never tired of the fact.

'Weed!' Kai said, as he flipped Jay on his back and drove a hand into his face, mashing his head down into the carpet.

Jay tried to break loose, but Kai was too heavy.

'Tell me how great I am,' Kai said. 'Then I *might* let you up.'

'You can't even write your own name, you dumb shit,' Jay said defiantly.

This line was meant to sting: Kai had learning problems and got heaps of abuse about being thick. Kai smashed Jay in the ribs before lowering his head until the boys' noses almost touched.

'I can have you any time,' Kai said, then spat in Jay's eye before rolling off.

Jay felt humiliated as he sat up. 'You'd better watch out,' he yelled furiously. 'One of these days I'll stick a knife in your guts.'

Kai laughed as he swung his beefy frame up on to the lower bunk. 'Try it,' he sneered. 'See where it gets you.'

7. Lemon with Sprinkles

Summer belted out of maths class when the bell went for morning break. The weather was still miserable, with a fine mist of rain glazing her face as she hurried through the school's main gate, trying to get out before a teacher arrived to guard it.

You weren't allowed off school premises at morning break, nor to use your mobile during school time. But Summer had to call the oxygen depot and figured it was better to risk a half-hour detention for going outside, than to have her phone confiscated until the end of the week.

Summer sat at a deserted bus shelter fifty metres from the school and fished a Nokia from her backpack. The battery cover was held on with tape and the display cracked, but it still worked. She just hoped they didn't put her on hold because she only had £2.72 credit, and no chance of finding a tenner to buy a top-up.

After Summer had given her nan's patient number and

explained that the oxygen cylinders hadn't arrived the day before, the woman on the other end said she'd call the delivery driver and took Summer's number to call her back.

As Summer waited a bus pulled up and a year eleven boy stepped off. He was lean, with shaggy black hair, and he had a white headphone cord running from the pocket of his jeans up to his ears. Cute in a geeky kind of way, she thought, and definitely a nice bum.

Summer was still eyeing him when the ringing mobile brought her back to reality.

It was a different woman. She sounded worn out, like she'd had similar conversations thousands of times before.

'I just phoned the driver for your area,' she explained. 'He tried delivering four oxygen cylinders yesterday afternoon, but the lift was out of order. Give us a call when the lift is fixed and he can be there in under an hour.'

Summer sighed. 'When the lift goes it's usually three or four days. My nan will need a new cylinder by tonight.'

'We can deliver if there's someone available to carry the cylinders upstairs.'

'I can barely lift one down the hallway to my nan's bedroom,' Summer explained. 'Why can't the driver carry them up?'

'It's all contracted out to a private company,' the woman explained. 'There's only one person in a truck, and they can only carry cylinders up a maximum of two floors. It's health and safety rules.'

Summer felt stressed. 'But my nan's a severe asthmatic. If she runs out she could die.'

'I understand,' the woman said. 'If your grandmother gets short of breath, you'll have to call 999 and have her taken to the hospital.'

This was obvious and unhelpful. Summer made a loud grunt.

'But there must be *something* you can do,' she snapped. 'It must be easier and cheaper to send over a few cylinders of oxygen than to wait for my nan to get sick, send out an ambulance and then have her in hospital for three days.'

'It's all different departments,' the woman explained.

'We had the ambulance in once before when the lift was out. It took forever to get my nan down the stairs. She got so upset she passed out.'

'I know it's a nuisance,' the woman said. 'But I didn't make the rules, did I?'

Summer's knuckles turned white as she clutched the phone tight with frustration. 'Not being able to breathe is a bit *more* than a nuisance,' she said angrily.

'Does your nan have a social worker, or health visitor?'

'I'm the only one who lives with her,' Summer explained. 'But someone comes in and does a bit of cleaning and helps my nan in the shower once a week.'

'All I can suggest is that you call social services and see if they can send a couple of people round to carry the cylinders upstairs.'

The thought of this made Summer groan. It was a

nightmare just getting social services to turn up regularly to give her nan a weekly shower. The chances of them having two people available at short notice were nil.

Summer sensed that she'd run into a brick wall. 'I'll try and sort something out,' she sighed, before ending the call.

She rocked her head backwards and looked up at bits of gum stuck to the corrugated roof of the bus shelter. She felt like screaming, throwing her phone, or kicking something, but that wasn't Summer's style.

She had no idea what to do now, except cross her fingers and hope the lifts were working when she got home at lunch-time.

A teacher would guard the school gate until break ended, so Summer waited, shivering from the cold and listening to the shouts of boys playing football inside the school grounds. She was starving, but the canteen would be closed by the time she got inside and the cafés and takeaways nearby were too expensive.

After the school bell, Summer gave it a minute for the teacher on the gate to clear off before walking back. She made it less than ten metres before Mr Obernackle yelled her name. Her head of year was crossing the street, holding a paper bag from the bakery on the corner.

'Well, well. Look who it isn't!' Obernackle cackled, delighted to have caught a pupil redhanded.

Summer hated Obernackle's rusty-gate voice and the way he was completely up himself. Every word and gesture oozed smugness and nothing you said could change the opinions he formed before you opened your mouth.

'It's time for *serious* discussions,' he said gravely, as he marched Summer up the ramp and through school reception.

Keys jangled as Obernackle unlocked his tiny office and threw the baker's bag on the table.

'Sit,' he said, sounding like he was instructing a dog. 'Your parents will have to be brought into school, but I have more important things than you to deal with. You'll have to wait.'

Obernackle's theatrics ended with a slam of the office door and his shoes clacking self-importantly down the hallway. The waiting was designed to intimidate, but looking after her nan had left Summer with a total lack of respect for adults on power trips.

She glanced around the office, wondering what she was missing in French class. There wasn't much to see and her eyes came back towards the desk top and the paper bag from the baker's. It had turned clear with grease, revealing outlines of two donuts. One was pink-iced, the other lemon-iced with sprinkles. It seemed like a curiously feminine snack for the strutting Mr Obernackle.

Summer thought about spitting on the donuts, or attaching a bogey to give herself some juvenile satisfaction, but she was starving and as Obernackle already had it in for her, she couldn't see what extra harm it would do if she actually did something bad.

Summer swelled with mischievous pride as she pulled out

the lemon donut. Sprinkles tumbled down her shirt as she tore out a huge bite. She'd never eaten from the baker's on the corner and found it surprisingly good. The dough was fluffy, with crisp sugary icing and a citrus bite from lemon curd inside.

As Summer ate, she calculated that the donut would save her £1.60 on lunch. If she could scrimp another couple of pounds from somewhere she'd be able to buy the phone top-up she desperately needed once her nan's benefit payment cleared.

Obernackle hadn't returned when Summer polished off the lemon donut, so she scoffed the pink one as well. She considered hiding the bag so that Obernackle would think he'd mislaid the donuts. But she wanted to make it clear that she wasn't intimidated, so she screwed the bag into a ball and left it in the middle of the desk with a multicoloured trail of sprinkles all around it.

'Right, let's deal with you then,' Obernackle said, trying his hardest to make Summer feel like an unimportant speck as he came back into the office.

His essential business had apparently been a quick staffroom gossip and a mug of filter coffee. He reached for the donuts as he sat down and his eyes shot open like a hot poker had been rammed up his butt.

'I *see*,' he hissed, as his body shuddered and his pointing finger wagged.

Obernackle's eyes darted in several directions as he sought a decision. Eventually he picked his telephone off the desk top and slammed it dramatically in front of Summer.

'Call your parents,' he demanded. 'I want to see them here at school *today*.'

Summer eyeballed Mr Obernackle, smiled slightly and spoke with a calm voice which she knew would annoy him. 'You can't.'

'Young lady, I can and I will.'

'I have no idea who my father is,' Summer explained. 'For my mum you could try the prison service, or ringing round a few rehab centres, but the last we heard she was living rough in London, sticking needles in her arm at every opportunity.'

'Then you have a carer,' Obernackle shouted, as he grabbed Summer's file, which was still on his desk from the night before. He found a mobile number and violently stabbed out the digits. 'Let's see, shall we?' he grinned.

Summer tried not to smirk as she pulled the ringing Nokia from her pocket. 'Hello?' she said. 'Who's that?'

Obernackle slammed down the receiver and pointed at Summer. 'Well, who do you live with?'

'I live with my nan. She has severe asthma and any kind of stress can lead to a bad attack. I'd rather you kept her out of this, but if you insist, you'll have to wait until the lift at our flats is fixed. Then you can call dial-a-ride and arrange for her to be picked up. They'll fit you in at some point during the week after next. But she needs oxygen with her at all times, so you'll also have to call a completely separate number and arrange for social services to deliver a portable oxygen supply and an escort to carry it. I'd love to do all that myself, but I've only got two pounds' credit on my phone and I might need that if there's an emergency.'

Mr Obernackle expected kids to be in awe of him. He had his *straighten up and fly right* speech all ready to rip but his lips made a stunned O as Summer's voice changed from calm to a tone of mild disgust.

'I've been here nearly three years,' she stated robustly. 'I'm always on time. I've only ever missed a couple of days when my nan was sick. I always hand in my homework and I'm not smart, but I try hard. I'm in the top three or four in my class on every exam.

'I got the giggles in class yesterday. I followed Michelle because I'd *never* been in trouble before and didn't know where the referral classroom was. I went out of school at breaktime because I had to make an urgent phone call to have oxygen cylinders delivered to my nan. If you don't believe that, you're welcome to redial the last number in my phone's memory. I ate your donuts because I was hungry, and because you're a silly little man who isn't nearly as clever or powerful as he likes to think he is.'

Summer stood up and finally raised her voice: 'If you don't like what I'm saying, then suspend me, or expel me or do whatever you like, because I've tried my hardest, but I don't give a *damn* about you or this stupid school anymore.'

'Now hold on,' Obernackle said, with a tremor in his voice.

He'd already spoken to a couple of Summer's teachers,

one of whom had mentioned something about her grandmother. They didn't have a bad word to say about her and the head of year would look very bad if it got around the school that he'd come down hard on a good pupil with a difficult home life.

'Summer, perhaps we've got off on the wrong foot . . . I think we need . . . I mean . . . I wasn't aware of your personal difficulties. I think I should speak with your form tutor and the school counsellor and sort out some kind of plan–'

'Do whatever you like,' Summer interrupted, as she waved her hand dismissively. 'I've got to go. I have much more important problems to deal with than *you*.'

8. Lazy Winter Afternoon

Yellowcote boarding school, near Edinburgh

Dylan Wilton glanced at his watch, before peeking out of his minuscule bathroom to make sure nobody was around. He was fourteen and handsome, with tangled bleached hair and a stud in one ear. His uniform was deeply traditional, with red piping down his trousers and waistcoat buttons straining over a flabby waist.

It was just past noon as he stopped hiding in his shower and moved cautiously into his bedroom. The space was originally a dormitory, where shivering boys slept under rough blankets, in between Latin prep and thrashings with a leather tawse. Fortunately, modern-day parents didn't hold with that sort of thing and the dorms had been partitioned into individual rooms, with each pod sharing half of a metal-framed window.

Dylan's narrow space had room for a wardrobe and a raised bunk, with a desk and chair beneath. Posters were allowed on the cork-lined wall opposite. He'd pinned up hundreds of postcards and flyers for rock bands, but pride of place went to a poster of the Mona Lisa smoking a huge joint, on which some anonymous wag had written *Dylan is a cock face.*

He sneaked a quick glance out at the playing fields. Little boys were setting out cricket stumps on the all-weather pitch, lads his own age lined up with curling breath, ready for a punishing afternoon running through mud, jumping gates and crossing streams.

The thought of all this suffering made Dylan feel deliciously warm as he sat on his deskside chair and unlaced his shoes. An amber flash passed by in the hallway, before skidding on socked feet and turning back. Dylan had been stupid to leave the door open, and the bandy-legged kid poked his head curiously inside.

He was called Ed and wore Yellowcote's wasp-striped PE kit, with football boots swinging from the laces clutched in his hand. Ed was the sort of kid who tried hard and grinned all the time, even though some of the tougher lads amused themselves by dangling him over banisters or chucking his books in the urinals.

'How come you're still here?' Ed asked. 'You're not even changed yet!'

'I have music, don't I?' Dylan explained, as he stretched into a lazy yawn. 'I expect I'll cruise down to the practice studios in a momento.'

'You're so lucky,' Ed complained. 'I'm gonna freeze

my nuts off out there. We're not even allowed tracksuit bottoms. By the way, thanks for putting that Black Flag stuff on my iPod. You were right, it's fricking awesome.'

'Told you,' Dylan smiled. 'Ten times better than all that twangy indie rubbish everyone round here raves about.'

'I'd better run. Last thing I need is a games master on my back and I'm already late.'

As Ed belted down the corridor, Dylan shut his door and opened his wardrobe. There was no lock on the room door or his wardrobe, so he kept his most illicit possessions in the ripped lining of an army surplus jacket.

The first thing he touched was a memory key loaded with all kinds of naughtiness banned by Yellowcote's internet filters, but he pushed deeper into the lining, slid out a small tin and flung it up on to the bed. He checked that his iPhone was already up there, before throwing off his tie, belt and waistcoat and climbing up.

Dylan was almost as tall as the bed and his sweaty grey socks left damp smears on the side of his wardrobe as he reached behind his head and opened the window. The metal lid flexed as it popped off the rectangular tin, revealing a lighter, cigarette papers and a compressed brick of strong Indian tobacco that he'd stolen from his stepmum.

He lifted everything out, hoping to find a remnant of marijuana resin, but he'd smoked the last piece the previous week and wouldn't get his hands on any more until the holidays.

Dylan sniffed inside the tin. He hated the dusty synthetic

taste of regular cigarettes, but loved the exotic pipe tobacco and craved the first hit of smoke as he laid a Rizla paper on the window ledge and sprinkled it with curly brown tobacco strands. Once it was evenly spread, he licked the gummed edge, rolled, lit up and drew a long, smoky puff.

This first hit was the pinnacle of cigarette smoking: the heat in his lungs and the first blast of nicotine. The wrongness made it even better. Yellowcote was a hotbed of hard work, Christian charity, rigorous competition and people trying their best. Dylan hated all of those things.

He was proud to be a bum. Screw healthy living, exam results and school spirit. Each puff felt like a big *up yours* to all the boys running ten kilometres and coming back with cow manure spattered up their legs. Who gives a shit about diseased lungs and heart attacks in some distant future?

Dylan held the burning cigarette end out of the window, keeping close to the ledge so that he couldn't be seen from below and trying to understand why it was so hard to blow smoke rings. Maybe he could get instructions off YouTube.

When his smoke was finished he planned to listen to something heavy on his iPhone, or maybe just curl up for a snooze.

Down on the all-weather pitch, a boy of about nine held a cricket bat all wrong. He looked worried as the ball flew at him and his white-trousered team-mates screamed abuse at his hopeless swing. Dylan felt sorry for the little guy as he took another puff of smoke and for some reason remembered a really hot girl he'd seen outside Harrods when he went shopping in London with his dad.

Then his door clicked. *Shit!*

Dylan flicked the last third of his cigarette, sending it pirouetting down the outside of the building as he rolled on his back to see how bad the situation was.

'Wilton,' a man shouted, as Dylan recoiled with shock. 'Get off that bed, you lazy turd.'

Dylan's worst nightmare was a huge man with muddy tracksuit bottoms tucked into striped socks. He had a pulped nose and a South Africa rugby shirt to go with his South African accent. He was Yellowcote's head rugby coach and he went by the name of Piet Jurgens.

Dylan's tobacco tin clattered as he shuffled to the side of his bed and jumped down. *Had someone grassed him up? Had Ed grassed him up?* The only sure thing was that his heart was thumping and his peaceful afternoon had just gone down the shitter.

'Can I smell smoke in here?' Jurgens shouted. 'In fact I'm not asking, I *know* I can smell smoke in here.'

'I can't smell anything, sir.'

'Then why is there a packet of cigarette papers on the floor?' Jurgens asked.

The distinctive turquoise Rizla packet had dropped to the floor when Dylan climbed down, and now he felt *mega-*screwed.

'Must have brought them in stuck to the bottom of my shoe,' he suggested hopefully.

Jurgens smiled as he closed in, his massive stubbly neck level with Dylan's eyeballs. 'My head has been bashed about over the years, but do I really look *that* stupid?'

'No, sir,' Dylan admitted, before coughing some tobacco-tasting spit into his mouth.

'It's a filthy habit. You're lucky they don't let me knock sense into you, because I'd smack your silly head from one end of this building to the other. That stuff killed my mother and grandmother. It will kill you too, understand?'

'Yes, sir,' Dylan said. He felt like a pussy doing *yes sir, no sir*, but nobody gave Mr Jurgens lip.

'Now, I want a straight answer. Where is your lazy butt supposed to be right now?'

'Music practice, sir.'

'Bull and shit, bull and shit!' Jurgens shouted, as he jabbed a finger into Dylan's chest, pushing him back against the bed. 'Miss Hudson told me you've been removed from the school orchestra because you were messing about in practice. What have you been doing for the last couple of Tuesday and Thursday afternoons?'

'I didn't have music so I stayed up here in my room.'

'Is that what you're supposed to do?'

'Isn't it, sir?'

Jurgens reared up. 'Don't play games with me, boy. You know as well as I do, if you don't have a special activity such as music, art or drama you come down to the playing fields with everyone else.'

'Oh,' Dylan said. 'Nobody told me that.'

'Well you're told *now*, so get into your kit. I'm running an elite training squad for year nine rugby, and you've just joined it.'

Dylan gulped. When he'd first arrived at Yellowcote he'd been ten years old and eager to please. He didn't like rugby and if he'd known better, he'd have dropped every rugby ball and missed every tackle. Instead he'd dug in, tried hard and showed a remarkable talent for a game he couldn't stand.

'Sir, I haven't played rugby since year seven, except a few knockabouts in games lessons. I'll be hopeless. I've got a fat belly. I smoke *all* the time.'

'I've knocked worse than you into shape,' Jurgens said, as he broke into a confident smile. 'I still remember that cup game you played in year six. You were beautiful, man. You would have been player of the season if you'd shown more enthusiasm in training.'

The main thing Dylan remembered about the cup game was bruised ribs and a trip to the school nurse to get mud syringed out of a clogged ear.

'Dylan, you've got fast feet, good ball control and you used to read the game better than anyone your age had any right to. I was bloody gutted when you joined the orchestra.'

'I thought all the rugby tournaments start after summer holidays,' Dylan said.

'Tournaments, yes. But my elite squads train year round. When you lot start year ten I'll have you sharp and ready to play the best rugby of your lives.'

'I've got exams next year, that's going to be a lot of work,' Dylan said, trying to keep the desperation out of his voice. 'And I'd be keeping someone who *wants* to play out of the squad. That's not fair if you ask me.'

'I'm not bloody asking you,' Jurgens boomed, making Dylan's stomach somersault as the South African's spit pelted his face. 'Your parents pay big money to send you to this school. All pupils are expected to partake fully in extra-curricular activities. You will train hard for the rugby squad and play to the best of your ability. If you slack off or muck about you'll make an enemy of me. Do you want to make an enemy of me, Mr Wilton?'

'No, sir,' Dylan said meekly, as he remembered Jurgens' shattering year seven rugby training sessions.

'You've got five minutes to change. Meet me downstairs on practice pitch C. Leave your cigarettes and bad attitude here. You're a rugby player now, my lad.'

9. Industrial Scale Slaughter

Summer didn't slam Mr Obernackle's door, but she banged it with a certain authority, making clear that it wouldn't be worth coming after her. She'd enjoyed putting Obernackle in his place, but there might still be consequences and she didn't want anything to happen that would stress her nan.

She'd missed two thirds of French class and wasn't in the right frame of mind to ask the time of the next train to Le Havre or the price of chocolate ice cream. Summer needed to get home and see if the lifts were fixed, so she headed straight towards the school gates. Breaking another rule by missing fifteen minutes of class hardly seemed to matter at this point.

To Summer's surprise Michelle Wei was hiding in the doorway of the girls' toilets. She was out of uniform, in ripped jeans and a bright green puffa jacket.

'I looked all over for you,' Michelle said, as she stepped in front of Summer.

'I thought you got suspended,' Summer said, as she carried on walking.

Michelle pointed. 'Yeah, but I live just across the street.'

'How come you never get expelled?' Summer asked bluntly. She wouldn't normally have risked setting Michelle off by speaking like that, but she was pumped after her confrontation with the head of year.

'S-E-N,' Michelle explained. 'Special Educational Needs. The shrink says my hilarious antics are caused by attention deficit disorder and boredom caused by my exceptionally high IQ. They can no more expel me for calling Mr Gubta a moose than they can expel a kid in a wheelchair for not doing PE, or a kid with dyslexia for writing slowly.'

'So we're stuck with you,' Summer said, half smiling as she pushed through a door and headed outside on to the ramp.

'I want to talk to you about Industrial Scale Slaughter,' Michelle said.

Summer was walking really fast, and because Michelle was titchy she had to do a little skip every fifth or sixth step to keep up.

'You what?' Summer asked.

'That's the name of our band.'

Summer held up her hands and groaned. 'I can't sing in any band. There's *nothing* to talk about.'

'Hear me out, fluffykins. I know I was pushy yesterday

and I landed you in doo-doo. I apologise, OK? But we've auditioned about twenty singers. There's nobody else half as good as you. What have you got to lose? What are you so afraid of?'

'I didn't say *no*,' Summer said irritably, as they reached the school exit. 'I said *can't*, as in *not possible*. My nan is sick. I have to look after her. I have to go home *right* now, because the lifts in my flats are dead. If they aren't fixed by this afternoon my nan can't get her oxygen delivered. And when that happens, I'm completely and utterly screwed.'

'Oxygen's a gas. Gas is light. Why can't you carry it up the stairs?'

Summer sighed. 'It comes in beefy metal cylinders, more than a metre tall. I'm on the fourth floor. It takes two blokes to carry them up the stairs and the delivery drivers won't do it.'

Michelle pointed at herself then at Summer, and counted. 'One, two. There's two of us. I've got nothing else to do. Let's roll.'

Summer shook her head. 'I can just about shift a cylinder from the hallway to my nan's bedroom, but stairs are really tough and neither of us are exactly butch.'

'My sister's butch,' Michelle said. 'Lucy pumps weights so that she can hit the drums harder. She's also got loads of boyfriends. I mean, what's the world coming to if two pretty girls can't get dumb boys to carry shit for them?'

'That's my bus,' Summer gasped, as she cut into the traffic and broke into a run on the opposite pavement, waving her arms for the driver to stop. The driver scowled as she fumbled for change, but Michelle reached around and put coins in the tray by the ticket machine.

'Two seventies, please.'

Summer clutched at a yellow pole as the driver hit the gas. She sat up the back and Michelle joined her.

'I'll make you a deal,' Michelle said, as she squeezed her mobile out of her jeans. 'I'll rustle up some people to carry the oxygen up the stairs if you come and jam at my place after school.'

Summer was relieved to have a route out of the oxygen crisis and lit up with a rare smile. 'That's fair,' she said. 'But one rehearsal, that's all.'

*

The year nine rugby squad was doing passing drills as Dylan came off the paved path between pitches. He'd dug an old gumshield out of his desk drawer, but his compression shorts were too small and he'd thrown out his headgear.

'Two-lap warm-up,' Jurgens ordered.

Some of the other squad members eyed the new arrival as Dylan set off at jogging pace. The two-hour training session was thirty minutes old and the squad was plastered in mud. Dylan had played with about half of them in year seven, but the rest had joined from different prep schools in year nine. They all looked tough and it wasn't just the wind that sent a chill down his back.

'Run, Wilton, you lazy piss streak,' Jurgens shouted, as

Dylan puffed his way into a second lap. 'I've seen year fours move faster than that.'

To emphasise his point, the big South African snatched a rugby ball and rifled it more than twenty metres through the air, hitting Dylan between the shoulder blades. The rest of the squad cheered as Dylan stumbled forwards, but he just managed to stay on his feet.

By the end of the second lap, Dylan was gasping for breath and his toes were hurting. If he survived this nightmare, the first thing he'd do when he got cleaned up was go to the school shop and buy every piece of protective gear he could lay his hands on.

'Line up, my boys,' Jurgens shouted, as the twenty-five-strong squad jogged back from their passing exercises, breathing deep with slippery balls tucked under arms. 'Not you, Dylan, you step up here with me.'

So Dylan faced off his new team-mates, gasping for air, with hands resting on his knees.

'This boy has talent,' Jurgens told the others, as he pulled Dylan's Indian loose-leaf tobacco out of his tracksuit pocket and tore away the foil in which it was wrapped. 'Those of you who played with him in prep school will remember that.'

Dylan was appalled as Jurgens sprinkled his tobacco over the grass, then squelched it all under the studs of his size thirteen.

'But Dylan is a delicate chap who'd rather be flower arranging or learning contemporary dance,' Jurgens continued, with a sneer. 'He tells me that he doesn't want to play rugby, because you're all a bunch of thick idiots.'

The lads all hissed and shook their heads as Jurgens broke into a wry smile. Dylan was really shitting himself now, but he laughed along, hoping his new team-mates understood that it was a joke.

'So I want you all to be extra gentle with our delicate flower, OK?'

The lads all roared, 'Yes, boss!'

Fists pounded into palms and boots stomped in the mud. Dylan was starting to wonder if Jurgens wanted to train him up to get back on the squad, or just wanted to make him suffer for having the temerity to quit his team two years earlier.

'Tackle drills, one on one,' Jurgens shouted. 'McGregor, you start out with Wilton.' He then turned towards Dylan and spoke more quietly. 'I take it you remember how a one-on-one works?'

'Yes, sir.'

'You call me boss out here on the field.'

Dylan nodded slightly. 'Yes, *boss*.'

The squad paired off at ten-metre intervals on opposite sides of the pitch. One-on-one was a tough but simple drill. Two boys stood on opposite sides of the pitch. The carrier had to get the ball to the opposite side, while the other boy tried to tackle him. After each successful tackle, the ball carrier stood up, while the tackling player retreated to the touchline for another attack.

'Hey,' Dylan said, trying to befriend McGregor, as they found a space near the far post. 'You know what Jurgens said about me was bull, right?'

McGregor had his gumshield in and just grunted. Dylan found it reassuring that his red-haired partner was one of the smallest on the squad, but he had massive arms and thighs.

Dylan picked a ball out of the mud on his way to the touchline. In one-on-one the first carry was your best chance to run the ball straight to the other side, because the distance between players was greatest and you could build up more speed.

When all the pairs were lined up, Jurgens moved to the halfway line and blasted his whistle. Dylan charged forwards, doing his best despite his toes hurting and a shortness of breath after the laps.

He glanced right, seeing the other boys from his side of the pitch powering ahead of him. McGregor closed in at unbelievable speed, his gumshield on display and eyes shut down to mean little slits.

When they were ten metres apart, Dylan faked left, but McGregor wasn't fooled. McGregor's tackle was high. His arms crushed Dylan's stomach making the ball pop loose. Somehow, McGregor pulled off an extra trick, violently jerking Dylan's torso to one side and lifting both feet high off the ground. Pain ripped up Dylan's right side as he slammed down hard on his back. His cheek spattered a brown puddle and the water sprayed up, filling his right eye and splashing into his mouth.

'Oh god,' Dylan moaned, struggling for breath as he looked up at the sky with one eye, while rubbing the muck out of the other. He'd suffered a few hard tackles in his time, but this was unbelievable.

McGregor laughed as he gave Dylan a hand up. 'Felt that one, did you?'

10. Domino's Full House

Michelle's big sister Lucy and a year eleven called Jack dropped the last oxygen cylinder in the narrow hallway of Summer's flat.

'Beats any gym workout,' Lucy gasped, as she wiped her brow on the sleeve of her school blazer.

Summer came out of the kitchen holding two plastic beakers. 'Sorry it's only squash,' she said. 'Thank you *so* much. You've no idea how stressed I was getting.'

'Happy to help,' Lucy said, before downing one of the juices in three gulps. 'I've driven past these flats loads of times. Always wondered what they'd be like inside.'

'It's cosy,' Jack said. He'd uncomplainingly carried two oxygen cylinders up four floors and kept agreeing with everything Lucy said. His intentions wouldn't have been plainer if he'd Biroed *I'm desperate to get inside Lucy's pants* across his forehead.

Summer glanced at her watch. 'I guess we'd better get moving.'

School lunch break was almost over, but as long as the bus turned up they'd only be a couple of minutes late for afternoon registration.

'Mind if I wash my hands first?' Jack asked, as he looked at paws blackened with whatever gets stuck to the bottom of an oxygen cylinder.

'In there,' Summer said, before opening the door directly behind her.

The doorbell rang as Jack latched the bathroom door.

'That's weird,' Summer said, moving towards the hall. 'You don't get a lot of callers up here.'

'Pizza,' Michelle explained, as she squeezed past Lucy and opened the front door. 'I ordered while Lucy and her love-slave carried the last bottle up.'

Summer gawped as she saw the delivery rider holding two pizza boxes, plus sides and a bottle of Fanta. She felt obliged to pay after Lucy, Michelle and Jack had helped out, but there was less than a tenner in the house.

'Put this towards some lotion for your zits,' Michelle told the delivery rider, tipping him a pound before booting the front door shut.

'Do you need money?' Summer asked warily.

'Nah,' Michelle laughed. 'I used the Dominos app on Lucy's phone.'

Lucy's eyebrows shot up. 'You mean this lot came off *my* debit card?'

'You're the one who wants a singer,' Michelle said, as everyone followed the smell of pizza into the living room.

'How long have you known my phone PIN?' Lucy asked sourly.

'1394,' Michelle explained. 'Justin Bieber's date of birth.'

Jack came back in, wiping wet hands on his trousers. 'I didn't know you liked Justin Bieber, Lucy. I *love* Justin Bieber.'

Michelle started howling with laughter as Lucy stared at Jack like he'd just landed from outer space.

'When I was *eleven*,' Lucy explained. 'I've just always used the same PIN for my mobile.'

Jack nodded frantically. 'I know, I'm joking . . . *Obviously*.'

'Ob-*veeeee*-ously,' Michelle repeated.

Lucy waited until Michelle put the pizza boxes on the coffee table before yanking her back by the collar of her puffa jacket and growling in her ear. 'You're paying me back.'

'I found us a singer, didn't I?' Michelle replied.

'This smells lovely,' Eileen said, cracking a big smile as Summer came in with a stack of plates. 'It's so nice to see Summer's friends.'

'What would you like, Mrs Smith?' Lucy asked, as she popped open the pizza boxes. 'Full House or . . . This one looks like Hawaiian.'

Summer had made another trip to the kitchen, returning with a stack of mugs hooked over her fingers. 'All out of glasses, I'm afraid.'

She smiled as her nan bit eagerly into a triangle of Full House. Jack settled in an armchair and the Wei sisters squatted on the floor around the coffee table. The room wasn't very big and Summer had to inch around Jack's sprawling legs to get to the table, but she was used to it just being her and her nan and liked having the flat filled with noise.

'This is fancy,' Eileen chuckled, as a strand of hot cheese dangled from her glasses. 'We've never had pizza delivered before.'

Jack looked surprised. 'Not ever?'

Summer was already embarrassed about the small and grotty flat and her nan's line about the pizza made her feel even more like a charity case.

'It's a bit pricy,' Summer explained.

One of the side orders was chocolate brownie squares, and Michelle theatrically dipped one of them in the chilli sauce that came with the potato wedges.

'Gross!' Jack protested.

'Ignore her,' Lucy said firmly. 'She just does it to get attention.'

Eileen spoke, as Michelle poked her brownie-smeared tongue at her sister. 'It'll be nice for Summer to sing in a band. I heard she was very good in *Evita*.'

'Didn't you see it?' Lucy asked.

'It's rough round here after dark,' Eileen explained. 'And if the lift breaks, I'm stuck out of doors for the night.'

'Everyone says I was good,' Summer admitted. 'But I was

so nervous. We did three performances and all I can remember about them is leaning over the toilet spewing.'

Jack spoke with his mouth full. 'Me mum works for the housing office. You should be able to get a place on the ground floor.'

'We're on the waiting list,' Summer said. 'Supposedly near the top, but they said the same thing two years ago.'

'This flat is so authentic,' Michelle laughed. 'I feel like I'm in one of those Channel Four documentaries about poor people.'

Lucy tutted and gave her sister a kick under the table. Summer understood that Michelle said things just for the hell of it, but she was embarrassed enough without being reminded.

'So what sort of tunes does your group play?' Eileen asked, at which point Summer realised that she didn't have a clue herself.

'Thrash metal,' Lucy said cheerfully.

'What's thrash, exactly?' Eileen asked.

'It's like heavy metal, only louder and faster,' Lucy explained. 'Have you ever heard any Metallica, or Slayer?'

Eileen laughed. 'I'm more of a Cliff Richard and David Essex girl myself.'

'We made a three-track demo,' Lucy told Summer. 'If you add me on Facebook I'll message them over and you can put them on your iPod.'

'Err,' Summer said, embarrassed that she didn't have an iPod or a computer to use Facebook.

'Our band's original name was Alien Rape Machine,' Michelle explained. 'But we got our dad to drive us to this battle of the bands thing and the name freaked him out, so we changed to Industrial Scale Slaughter.'

'I went down to watch them,' Jack said, as he licked his fingers. 'They're a good band. Finished runner-up. You should enter more battles. Or try getting some gigs.'

'You can't do gigs without a singer, divvy,' Lucy said. 'We would have if Grainne hadn't gone back to Ireland.'

'Now we've got Summer we should go online and look up any competitions or showcases that are going on,' Michelle said.

'I haven't even done *one* rehearsal yet,' Summer gawped. 'You've all been *really* nice and I'll keep my promise to rehearse with you, but let's see how it works out, yeah?'

Lucy scowled at Michelle. '*Don't* pressure her.'

'Can I take the last piece of Hawaiian?' Jack asked.

'If you don't ask you don't get,' Michelle said. 'If I hadn't been a pain in Summer's butt we never would have got this far.'

'I certainly hope it all works out,' Eileen said. 'Summer spends too much time here fussing over me. It's not that I don't appreciate all that she does, but she needs her own life too.'

Summer was relieved to hear her nan speak like that. She liked the idea of having something in her life away from school and the dreary flat, but it also scared her.

The Wei sisters and their band mate Coco came from posh backgrounds and already knew each other well. Would someone like her ever fit in with them?

11. We Have Ignition

There were photos of Salman, Tristan and Jay making sandcastles on Southend beach aged four. They'd stayed friends from nursery up to year eight, despite rowing over everything from the Playmobil pirate ships to PC death matches.

The trio had done a routine Thursday of double games, art, lunch, maths and finally combined science. They were supposed to do an experiment to measure the boiling point of different liquids, but the class went a bit nuts, two beakers got smashed and Mrs Voolt made everyone put their equipment away and copy her results off the blackboard. Then she kept the class back for ten minutes after the day ended, sitting in silence with arms folded.

'I hate that old bag,' Tristan moaned, as the class filed out. 'You guys wanna go to mine and play Xbox?'

The late finish meant that the corridors were deserted.

'I'll come round,' Salman said. 'But only for an hour or

so. I've got a load of work from the lessons we missed yesterday.'

'Making us catch up is taking the piss,' Tristan said. 'If none of us do it I bet the teachers won't even remember.'

Jay tutted, as the three boys walked slowly down the hall. 'If we don't catch up we'll never be allowed time off to enter another competition.'

'Competition was totally fixed anyway,' Tristan said. 'So are you coming round for Xbox or not?'

Jay shook his head. 'I wanna pop upstairs and see if I can talk to Mrs Hinde about that mural project.'

Salman laughed. 'You're not seriously gonna get involved in painting the school, are you? It's *so* lame.'

'Completely bent,' Tristan agreed. 'You're not even any good at art. She's just scraping the barrel because nobody wants to do it.'

'I just want to find out a bit more,' Jay said. 'I'll see you guys tomorrow.'

'How long will you be?' Salman asked. 'We can wait if it's only a few minutes.'

'I don't fancy Xbox, anyway,' Jay said, as he raised one arm and made out like he was sniffing his armpit. 'I wanna get home and take a shower. I stink from games and I've got about ten hours' homework backed up.'

'Sod you then, misery guts,' Tristan said.

Jay went upstairs towards the art studios. He had no intention of painting any murals and gave it two minutes for Salman and Tristan to clear off before doubling back towards the music block. The quickest route was across the play-ground, but his mates might have stopped to chat or something, so he took an indirect route through the core of the school.

He felt guilty about lying to his two best mates. Deep in thought, Jay ignored a couple of distant shouts and turned a corner into a group of psycho year tens. Two rough girls and a fat kid looked on as a pair of toughs held a mouthy year eight called Wallace against the wall. His face was bright red after being smacked around and he was fighting back tears.

'You speak to her like that again . . .' one of the bullies warned, as he bent Wallace's fingers back. Then he grabbed Wallace's head and showed it to one of the girls. 'Mel, you wanna come over and give him a slap?'

Jay froze, knowing he'd landed right in it. He couldn't carry on walking because the yobs were blocking the corridor. He'd become a target if he stood and gawped, but if he turned back they might think he was heading off to get help.

'What you staring at?' the fat kid hissed, as he lumbered towards Jay.

Mel slapped Wallace hard across the face, then the bully brought his knee up into his guts and let him crash to the floor with a big *ooof* sound.

Jay thought fast. He'd outrun the fat kid, but not the other two. And for guys like them, running off was proof of guilt. Jay didn't rate his chances, but his mouth was his best shot at a pain-free escape.

'I asked what you're staring at!' Fatty shouted.

Jay pointed to a door at the end of the hallway and tried to sound cool as Wallace snivelled. 'Just heading for the music rooms, mate.'

'Do you know that prick?' Fatty asked, pointing at Wallace as the thugs unzipped their victim's pack and tipped all his stuff out.

'We're both year eight, but I don't know him,' Jay said, as the fatty got so close that he could smell hair gel and bad breath.

'Got any money?' Fatty asked.

A hand shot upwards, grabbing Jay's tie and shoving him against the wall.

'I've got thirty p,' Jay said. 'Just take it, I won't say anything, I swear.'

'You think I want thirty pence?' Fatty sneered, as he lifted Jay off the ground. 'Are you saying I'm poor?'

'No offence,' Jay squirmed, as he looked desperately up and down the corridor.

The two thugs were heading his way, as Wallace scuttled about picking his books and PE kit off the floor. There were no staff around and Jay had lowered his expectations: the best outcome now looked like a couple of slaps and a warning to keep his mouth shut. The worst didn't bear thinking about.

'What do you reckon?' Fatty asked the other lads.

'Come on, guys,' Jay begged. 'What good's this gonna do?'

The girl who wasn't Mel enjoyed watching Jay squirm. 'Listen to his voice,' she cackled. 'He's *wetting* himself.'

'My dick weighs more than this streak of piss,' Fatty laughed.

Mel turned towards Jay. 'I've seen you serving in the chip shop by our flats, ain't I?'

'Yeah,' Jay croaked, as his entire bodyweight hung painfully from his tie.

'You what?' one of the thugs said urgently, as he gave Fatty a shove. 'Shit!'

'Paul, let him go,' the other one gasped.

Jay's feet touched down and he coughed to clear his throat as Fatty stumbled away.

'What you shoving me for?' Fatty demanded.

The thugs ignored him as they looked warily at Jay.

'You're Adam and Theo's brother, ain't you?' one asked.

Now Fatty understood and he sounded stressed. 'Theo *Richardson?*'

'Is he the one who got expelled for sticking that guy's head through a window?' Mel asked.

The two bullies and the fat guy now surrounded Jay, but instead of being scary they couldn't have been more eager to please.

'Sorry, little man,' Fatty said, as he patted Jay's shoulder. 'No disrespect. I didn't know who you were.'

'We'd really appreciate it if this misunderstanding *didn't* get back to Theo,' one of the bullies grovelled.

Jay tried not to smile as he straightened his shirt and tie.

His older brothers Adam and Theo had a reputation. Adam was actually pretty harmless, but sixteen-year-old Theo had been expelled from four schools, won a dozen boxing belts and done two months in young offenders after a group from his gym wheeled an ice cream van into a duck pond with the driver still inside.

'We're all sorry, mate,' the bully standing opposite added. 'We didn't mean any disrespect. Is there anything you need? I think we popped a button off your shirt.'

'What size are you?' Fatty babbled. 'We can get you a new shirt. Or give you money for a shirt.'

Theo would probably just laugh if he saw a couple of year tens slapping Jay around. So Jay didn't want to push his luck, but he didn't like what he'd seen happen to Wallace.

'Forget about my shirt,' he said. 'But Wallace is harmless. Give him a slap if he disses your girl, but don't beat him like that.'

All three lads nodded. 'Right, right,' Fatty agreed.

'Now I wanna go by to the music rooms. And we're cool, OK? I expect Theo's got enough enemies without worrying about you guys.'

'Appreciate it,' one of the bullies said. 'You the man!'

Jay gasped with relief as he pulled his backpack up on to his shoulder and headed off. Coming from a large family of lunatics caused him all sorts of problems – from having no money to teachers assuming you were a nutter – so it felt good having his family connections get him out of trouble for a change.

The swinging doors at the end of the corridor led outside into a grey sunset. Wallace's hunched silhouette limped over a stretch of grass fifty metres ahead. Jay thought about catching up and checking he was OK, but they'd never exchanged more than a couple of words and he'd be embarrassed, so he went in the other direction towards the music rooms.

The school had a dozen small practice rooms, which opened directly on to a paved courtyard with a buckled goalpost at one end. Jay peered inside each room as he passed, waving at Mr Currie who was teaching keyboards to a group of year sevens. Some of the other rooms had one-on-one music lessons, a few were dark and a couple had been booked by groups or individuals for solo practice.

Jay thought he'd misread the practice timetable when he reached the last room and saw the lights on, but nobody at the drum kit. Then a kid stood up just inside the window and made him jump as their eyes met through the glass less than twenty centimetres apart.

Babatunde Okuma had extremely dark skin and gold-rimmed aviator-style glasses with green tinted lenses. He wore a black hoodie over his school shirt and tie, with the hood drawn tight around his face. He was Jay's height, but about three times the chest measurement.

'Sorry, wrong room,' Jay said, smiling weakly before scuttling away. There was nowhere to go, except under a little canopy with metal ducts that vented the smell of stale food from the back of the school kitchens.

Jay's brain spun as he stood there. Why had he chickened out when he'd seen Babatunde? Partly it was because the kid looked pretty menacing, but he was also torn about the whole idea of flirting with a new drummer.

Tristan *was* rubbish. But what came first, the quality of Brontobyte's music or their nine-year friendship?

Jay's life goal was to play in a band and make his living as a rock musician. But that was a dream, whereas having mates like Tristan and Salman was what made school life bearable. Someone to talk to, to sit with in lessons, hang out with at lunch-time and not be the poor loner who gets picked off by the bad guys.

Jay took three steps towards home before the drumming started. It was loud, even though the practice rooms were soundproofed. Anyone with ten fingers can play a guitar or keyboard, but drums also have a physical element. You need power to hit them hard and endurance to keep hitting over the course of a two-hour jamming session or gig.

Drawn to the noise, Jay crept back towards the glass. Babatunde was on the kit Tristan had used in the competition the day before, but it sounded a million times better. He was side on to the window and had no idea Jay was watching as his arms flailed, head rocking from left to right. Sweat drizzled off his brow as the oversized sunglasses slid down his nose.

When Jay opened the door the noise crushed his eardrums. Babatunde wasn't just good, he was *epic*. No reasonable person wouldn't want him in their band. Jay stood at the edge of the room for a full minute before the drummer looked around.

When Babatunde saw his company, he showboated by twirling his sticks between his fingers without losing the beat, then he threw them down and played the toms bare-handed.

Jay's ears rang when the noise stopped. Babatunde peeled back his hood, revealing streams of sweat running through his close-cropped hair. After turning his stool towards Jay, he pushed the sunglasses back up his nose and scowled.

He looked like some crazed military dictator and Jay suspected he was about to get killed for interrupting the practice, but Babatunde raised one eyebrow mischievously.

'So you decided to come back,' he said, his voice as strong as his enormous arms.

Jay was nervous as hell. 'I just . . . I was just walking by. I heard you play and I had to come in and listen. I didn't mean to interrupt. You're a *mental* drummer.'

'Appreciated, Jay,' Babatunde said, with a nod.

'How'd you know my name?'

'Mr Currie said you might drop by to hear me.'

'Ever been in a band?' Jay asked.

'A couple,' Babatunde said. 'But they never took it serious. It was all about swaggering and trying to impress girls, so I quit. I'm about the music.'

Jay smiled, feeling like he'd found a soul mate. 'I know *exactly* what you mean. There's a lot of posers out there, but the only thing I've ever wanted to do is be in a band. God knows what I'll do with my life if it doesn't work out.'

'Same as,' Babatunde nodded, as he bent forwards to pick up his sticks. 'Your band's Brontosaurus, right? I've heard people say you're pretty good.'

'Bronto*byte*,' Jay corrected. 'Don't ask why, it's a shit name. Our singer Salman has a weird voice, but I really like it. We've got a bass player called Alfie, who's a titchy little year seven, but he kicks ass. I like to think I'm a pretty decent lead guitar. Only trouble is, our drummer Tristan sounds like a drunk man falling over metal dustbins.'

'So Tristan's getting the boot?'

Jay looked awkward. 'He's a mate. He can sing a bit and play some keyboards. I'd like to find a way of keeping him in the band, but getting him off that drum stool. Do you think you'd be interested?'

'Definitely,' Babatunde agreed. 'I'd have to get to know your music, but if the suit fits I'll wear it.'

Jay pulled a fancy Android phone out of his blazer. 'I've got to break this thing gently to the others,' he explained. 'Do you mind if I make a little video of you drumming? The microphone on this isn't great, but they'll be able to see your moves.'

12. Shameful Display

Boarders at Yellowcote were allowed to wear casual clothes out of school hours. Dylan looked pretty cool in Vans, baggy jeans and a striped Abercrombie polo shirt, but the smart clothes papered over cracks. He felt like death as he dragged himself towards the music block, with a split lip, cricked neck, torn stomach muscles and massive stud-shaped gashes down his right calf.

'What brings you here?' Miss Hudson said cheerfully, when Dylan found her in the hallway outside her office, running off bright yellow sheets on the photocopier.

Hudson was the head of music. She was nearly forty, but wore the years well. She had big frizzy hair and armfuls of silver bangles. She always walked around barefoot and Dylan – along with about a hundred other horny teens starved of girls their own age – had a bit of a thing for her.

'Do you mind if we talk for a minute?' he asked, trying to

win sympathy by sounding needy and depressed, while competing with the noise of the photocopier.

Hudson seemed suspicious. 'What about?'

'I want to get back into the music programme,' he explained. 'I *love* music. Somehow my life doesn't feel complete without it.'

'Is that so?' Hudson said, smiling slightly. 'The thing is, Dylan, I already gave you every chance to stay in the orchestra. You had countless informal warnings about your behaviour during class time. On two occasions I even sat you down in my office to discuss your attitude.'

Dylan nodded solemnly. 'Miss, I know I didn't work hard enough and I mucked around during orchestra practice. But you kicking me out has really set me straight. I swear, if you let me back in I'll practise *really* hard and never backchat or mess about.'

The photocopier had finished its run. Miss Hudson grabbed the warm yellow sheets and turned towards her office, making a gesture for Dylan to follow.

'Close the door,' she said firmly.

There were mounds of different-coloured sheets on Miss Hudson's desk and she began taking one of each colour and fixing the multicoloured bunch together with a staple.

'Dylan, you've had your second chance. And your third, your fourth, fifth and probably sixth. You're a talented musician, but frankly you're bone idle. In case you haven't noticed, this school devotes a lot more resources to sport than it does to my department. I have to focus what

I have on musicians who apply their talent, instead of squandering it.'

'But, miss,' Dylan said pleadingly, before his teacher cut him dead.

'If you want to be reconsidered for admission to the music programme, you can apply along with everyone else when you start year ten in September.'

'Oh come on,' Dylan grovelled. 'Music is my life.'

'Well, you could have fooled me over the past two terms,' Miss Hudson laughed.

'I'm not that bad, am I?' Dylan asked, giving her big pleading eyes.

'I suppose this sudden burst of enthusiasm for the school orchestra has nothing whatsoever to do with the conversation I had with Mr Jurgens in the staffroom this morning?'

Dylan's heart sank as he realised she'd been playing him along.

'Piet tells me you were an outstanding rugby player in year seven,' Miss Hudson said. 'It's almost as if you've chosen to specialise in wasting your talents.'

'OK,' Dylan said. 'I admit it, I'm *desperate* to get out of rugby. It's freezing cold and it's muddy. I haven't played for two years, so I'm unfit and the other members of the team take great pleasure reminding me with their metal-studded boots.

'What I don't get is, how can it be against the law for a teacher to hit me with a belt or some little stick, but nobody bats an eyelid if Jurgens sends me out to play a game where some nut job gets to splat me in the mud and dance on my head?'

Miss Hudson could see Dylan's point, but it didn't change her mind. 'Dylan, I take no pleasure from the fact that Mr Jurgens is making you play rugby, but I warned you a dozen times. You made your own bed.'

'I'm begging you, miss,' Dylan pleaded, as he put his hands together in prayer. 'I'll do *anything*. I'll sweep the floor. I'll make you coffee. I'll do your photocopying, tidy up, vacuum, wash your car, run your errands, worship the ground you walk on. You've *got* to save me, miss. I'm a musician, not a battering-ram.'

'Dylan,' Miss Hudson said firmly, stifling a slight smile as she continued dividing and stapling the coloured sheets. 'If I let you back in the orchestra after kicking you out, I'd lose the respect of the other members. Mr Jurgens wouldn't be too happy either.'

Dylan sighed, then smiled as he had another idea. 'You don't earn much as a teacher, do you?'

Miss Hudson looked startled. 'I don't think my salary is any of your business.'

'I can easily get my hands on ten grand of my dad's money,' Dylan said. 'He's rich. He'll never even notice. Think about it. You could buy a new car, or do up your house. All you'd have to do to make ten grand is get me out of rugby.'

Miss Hudson laughed noisily. 'You're trying to bribe me?'

'No messing about,' Dylan said. 'I can easily lay my hands on ten grand.'

'I'd get sacked and you'd be expelled. And if I mentioned what you just suggested to one of the senior staff you'd be in *serious* trouble.'

'More serious than getting stomped under a size ten boot?'

'Dylan, stop being so melodramatic. You're only talking about a few games of rugby. You make it sound like Mr Jurgens is going to chain you up and pour boiling oil over you.'

Dylan ground his teeth with frustration. 'There must be *something* you want, or something I can do for you.'

Miss Hudson sighed. 'The only thing I want right now is for you to leave this office. You're being ridiculous.'

'I'll kill myself then,' Dylan said desperately.

'I don't happen to find that very funny,' Miss Hudson said, as she put her hands on her hips. 'I've had to deal with depressed and suicidal pupils in the past and it's not something to joke about. And besides, if you're suicidal, you'll need the school counsellor not the music department.'

'Do you think that might work?' Dylan asked seriously.

Miss Hudson finally lost her patience and raised her voice. 'Dylan, get out of here! I have a million things to do. There's a prep school parents' evening on Friday, I've got a concert in two weeks, we've lost a tuba and my five-year-old is having a birthday party on Saturday.'

'I could help with all of that if you let me,' Dylan said.

'Scram!' Miss Hudson shouted as she pointed at the door.

'I don't want to see one bleached hair of you until winter term.'

She slammed a set of papers down on the pile, causing the rest to topple off the edge of the desk and spill across the floor. Dylan dived down on one knee and started scooping them up.

'I'll do it,' Miss Hudson growled.

Dylan finally got the message and backed off. His thighs ached and, as he used the desk as a lever to stand up, Miss Hudson saw a dark patch on the back of his jeans.

'Is that blood?' she asked, craning her neck.

Dylan looked behind and saw that blood had soaked through the denim where he'd been studded.

'You should probably go and see the nurse,' Miss Hudson said.

Dylan pulled up the denim, revealing a partial scab and trails of blood running down from the wound and soaking into the top of his sock. 'Mr Jurgens reckons it's only a scratch.'

Miss Hudson felt a twinge of compassion. 'Go and get that leg looked at,' she repeated, before sighing. 'And you'll have to put up with rugby training for now, but I'll see what I can do when you start year ten in September.'

13. Wei and Wei

Summer had never paid much attention to the vaulted brick building opposite her school, sandwiched between a Nissan dealership and a boarded-up carpet store. From outside it was bland, with the name of the long-deceased *Dudley to Stourbridge Tram Corporation* carved into the limestone frontage. The only clue to its present role was an engraved sign beside the main door which read *Wei & Wei Architects RIBA.*

Summer gawped at the large space, as Lucy led her inside. The vaulted roof of the former tram shed had been carved open with skylights. The two dozen employees of Wei & Wei worked on large-screened Macs, amidst trendy office furniture, split between the cobbled ground floor and modern yellow gantry that ran around two sides.

Lucy, Michelle and Coco led Summer past a huge wooden meeting table under the main skylight, surrounded by architectural models.

'Hello, girls!' an Asian man said, as he took turns to kiss his daughters. 'Lovely to see you again, Coco.'

Mr Wei was like a fantasy dad: tall and healthy-looking without being too scary, and he dressed well, in handmade loafers, chinos and a striped shirt with the sleeves rolled up. Summer didn't know about watches, but the chronograph on his arm must have cost a few bob.

'This is Summer,' Lucy said, as she held out crossed fingers. 'She's got a great voice and we're hoping she's going to be our singer.'

'They've been hunting for a singer since last Christmas,' Mr Wei said, as he reached out to shake Summer's hand. 'Call me Lee.'

Summer was slightly awed. 'I had no idea this place was right next to our school. Everything else round here is so grotty.'

'You like it?' Mr Wei smiled.

Summer nodded. She wasn't sure what you were supposed to say to an architect and finally settled on, 'Are any of your buildings famous?'

Mr Wei held his hand out towards the models on the surrounding tables. 'Not much call for museums and skyscrapers here in the West Midlands. We grind out a living doing retail parks, leisure centres, that sort of thing.'

'You and Uncle Mike won that award for the eco houses,' Lucy noted.

'It's handy being so close to our school,' Summer said.

Mr Wei laughed and pointed at Michelle. 'It is, the

number of times I have to go speak with madam's teachers.'

'I'm officially bored,' Michelle said, as she tugged Summer's arm. 'Let's go make noise.'

'Nice to meet you,' Summer said, as they headed away. Then she turned to Lucy. 'So you live here?'

'You'll see in a second,' Lucy said.

The back of the refurbished shed opened out into a shaggy lawn, rutted with the old tram tracks. Beyond this was a car park and a row of modern houses, with large glass balconies and living roofs. They looked like something you'd see in a magazine and made Summer even more paranoid that she'd never fit in.

To Summer's surprise they didn't head for the houses, but towards a narrow shed, designed to house a double-deck tram.

'This is the pit,' Lucy explained as they entered a brightly lit space.

A couple of staff members sat at a long dining table drinking coffees. At the far end was a pool table with purple felt and along the side wall were coffee machines and glass-fronted refrigerators filled with water, Coke and juice.

'There's a kitchen out back,' Lucy explained. 'They do a cracking lunch for all the staff. Our mum can't cook so we eat here loads too.'

Summer smiled. 'Your dad must be a great boss. It must be really cool working here.'

'It's a con,' Michelle grunted. 'He shells out for a trendy office and a free lunch. In return he gets obedient little worker drones who earn a pittance for twelve-hour days.'

The four girls reached the top of a narrow stone staircase, and headed into a basement. Only Coco had to duck for the *Mind Your Head* sign.

Lucy explained to Summer as she flipped a pair of light switches, 'This was the inspection pit. In the old days there was no floor above. The trams would have driven in and mechanics would have gone down here to do repairs and stuff.'

Summer smiled as a row of uplighters illuminated a long space less than three metres wide. The pit had a rubber floor and bare brick walls covered with framed music posters. Lucy's drum kit was set up, along with guitars, amplifiers, two Yamaha keyboards and a recording console linked to an iMac. There were dozens of beanbags spread about and the place was littered with clothes, CDs, magazines and empty drink bottles.

'This rocks,' Summer grinned, scarcely able to believe how lucky some kids were.

Michelle had gone straight to the far end and fired up iTunes to play a Sonic Youth track. The computer was linked to a powerful amp and studio monitors, making the sound deafening.

'Shut that off,' Lucy shouted, as she threw a cushion at her sister's head.

'I'm getting my groove,' Michelle shouted.

Coco was the last one down, because she'd stopped by the fridges to grab bottles of drink.

Michelle turned Sonic Youth down to background level as Summer dropped her backpack and sank on to a leather beanbag.

'We've been working on a bunch of songs,' Lucy explained to her, as she passed over a pile of lyric sheets. 'Mostly covers, but also some stuff of our own. I don't know exactly what the best way to do this is. Usually we just sort of stop and start and yell at each other until it seems to work. Does that sound OK to you?'

Summer nodded as she unscrewed a lid on a bottle of sparkling water. There was a hiss as the water spewed up over her hand and spattered the lyric sheets. 'Balls . . . Sorry.'

Michelle came to her aid, drying off the pages with someone's discarded T-shirt. When she handed them back she made sure that the lyrics to a song called 'Bears, Bikes, Bats and Sex' were on top.

'I think we should start with this one,' Michelle said.

Summer laughed as she read through the lyrics:

> Bears, bikes, bats and sex,
> Dreaming in my bed,
> Of a boy named Mike,
> He's got a motorbike.
>
> On the following night,
> I get in a fight,
> With a polar bear,
> It's icy out there.

Black bats all around,
As I dream away,
Mike saves the day,
I let him have his way.

Bears, bikes, bats and sex,
Dreaming in my bed,
The dawn awakens me,
I must get up and pee.

When I get to school,
I realise Mike is real,
He's in my physics class,
But he's a total arse.

Summer looked at Michelle. 'You wrote this?'

'How'd you know that?'

'Wild guess,' Summer said, smirking as Coco switched on guitar amplifiers which filled the air with a faint buzzing sound.

'It's kind of a fast song,' Lucy explained, as she sat behind her drum kit and began spitting out words. '*Bears, bikes, bats and sex. Dreaming in my bed. Of a boy named Mike. He's got a motorbike.* Try making it really heavy and in your face.'

'How about I just try getting the words in the right place to start with?' Summer said as she realised it would have been easier to have started with a song she already knew.

Coco came across holding an acoustic guitar and squatted

on the next beanbag. 'I can play the tune through a couple of times so you get a feel for it?'

'OK,' Summer said, then she cleared her throat and sang a couple of lines just to get her vocal chords going. '*I'm on the top of the world. I'm on the top of the world.*'

Her rich tone filled the cramped space. Summer felt embarrassed as Lucy and Michelle grinned at one another.

'What's wrong?' Summer asked.

'Nothing,' Lucy laughed. 'It's just, when I try and sing like that it sounds awful. You open your mouth and it's like, I don't know . . .'

Coco finished Lucy's sentence. '*Angelic* or something.'

'Exactly,' Lucy nodded.

Summer put her hands over her face. 'I can't sing if you embarrass me.'

Coco tapped a beat on the side of the acoustic guitar and began the song.

'Hold up!' Michelle shouted, as she sat over by the computer making a frantic series of mouse clicks. 'I want to capture the moment: the first sounds made by Industrial Scale Slaughter with the line-up that went on to sell ten billion records.'

'Why so few?' Coco laughed, as Summer studied the lyric sheet.

Coco played and Summer started to sing. She tried singing fast and aggressive like Lucy had asked, but it sounded awful with an acoustic guitar, rather than a full band. After one verse Summer reverted to her regular singing voice. The high tempo meant it took less than ninety seconds to get through the five short verses.

'Well?' Summer asked nervously, as she looked at the others.

Slow claps came from the top of the staircase as Mr Wei walked down. 'Awesome,' he said. 'I think you've found your singer.'

Then he ducked as Michelle's trainer skimmed over his head. 'Get out of our pit, you nosy sod!'

'What did you call me?' Mr Wei shouted. But he was smiling so you could tell he wasn't really angry as he hurdled a beanbag and snatched Michelle's ankle. 'I seem to remember a certain little girl being quite ticklish around here.'

Mr Wei ran his fingernail along the length of Michelle's sole, making her whole body shudder.

'Dad, no!' Michelle begged.

But Mr Wei couldn't resist having another go before freeing his daughter and then making a lunge like he was going to dig her in the ribs.

Lucy and Coco laughed as Michelle dived under a beanbag so that her dad couldn't get at her. Summer drank some water, tipped her head back and felt happy. It was like a door had opened into a new world.

14. Cutlery Incident

Dylan was eating lamb curry in the Yellowcote dining room. He always sat in the same spot near the window, as far as he could get from the high-pitched prep school voices in the room next door. Ed often sat with Dylan, but he wasn't around so Dylan was listening to Nirvana's 'Unplugged' album on his iPhone when a lad called Owen came over and offered his hand.

Dylan shook, noticing the hand's massiveness and the fact that half a rugby pitch was packed under its fingernails.

'Welcome back to the squad,' Owen said, trying to sound extra friendly as Dylan took his headphones out. 'Jurgens runs a pretty tough practice, don't he? I'm sorry I tramped the back of your leg.'

'Didn't even know it was you,' Dylan said, with a shrug. 'I was face down in a puddle at the time.'

'Our squad was piss poor this year,' Owen explained. 'Played twelve, lost seven. We've got loads of big guys, but no flair players. I had an eye on you today. You're weak and out of shape, but you showed flashes of brilliance. I can see why Jurgens is so keen to have you back. A creative player like you could turn games for us.'

Dylan laughed. 'I'm at my most creative when someone your size is trying to crunch me.'

Owen couldn't work out if this was an insult. He processed for a few seconds before continuing. 'I came over here because me and the guys are hitting the weight room at seven. We usually have a laugh and you *really* need to bulk up a bit and lose the puppy fat.'

'I'm quite fond of my puppy fat,' Dylan said shaking his head, as he bit the last cube of meat off his fork. 'Besides, I can barely walk.'

Owen pulled his T-shirt up to his chin, showing off a six-pack and big pectoral muscles.

'You need to get hard like me,' Owen advised. 'I haven't grown in almost a year, but I've packed on ten kilos of muscle. It's like armour plating. We play in a tough league. Everyone is pumping weights. They'll whack you a couple of times at the start of a game. If they sense weakness they'll smash you every chance they get.'

Dylan was slowly resigning himself to playing rugby. But that didn't mean he wanted to spend his spare time hanging around with his squad mates. He wanted to get back to Kurt Cobain singing about birds and tried to think of the quickest way to get rid of Owen without offending him.

'Maybe another night,' Dylan suggested. 'I've got stuff arranged with other people.'

Owen's tone suddenly turned aggressive. 'What people?' he sneered, before thumping the table. 'We're your people now, Dylan.'

The intrusion was starting to piss Dylan off and he returned the anger. 'I don't want to play rugby, Owen,' he snapped. 'I can't stop Jurgens making a monkey out of me in practice. He can even pick me for the squad and make me waste my Saturdays sitting on a bench, but he can't make me play *well*, can he?'

'What you saying?' Owen asked, as he leaned across, pressing his bulk against Dylan's side.

Dylan wasn't sure where his big mouth was taking him, but it kept on talking. 'If Jurgens makes me play, I might have a couple of little accidents, you know? Maybe the ball will get dropped, or I'll pass it into the wrong hands.'

Dylan felt a hand on the back of his skull. Before he could react, Owen pushed his head forwards until it smacked against his plate. The blow made cutlery clatter. Boys at surrounding tables looked and laughed as Dylan sat up with grains of rice stuck to his forehead.

Dylan moaned as starbursts erupted in front of his eyes.

'Do you think you can mess with Mr Jurgens, plus all of us lads, and come off best?' Owen hissed.

Dylan glanced around and was disappointed to see that the only teachers were on the staff tables down the opposite end of the hall. He wasn't an aggressive person, but a cornered animal is always the most dangerous and the voice in his head reminding him that this was all his own stupid fault wasn't helping.

'Eat your pudding,' Owen growled, as he placed his hand on Dylan's head again to remind him of what might happen if he talked back. 'Find some kit and get over to the weight room for seven o'clock. If you don't show we'll pay you a visit after lights out.'

If Dylan gave in to the threat he'd be Owen's bitch. And he reckoned it was better to stick up for himself here and now than alone in his bedroom, or surrounded by thugs in the weight room.

'Guess I haven't got any choice,' Dylan said submissively. 'Can I just ask one question?'

Owen smiled, enjoying the fear in Dylan's voice. 'What?'

'Does this hurt?'

On *this*, Dylan clutched his fork and thrust it deep into Owen's thigh. Then he stood and tipped Owen sideways out of his chair. Boys at surrounding tables *ooh*ed and *ahh*ed as Dylan bolted down the hall towards the teachers.

'You're dead!' Owen roared, as he sprang up and started running with the fork still embedded in his thigh.

The tables were closely spaced and Dylan had no power in his aching legs as he dodged between them. Owen was faster and had the advantage of a pre-cleared path.

Despite getting knocked down and being in pain, Owen got his arms around Dylan's waist and tackled him less than five metres from where they'd started. Dylan hit his chin on a tabletop and smacked the floor hard, landing with someone's trainer in front of his nose.

Owen hadn't considered the effects of tackling with a fork embedded in his leg. The four metal prongs twisted as he landed, enlarging his wound and sending a spasm of agony through his body. Dylan swung around at the shoulders, smashing his elbow hard into Owen's nose as the big lad roared with pain.

'Break it up,' a teacher shouted, as kids sprang up from their seats, letting him through.

A scrawny year ten at the adjacent table squealed. Dylan rolled on to his back and saw that the kid's face was spattered with Owen's blood. He'd fluked such a perfect elbow on Owen's nose that it looked like he'd been shot in the face.

Dylan was braced for hard punches or a knee in the balls, but his opponent was dazed. Owen crawled forwards, taking a hand up from a sixth former before stumbling into the arms of a scowling teacher. Dylan's collar got grabbed and the teacher yanked him to his feet.

'Wilton, headmaster's office, right now!'

A female teacher had cut through to the other side of the table and knelt over Owen as Dylan got frogmarched out of the room with a hundred eyeballs on him. 'It's a bloody mess here,' she shouted urgently. 'Who's got van keys? I'll drive him straight up to the infirmary.'

15. Sausage Dog

The headmaster had gone home, so Dylan's judgement had to wait until morning. He blocked his bedroom door with a chair and stacked a bunch of heavy stuff on it, so he'd at least get an audible warning if a dozen vengeful lads steamed in to clobber him during the night.

His chin ached where he'd hit the dining table, competing in the pain stakes with the weeping scabs on the back of his leg. He thought about running away, but the school was miles out of the city and just walking up to his room had half killed him.

Dylan needed sleep, but he was too wound up. When he wasn't worrying about the possible arrival of the rugby squad, he held imaginary telephone conversations with his dad.

Dad, I've been expelled.

Hi, Dad, there's been a touch of trouble at school.

How's your golf going? Birdie on the sixth hole, way to go, Dad!

Err, just so that you know, I stabbed some kid with a fork, busted his nose and for some reason everyone seems quite miffed about it.

The last one made Dylan laugh for two seconds, before he heard someone walking by in the hall outside. He grabbed his trombone ready to whack them if they came through the door, but they walked on by.

*

Summer got woken by the toilet cistern in the flat next door. It was Friday, 7:30 a.m., and she caught a whiff of BO from her own armpit as she stretched into a yawn. Low sun blazed through thin curtains as she swung out of bed, placing her feet to avoid new pumps and a carrier bag stuffed with clothes.

The gifts were from Lucy, who'd gone off while Summer learned a song with Coco and returned with mounds of cheap Primark stuff that she'd bought but never worn. It was embarrassing being so raggedy that people gave you bags of cheap clothes without asking, but Summer had too many chafe marks to turn down plimsolls and bras that fitted.

The rehearsal had been the most fun she'd had in ages. Coco and Lucy raved about her singing, and spoke about changing Industrial Scale Slaughter's sound to fit with her voice. The only downer was Michelle being Michelle and throwing tantrums whenever she got bored or something didn't go her way.

Nothing overlooked Summer's fourth-floor bedroom, so she whipped her curtain across and stood naked at the window, enjoying sun on her neck and goose bumps as she touched the cold glass.

Her new friends made her feel liked, comfortable and grown up. She worried that for them the novelty of her friendship would wear off, but for now it felt great knowing that she mattered to someone other than her nan.

*

Breakfast was always chaos at Jay's flat. Kai was being even more annoying than usual, while a screaming battle between five-year-old June and six-year-old Hank was enough to make Jay head out early and walk two streets across to Salman's house.

His mate was shirtless when he opened the door, so Jay waited in the hallway while Salman brushed teeth and hunted down a missing school tie.

'I heard a story about you last night,' Salman said, grinning ear to ear as the two lads walked out of the front gate and swerved around the postman's trolley.

'Did you?' Jay said weakly, already pretty sure what it would be.

'Something involving naughtiness between your mum and a police officer in the back of a stolen van,' Salman explained. 'Roughly nine months before you were born.'

Jay tutted. 'I wish my mum could keep her trap shut.'

'Shamim told my brother,' Salman laughed. 'It's *such* a good story. I always wondered why you were weedy while your brothers scare the shit out of everyone.'

'Don't spread it at school,' Jay begged. 'If Tristan finds out, I'll never hear the end of it.'

'How much is my silence worth?' Salman teased.

Jay pulled a bunch of coins out of his pocket. 'Forty-six pence and my eternal gratitude.'

'Nah,' Salman laughed. 'I won't take your money. It's gonna be *too* sweet dangling this over your head.'

Jay sighed as the pair turned a corner. 'I wish I could be hard like my brothers, just for one day,' he moaned. 'I'd love it if Tristan opened his big gob and I could just slap him down.'

'Get some steroids,' Salman joked. 'Like Cartman in that *South Park* episode.'

'I *love* that one,' Jay said. 'I think I've still got your *South Park* DVDs.'

'So are you really getting involved in Mrs Hinde's mural painting?'

Jay shook his head and dug his phone out of his blazer. 'I went to see a drummer.'

Salman turned Jay's phone over in his hand admiringly. 'This handset kicks ass. How'd a pov like you get the cash for one of these?'

'Only cost thirty quid,' Jay smiled. 'A guy who drinks in my aunt's pub ram-raided a Carphone Warehouse.'

'Can he get me one?' Salman asked, as Jay took his phone back and set it to play the video of Babatunde.

'It was months ago. Last time I saw him he was flogging off satnavs,' Jay said. 'Now, watch this badass drumming.'

There were reflections all over the screen, so Salman stopped walking and made a visor with his hands. It took a second to recognise that it was one of the practice rooms at their school and even through the tiny phone speaker it sounded impressive.

'I think I've heard about this guy,' Salman smiled. 'He's a new kid. Year nine.'

'Babatunde,' Jay explained. 'I met him last night. He's not in a band or anything. He looks kind of psycho, but he seems really nice.'

Salman saw where this was going and sucked air between his teeth as he passed back the phone. 'I wouldn't want to be in your shoes if Tristan finds out you've gone behind his back looking for another drummer.'

'We've got to do it the right way,' Jay said, as they started walking again. 'Alfie won't go against his brother, but you and me could pull it off if we approach Tristan together. We'll tell him that we don't want him to leave the band, but he can play the keyboards or something.'

Salman turned up his nose. 'Tristan's not gonna buy that. None of our songs even have keyboard parts.'

'We can add some. I can write new songs.'

'Tristan can hardly play the keyboards though.'

Jay laughed. 'He can hardly play the drums and that hasn't stopped him.'

Salman burst out laughing. 'You're so harsh. He's not *that* bad.'

'But it's a stone-cold fact, Salman. You can't be a good band with a shit drummer.'

'You're too serious,' Salman said. 'Us three go back to the dawn of time.'

'I know,' Jay admitted. 'I've thought the same thing myself. But music's really important to me. You, me and Alfie are good enough to be getting some little gigs and winning competitions like the one on Wednesday. We shouldn't be losing to a bunch of jerks singing over a backing track.'

'I tell you what,' Salman said. 'If you raise it with Tristan, I'll cover your back. Just say you've met another drummer and you think we should give him a trial. We'll see how Tristan reacts, but I'm not prepared to start World War Three over this.'

'Right,' Jay said, though Salman's tepid reaction wasn't what he'd been hoping for.

*

Sir Donald Donaldson had been headmaster of Yellowcote school for more than three hundred years. Or at least he looked like he had.

He always wore a traditional black teacher's gown and trailed a whiff of Scotch whisky at whatever time of day you encountered him. He wafted in at eight thirty, driving the school's ancient Bentley, with his long-bodied dachshund Max curled up on the passenger seat.

The headmaster's eyebrows had a compelling hugeness and Dylan imagined birds and squirrels living in them as he sat across the elderly man's desk. To Dylan's left was the chief sports master, Mr Burton, and the pair waited in silence as Sir Donald flipped through the folder containing Dylan's personal records and school reports.

'Not much,' Sir Donald said finally. 'Some boys root themselves into the history of our school. Others pass by, scarcely noticed. Barring a rugger citation from year seven, you seem to be one of the latter.'

Dylan wasn't sure if he was supposed to respond. He'd been at the school for almost three years, and hadn't spoken to Sir Donald since his prep school interview with his father and stepmother.

'Nothing to say, eh?' Sir Donald said, unscrewing the nib of a fountain-pen before deciding not to write anything. 'The question here is one of discipline, Mr Burton. Far too many incidents with members of the rugby squads of late.'

Mr Burton nodded solemnly. 'They're aggressive on the pitch. It can be hard for a young man to temper that, Sir Donald.'

'Well, I'm thoroughly fed up with it,' Sir Donald said, as he thrust out his arms so that his cape hung down like wings. 'Sick and tired of incidents involving boys who play rugger. The game is important, but I fear that these exotic coaches you're bringing in are teaching our boys to win at the expense of their humanity. I remember when Yellowcote only played rugger in the winter term and to my mind we were the better for it.'

Dylan was relieved that it was the sports master on the defensive, rather than himself.

'Our leagues are very competitive, Sir Donald,' Mr Burton said. 'All of the top schools train elite athletes year-round and we'd be unable to attract the very best players if we didn't offer international-standard coaching.'

'But we're here to create distinguished young men, not machines for playing rugger,' Sir Donald said, raising his voice slightly and giving an impressive eyebrow flicker. 'Incident after incident. More than a dozen altercations involving rugby players within the last year. It *will* stop. I'm going to make an example of these two boys that will be adhered to for future incidents, however minor.'

Dylan had been about ninety per cent sure he was going to be expelled, but he still gripped his chair's velvet arms, awaiting Sir Donald's verdict.

'There will be a clear line in the sand,' Sir Donald said, as he leaned sharply across the desk towards Dylan. 'Both yourself and Owen Carter will be banned from representing this school in competitive sports and taking part in all levels of rugby for two years.'

While Dylan found it hard not to smile, Mr Burton was outraged.

'Sir Donald, with the greatest respect, Owen Carter is an *outstanding* player. He may even represent Scotland someday. If we stop him playing he'll be snapped up by any one of a dozen schools, here or south of the border.'

'Let them have him,' Sir Donald said, as he wagged his finger in Dylan's face. 'And let every one of your former team-mates know that we're returning to the old-fashioned system. Only boys of unblemished character will represent Yellowcote at sport. This win-at-all-costs mentality has done us no credit and I draw a line under it forthwith.'

Dylan nodded with appropriate solemnity. The old buffer clearly had no idea that his training session the day before was the first one he'd attended since his citation at the end of year seven.

'I respect and understand your decision, Sir Donald,' Dylan said.

Staying calm was some feat because on the inside Dylan was punching the air and screaming *yessssssss* at the top of his voice.

16. Indian Microwave Platter

Tristan and Alfie Jopling lived in a semi-detached house in Hampstead, a posh area a couple of kilometres from Jay's and Salman's neighbourhood. Their dad was managing director of a big office supplies company. Mrs Jopling had her own business selling fancy wedding invitation cards, though it seemed more like a hobby because whenever Jay visited she always had time to fuss over her boys.

The three-storey home was a mad outpouring of Mrs Jopling's over-the-top taste. From her orange Porsche Cayenne on the driveway, through rooms filled with frills, tassels, flock wallpapers, marbled paint effects and a sixty-grand rustic kitchen with wood-fired oven and dual microwaves so she could heat two ready meals at once.

One of these microwaves was nuking a platter of Indian nibbles, as Mrs Jopling stood by the counter top unpacking a Waitrose sandwich platter and tipping hand-cooked crisps into a wooden bowl.

When the microwave pinged, she loaded the sizzling nibbles on a tray, along with the crisps, sandwiches, cans of Coke and bottles of fruit juice. Tray in hand, she kicked the back door open with her furry slipper and trotted over the lawn towards the Canadian-style log cabin, where Brontobyte were jamming.

The four lads usually messed around jamming random tunes, sometimes giving up and playing video games if they got bored. The cabin had been built as a den for Alfie and Tristan, complete with heating, electricity and the old TV and hi-fi from before the living room got refurbished.

Alfie saw his mum coming and slid the glass door open. Mrs Jopling put the tray on a plastic table. The music stopped and the wolves descended, grabbing handfuls of food and cramming it down the way only teenage boys can.

Salman got a tap on the wrist as he lunged. 'They're Alfie's,' Mrs Jopling said. 'Made special with no mayonnaise.'

She sat on a plastic garden chair, knowing her welcome wouldn't outlast the food. The four lads had all spent a day at school and left their muddy shoes at the door. The cabin wasn't well ventilated and they'd all been jumping around. The result was a stench of trainers and pits, but Mrs Jopling kind of liked it. She lived for her boys. She liked their company and it made her sad that they were turning into men and growing away from her.

'So, what are you working on?' Mrs Jopling asked.

Tristan rolled his eyes. She always asked the same lame

questions. 'Just putting a couple of new songs together.'

Jay baulked at this, but didn't say anything. They'd been here over an hour and all they'd done was muck about. He'd tried getting them to practise 'Christine' after the disaster on Wednesday, but Tristan got pissy and the others ignored him.

'You always look after us so well, Mrs Jopling,' Salman said, as he scoffed a tuna mayo sandwich and cradled onion bhajis in his palm like eggs in a nest.

'Always my pleasure, Salman. How's your mum by the way? She had that foot operation, didn't she?'

The boys had been friends for so long that all their parents knew each other.

'She's OK,' Salman said. 'Cyst was benign. She's back at work.'

'You should get a job, Mum,' Alfie said. 'You must get bored, sitting around the house all day.'

Mrs Jopling looked furious. 'I have my own business and you lot to look after. I swear you two think I just sit on my backside all day.'

Salman smiled. 'And Brontobyte wouldn't get fed properly if you were out working.'

'I think my aunt Rachel's looking for a new barmaid,' Jay said, making it sound genuine but knowing the offer would get up Mrs Jopling's snobby nose.

'I think I'm rather highly qualified for bar work,' she snapped. 'I'm a certified nail technician *and* I did a business administration course.'

Alfie chimed in. 'And Dad says you've got a PhD in shopping.'

Anger flashed across Mrs Jopling's face as she wagged her pointing finger at Alfie. 'Don't think you're too old for a whack on the bum, mister.'

Salman made a whip-cracking sound and laughed. 'I definitely think your boys need stronger discipline.'

'Too right,' Mrs Jopling said, smiling with bleached teeth as she stood up. 'Anyway, I expect I've outstayed my welcome. Bring the tray and the empties back to the house when you're finished, and open a sodding window. It reeks to high heaven in here.'

The boys had all been drinking Coke and as soon as Mrs Jopling was gone, Tristan did a huge belch.

Alfie looked at Salman. 'Why do you always suck up to our mum?'

'I'm nice to anyone who feeds me,' Salman said, as he rubbed his fat belly. 'You wouldn't get food platters at my house. You two don't know you're born.'

Tristan ripped off another belch before speaking. 'I reckon you fancy her.'

'Wouldn't say no,' Salman said cheekily. 'Your mum might be thirty-whatever but she's got an *epic* rack.'

Tristan and Alfie were suitably outraged. 'Shut up!' Tristan shouted. 'Mind you, you're so hopeless around girls I bet you'd bonk anything that hasn't got a dick.'

'And quite a few things *with* one,' Jay added.

Salman made a little *nee-nah* police siren noise, which

shut Jay up.

'Mum's tits are fake,' Alfie grinned. 'Cost my dad six grand per boob to get them done.'

'Don't spread our family business,' Tristan said angrily.

'Besides, Tristan,' Salman laughed. 'You can't afford to be so fussy yourself. You snogged that girl one time and you act like you're bloody Casanova.'

Jay threw his empty Coke can at the food tray. 'My cousin Erin has a thing for you, Tristan,' he said. 'You should ask her out.'

Tristan shrugged. 'She's a girl and I'm a total stud muffin. It's only natural that she has a thing for me.'

'You're so full of it,' Alfie laughed.

'I mostly like older girls, anyway,' Tristan said.

'Who doesn't?' Salman asked, as he made the shape of two large breasts around his chest. 'But it's a fact of life: girls like older guys. No girl in year nine, or year ten, would go near any of us.'

'But I'm big for my age,' Tristan said. 'At our school everyone knows what year I'm in. But I bet if I went somewhere where they didn't know me, I could *easily* get off with a year ten girl.'

'No way!' Alfie scoffed. 'You spent two days drooling over that girl when we were in Dubai at Christmas and she blew you out like a candle!'

Jay's and Salman's faces lit up. 'This is news,' Jay said.

'Tell us more, little Alfiekins,' Salman added.

'You can't listen to Alfie,' Tristan said. 'He's never even

kissed a girl. He hasn't even got pubes yet.'

Alfie looked embarrassed and went on the attack. 'What do you know?'

Tristan laughed. 'So you have kissed a girl then, pubeless wonder?'

Salman moved closer to Alfie and teased. 'You haven't, have you?'

'Look at him turning bright red!' Tristan laughed.

Alfie had Tristan and Salman standing right in his face. 'You know I haven't,' Alfie squawked, before storming off to the back of the cabin and pretending to tune his guitar.

The food was gone, apart from a couple of samosas that had blown up in the microwave. Tristan headed back towards his drums, indicating that the break was over.

'Do you reckon we should run through a couple of proper songs?' Tristan asked.

Normally, Jay would have agreed eagerly, but the break was his best chance to talk to the others. He took a deep breath and pulled out his mobile.

'Before we start playing, I've got something I want to say.'

'Sounds serious,' Tristan mocked. 'Your mum's not having another five babies, is she?'

Jay didn't bite back because he was trying to be tactful. 'I went to see a drummer after school last night,' he announced.

Salman looked down at the floor, like he didn't think this was a good idea. Alfie looked curious and Tristan looked like he knew what was coming.

'Oh do let me guess,' Tristan said irritably. 'You think he's better than me.'

'I *don't* want to start another fight,' Jay said.

Tristan raised his voice. 'Because you know I'll kick your weedy arse.'

'We can't gloss over what happened on Wednesday,' Jay shouted back. 'Just watch this guy play. He's a megastar.'

Salman had seen the video already, so Jay held it in front of Alfie.

'Look at his arms go!' Alfie said enthusiastically. 'He's *way* better than you, Tristan.'

'Who says I'm the best drummer in the world?' Tristan asked. 'But I *am* the drummer in this band, Jay. I can't believe you!'

'I don't want you out,' Jay said, trying to control his nerves and seize the moral high ground by staying calm. 'You're one of my oldest mates. You could sing, you can do some keyboards. We wouldn't be the first band in the world with five musicians.'

Salman looked shocked. 'You never said anything to me about Tristan singing.'

'I mean . . .' Jay said weakly. 'What I meant was . . .'

Tristan glowered at Salman. 'So *you're* trying to stab me in the back as well?'

'No,' Salman shouted. 'Jay showed me the video on the way to school this morning. I just said that he should bring it up openly at practice, instead of sneaking around.'

Alfie had finished watching the video and took great

pleasure in teasing his big brother. 'Tristan, if drummers were cars, this guy would be a stretch limousine with champagne and topless birds in the back. You'd be a clapped-out minicab with dried sick on the back seats.'

Tristan reared up, not sure whether to go after Jay or Alfie first.

Jay realised it was going badly wrong. Alfie seemed all in favour, but he was the least powerful member of the band and hankering for revenge over Tristan's comments about pubes and kissing. It was Salman who mattered. He'd been less keen than Jay had hoped before school and the comment about Tristan doing some of Salman's singing was a major tactical error.

'Babatunde's a really nice guy,' Jay said. 'Why don't we all just meet him and see how it goes?'

Tristan flung his arm out, knocking his cymbal stand flying before gritting his teeth and closing on Jay. Jay was scared enough to back up against the wall, but all he got was a shower of spit as Tristan shouted.

'I thought you were my mate,' Tristan yelled. 'We all go way back. But you're digging, digging, digging at me the whole time. You're going behind my back, meeting people and making videos. I'm only in this band because it's a bit of fun. I don't need all this cloak and dagger bullshit.'

'Guys,' Salman said, trying to act as mediator. 'Jay had an idea. If you don't like it, let's forget about it. Is it really worth falling out over?'

'I can't be in a band with this puny dick anymore,' Tristan

said, as he eyeballed Jay. 'Either Jay goes or I go. We vote right now. Him or me?'

Alfie looked at Tristan. 'If Jay goes, how are we going to play?'

'We'd find someone new,' Tristan said. 'But this is my cabin, so if I'm kicked out you can't practise here.'

'Our cabin,' Alfie corrected. 'Mum and Dad built it for both of us.'

Tristan moved away from Jay and faced off Alfie. The age gap between the brothers was eighteen months, but looked bigger.

'Him or me?' Tristan asked furiously, pointing at Jay. 'Vote.'

'Sort it out amongst yourselves,' Alfie said. 'I abstain. I just want to play music.'

Tristan grabbed Alfie by the shoulders and shook him.

'How the hell can it be a fair vote when you're about to batter him?' Jay shouted.

Salman spoke next. 'Everyone shut up. Tristan, leave Alfie alone. You and Jay are my oldest friends and I hate having to do this. But for me, this is about hanging out, jamming, having a laugh. Yes, Babatunde's a better drummer than Tristan. But he's *not* our mate. Jay, you're taking this all too seriously.'

Tristan smiled. 'So you're voting with me?'

Salman raised his hand. 'I don't *want* to vote at all. But I'd rather chill with Tristan and Alfie than get mega-serious with some crazy drummer I don't even know.'

Jay felt like he'd been stabbed. With Salman leaning towards Tristan, Alfie caved.

'Mum would freak out if we brought a black guy round here anyway,' Alfie noted. 'She'd be hiding all the expensive ornaments and shit.'

Salman broke into tense laughter. Tristan looked pretty smug as he picked up his cymbal stand. Jay had a lump in his throat as he unplugged his guitar and looked around for the case.

'Guess this is it then,' Jay said, choking back tears.

'Maybe we can sort something out when things have calmed down,' Alfie suggested.

'Screw that,' Tristan said nastily, as he pointed at Jay. 'I'm past trusting him.'

Jay stood on the edge of the cabin, holding his guitar, as he slid his feet into his school shoes and grabbed his backpack. 'See you at school then, I guess.'

'Sorry, man,' Salman said. 'See you.'

Jay lost it as he waited for the bus home. Tears started flowing, and after a minute he looked so upset that the woman sitting alongside gave him a tissue and asked if he was OK.

17. Friday Night Live

As Brontobyte disintegrated, Industrial Scale Slaughter showed signs of becoming something special.

Lucy and Coco were the brains of the operation. The two sixteen-year-olds reworked songs, slowing up their thrash metal tempos and mellowing the sound to make room for Summer's voice. Michelle got frustrated with the monotony of playing bass, until Summer suggested that she sing backing vocals.

Coco and Lucy resisted on the grounds that Michelle couldn't sing to save her life. But Michelle plugged in a second microphone, and the combination of Summer's throaty blast, interspersed with random chants, wails and the occasional animal noise from Michelle, was oddly successful.

The slower tempos, Summer's extraordinary voice and Michelle's quirky counterpoint changed Industrial Scale Slaughter from a derivative all-girl metal band into a group with a distinct sound of its own. Now, they didn't just play covers of Guns N' Roses or Rage Against the Machine, they created their own versions.

After three hours together on Thursday, Summer was back the following night, sitting with Coco and Lucy in the centre of the pit and enjoying every moment as they played, rearranged, made notes, changed words. It was an intense kind of creativity that Summer had never experienced and she loved being able to talk and suggest ideas without fear of being shot down.

Michelle was the band's outcast. While the trio sat together, she was always pacing on the edge, scrawling out lyrics and screwing them up, or sitting at the computer at the far end, surfing the net. When she wasn't buggering about with her Facebook page, Michelle surfed websites for wannabe rock bands, trying to work out what they ought to do next.

Once you got a band together and learned to play a few songs, all the websites that were worth reading agreed that the next step for a group was to find ways of promoting themselves and playing in public.

Promotion comprised making a website or Facebook page, recording demos and letting people download them, putting videos on YouTube, starting a blog and stuff like that.

But to really get known you had to play in public. Bands could set up their own small gigs in a pub or a local hall and invite friends, audition for a venue's open mic night when six or seven bands played a short set, or enter a battle of the bands competition.

Michelle scanned websites and threads on internet forums trying to pick up tips. Their biggest disadvantage was their youth. Most venues excluded school-age bands. And even if they did land a gig in a pub or club, almost everyone they knew would be too young to get in.

The main options open to younger bands were nappy nights – where clubs and venues ran alcohol-free concerts for kids – or competitions, some of which were open to all age groups and some of which were exclusively for school kids.

Michelle waited for Summer to stop singing Industrial Scale Slaughter's heavy rock version of the national anthem before shouting across the pit.

'There's nothing at all in Dudley and all the ones in Birmingham look crap,' Michelle said, before turning towards a computer screen. 'But this one sounds pretty cool: *Rock the Lock, battle of the bands, sponsored by Terror FM. Open to rock bands with members aged up to eighteen. Venue: the Old Beaumont, Camden Town, London. Winner will receive prime-time air play and live interview on Terror FM, plus a hundred pounds in cash. Runners-up get fifty- and twenty-quid iTunes vouchers. Bands must fill in form, parental consent blah, blah, blah, etcetera, banana, gonads.*'

'When is it?' Lucy asked.

'Three Wednesdays' time, but the application has to be in by next Tuesday.'

'That's a schoolday,' Summer noted. 'And how would we get all this equipment down to London?'

'Do I look *completely* stupid?' Michelle asked. 'It's the first week of Easter holidays. I'm sure someone could drive us down there. We'd need a big car to move Lucy's drums though.'

'My mum's got a people carrier,' Coco said.

'I've always wanted to go to London,' Summer said.

The other three stared in amazement.

'You've *never* been to London?' Lucy said.

Michelle spoke in a posh voice. 'But one simply can't find designer gowns in Dudley.'

'OK, I'm as poor as dirt and I've only ever left Dudley about six times,' Summer confessed, red with embarrassment, but laughing because she was starting to feel comfortable with her new friends. 'And just to get it all out in one go: I've never left Britain, I've never been on an aeroplane or a boat, unless you include a dinghy when I was in Brownies, I've been to Birmingham three times when my nan had an operation, my mum is a junkie, I only have three pairs of knickers that fit properly and I've never kissed a boy.'

Coco smiled as she reached over and gave Summer a hug and a back rub. 'Poor old you,' she said, half jokingly.

Lucy hugged her too, and Michelle got annoyed that nobody was paying her any attention and threw her trainer at them. 'So are we gonna go for this competition or not?'

'How will we get there?' Summer asked. 'And will you all be allowed to go?'

Michelle spun her office chair and gave an evil laugh. 'Daddy does what he's told if he knows what's good for him.'

*

Jay sat on the living room carpet eating burger and chips cooked in the shop downstairs. Every so often he had to lean over and assist his two youngest siblings in some vital task, like cutting a pickled onion in half or squeezing ketchup without flooding the paper sheets in their laps.

The room was rammed: Big Len in the armchair with four fishcakes and a green salad smothered in brown sauce, June, age five, and Hank, six, on the carpet with Jay. Patsy, age eight, ate behind the couch in her private *do not enter on pain of a major screaming fit* den.

Twelve-year-old Kai sat on a dining chair, winding everyone up by blocking the TV with his feet. Adam, fourteen, and Theo, sixteen, were on the couch with a cousin from next door squashed between them. The only absentees were Jay's mum who was working in the shop downstairs, and his nineteen-year-old brother Danny, who'd be a guest at a young offender institution for another eight and a half months.

Although it was loud and cramped, Jay usually liked the banter over dinner. With such a big family there was usually some drama, or something funny that had happened.

Today Patsy was getting all the attention. She was big for eight, and Len had been called in by her teacher after she'd pinned a boy and drawn over his face with a marker pen.

Everyone teased Patsy, saying that the lad was her boyfriend, and she kept yelling *Bog off* or *Leave me be* from behind the couch.

But Jay was too down to join the fun. Being in a band meant everything to him. Getting kicked out stung and he didn't want to tell his family because his brothers would never let it go.

*

The tone of the rehearsals became less serious at seven, when Coco's boyfriend Prakash, Lucy's non-boyfriend Jack and a bunch of other year ten and eleven kids arrived at the pit. Mr Wei didn't like his daughters going out late, but he was happy to let the girls have friends over and the pit had become a Friday night fixture for their mates.

Always shy, Summer felt awkward being introduced. Everyone knew about Industrial Scale Slaughter's long search for a vocalist and wanted to hear her sing. Summer's cheeks burned as she grabbed the microphone and she didn't know where to look because faces stared from every direction.

Coco cranked up the amplifiers for maximum effect and Summer dripped sweat as she belted through 'Bears, Bikes, Bats and Sex'. After five sweaty verses everyone clapped and said how good she was.

As the chatter continued, Summer retreated to a beanbag up back near the computer. She thought about her nan sitting home alone eating microwave macaroni. They usually played Scrabble or watched a DVD on a Friday night and she felt guilty for abandoning her.

'You were great,' a boy said.

Summer did a double-take as she realised it was the lad with the nice bum she'd seen getting off the bus, just before Mr Obernackle caught her off school premises.

'Thank you,' she said warily.

'Mind if I sit down?' he asked, pointing to bare carpet next to the beanbag. 'I'm Sebastian.'

Summer gave a shy nod as Sebastian sat down. The pit was full of cushions so most people took their shoes off. Sebastian was barefoot and Summer was fascinated by the way he had wiry black hairs growing out the top of his big toe.

'My mum says I'm a woolly mammoth,' Sebastian said, wriggling his toes. 'I haven't seen you around in school.'

'I'm a year nine,' Summer said, feeling all embarrassed again.

Sebastian looked awesome, with tight jeans hugging long athletic legs and biceps bulging under his shirt-sleeves.

Summer couldn't stop sweating and her mind churned through questions: *Was Sebastian attracted to her or just being friendly? What would she do if he tried something? Had he been with lots of other girls? How far had he gone with them? How far would he want to go with her? Would everyone think she was a slut if she let him kiss her? Was Sebastian even interested in kissing her? Would all these older kids think she was just a kid if she read the situation completely wrong and made a fool of herself? Wasn't it dodgy that he was two years older than her? Was all that body hair sexy, or maybe a bit OTT . . .*

'So what else do you like to do apart from singing?' Sebastian asked.

'Not much, really,' Summer said. 'I have to spend a lot of time looking after my nan. I used to go to a swimming club, but I got bored of it.'

Sebastian's face lit up. 'I used to swim, but I'm the same as you. Too monotonous.'

'So what do you do now?' Summer asked. 'You still look pretty fit?'

She cringed as the words left her mouth. It was meant as an innocent question, but it sounded like a come-on.

'You're not so bad yourself,' Sebastian said, casually brushing his hand against Summer's leg to see how she reacted.

So now it was out in the open: they fancied each other. But was that a good thing, or did it just move Summer closer to an even more awkward situation? She was so wound up in her thoughts she didn't see Lucy striding over bodies and cushions towards her.

'You OK, Summer?' Lucy asked. 'It's time we got slammed, so I'm going over the supermarket to get a couple of bottles of tequila. Is there anything you want?'

Summer wondered what Lucy thought about her being with Sebastian. He was cute, but she felt nervous and this might be her only chance to escape before things got serious.

'Actually, I really need to get home,' Summer blurted. 'I haven't seen my nan since lunch-time and she's all on her own.'

'Aww,' Lucy said. 'Party's just starting.'

Summer stood up and turned towards a disappointed Sebastian. 'It was really nice talking to you.'

Lucy led the way out of the pit, followed by Michelle and Jack. They cut through the Wei & Wei offices, which were now in darkness apart from one mezzanine office where a couple of draughtsmen were carving up sheets of polyboard for an architectural model.

Lucy spoke to Summer as they walked. 'Sebastian wasn't being weird, was he?'

'He seems nice,' Summer said. 'It wasn't him. I just can't keep leaving my nan on her own.'

'He went out with Coco for a while,' Lucy said, with a smile. 'I'll get her to text you his number.'

'Right,' Summer said uncertainly, thinking about how quickly your credit gets eaten up when you get into a text conversation. 'He's a year twelve. Is that too old?'

'Age is just a number,' Lucy said wisely. 'What matters is that you're comfortable with what's going on.'

A blast of cold hit as Lucy opened the big door on to the street. It was gloomy, with the black outline of their deserted school across the street and wind strong enough to send a Heineken can clattering down the pavement. The bus stop was less than ten metres away. There was no one else waiting and Lucy looked up and down the street.

'It's a bit of a ghost town around here after dark,' Lucy warned, as she pulled her mobile out. 'I've got Wei & Wei's account number, I can easily call you a minicab.'

Summer wouldn't have minded, but she was conscious that she'd already accepted free food, drinks and clothes from Lucy and Michelle. They could clearly afford it, but she hated seeming like a sponger.

'I've done this trip a million times,' Summer said, shaking her head and smiling. 'I'll be fine.'

Jack and Michelle were already walking towards the supermarket in the next street as Lucy gave Summer a little wave. 'I'll give you a call to confirm when we're rehearsing on Sunday.'

'Brilliant,' Summer said. 'I'll get all my homework done tomorrow. Then I'll be free the whole day.'

18. From the Ashes

Kai had gone to boxing club, which meant Jay had the bedroom to himself. He played Connect Four and Battleship with Hank, letting him win until Len called him downstairs for a shower and pyjamas.

After packing up the game Jay flicked off his light, lay on the bottom bunk, stuck his pillow over his face and felt sorry for himself.

He relived the scene at Tristan's house, wondering if he could have played it better. But the more he thought, the more he realised he'd been naive: Tristan wouldn't have quit drums no matter what he'd said.

Jay also wondered about school on Monday. He sat with Salman and Tristan in every lesson and that was going to be awkward. He thought about calling Salman to ask what was said after he'd left, but he didn't want to seem desperate to get back in the band, even if he was.

'You all right, Jay?'

Surprised, Jay shot up and saw his fourteen-year-old brother Adam standing in the doorway. Hank was in an identical posture down by the doorknob.

'Rough day,' Jay confessed, throwing the pillow aside and hoping there wasn't enough light to see the red rings around his eyes. But he'd already been rumbled.

'Hank said you were crying.'

'He *was* crying,' Hank insisted. 'He didn't hear when I came to say goodnight.'

'You wanna talk?' Adam asked, though he didn't sound keen to get involved.

Jay was fond of his three younger siblings, but of the four boys spawned by his mum and Chainsaw Richardson, Adam was the only one he got on with.

'I guess you'll find out soon enough,' Jay sighed, as he sat up. 'I got kicked out of Brontobyte. I wanted to bring in a new drummer. Tristan said it was him or me and the others picked him.'

Adam knew the band meant a lot to Jay and he came inside and flipped the light switch. 'Harsh,' he said.

The light blinded Jay temporarily, as Adam sat on his bed. He had a handsome face a lot like Jay's, and the same spiky hair only in blond. But the family resemblance ended at the neck. Adam didn't box like Kai and Theo, but he did some weight training and a naturally bulky physique meant nobody messed with him.

'If it's any consolation, I heard you play a couple of times and you'd never get anywhere with that shitty drummer,' Adam said.

Jay half smiled. 'It's OK for you,' he said, eyeing Adam enviously. 'You play a bit of music, but you've got other stuff going on: girls wetting their knickers over you, parties, mates, football. I'm a nobody. I had two friends and a band and now I've *totally* screwed that up.'

'I'm your friend,' Hank said earnestly, but pity from a six-year-old wasn't the boost Jay needed.

'Did you have a drummer in mind?' Adam asked.

'I've got a video on my phone. You know that new black kid in your year?'

'Babatunde?' Adam asked.

Jay nodded.

'We do PE with Babatunde's class,' Adam said. 'Didn't know he was a drummer. I can't work him out. He got in this massive row with Mr Gilmore because he wouldn't take his hoodie off when we were playing table tennis.'

'He drums with the hoodie on as well,' Jay noted.

'Can I check the video?' Adam asked.

Adam sat between Jay and the window ledge where he kept his phone and door keys, so he asked Hank to fetch it.

'Give us then,' Jay said, as Hank stood in front tapping the phone's touchscreen. 'You don't know how to do it.'

Hank pulled the phone in close and gave a superior smile. 'I do,' he said. 'I watched Theo's phone. One had this girl wearing furry knickers, and a man was—'

Adam interrupted, and pointed sternly at Hank. '*Don't*

tell your dad you saw that,' he warned. 'He'll go ape.'

Hank nodded solemnly. 'Theo said he'd put mustard on my tongue if I touched his phone again.'

The drumming started out of the phone's speaker as Adam grabbed the handset.

'I wanna see,' Hank whined, before squeezing between the older boys on the bed.

'Not too shabby,' Adam said enthusiastically, as Hank looked baffled. 'Someone's gonna snap him up if you don't.'

'Well, that's not how Tristan and Salman see it,' Jay sighed.

'What about a new band?' Adam asked.

'Eh?' Jay asked.

'You on lead guitar, me on bass and this bad boy hitting drums.'

Jay calculated: Adam was a decent guitar player. Maybe not as good as Alfie, but with Babatunde on drums they'd still own Brontobyte.

'Are you serious?' Jay asked, tantalised.

'It's been on my mind for a while,' Adam said. 'If I don't join a group, what's the point practising my guitar?'

'We'd need a singer,' Jay said.

'Keep it in the family,' Adam suggested. 'Wanna go next door and talk to Erin?'

Jay considered for a couple of seconds. His cousin Erin was two months younger than him and in the same year at Carleton Road school. Len used to give them guitar lessons together when they were little and although Jay wouldn't admit it if you stuck hot needles under his fingernails, Erin was the better player.

'She doesn't play these days,' Jay said. 'I like girl singers a lot, but she's in that drama club. She's more into being an actor than a rock star.'

'No harm asking,' Adam said, with a shrug. 'If she's not interested we'll try and find someone else.'

As Jay said this, Big Len came through the open door and eyeballed Hank. 'I *told* you to say goodnight. June and Patsy are already in bed, now scramble!'

Hank got frightened when his dad got strict and went all stiff. He gave Adam and Jay goodnight bear hugs before belting off to his room.

'Don't keep him up late,' Len said firmly. 'He's got football in the morning.'

'Sorry, Len,' Jay said. 'I didn't see the time.'

Len looked down the hallway, making sure Hank had gone straight into his bedroom before looking back at Jay and Adam with a smile. 'So you're forming a group? I expect you'll be wanting a manager . . .'

*

Summer's bus was packed, and rowdy with people dressed up for Friday night. A group of lads up back swilled lager and had a go at a tired-looking nurse. It was tense, but no worse than riding home when the bus was rammed with kids from her school.

It was eight when Summer got off by her flats. Her nan had been home alone since she'd left for school that morning, so she went into Spar and bought a white Toblerone to cheer her up.

A man came out of the shop at the same time and started walking behind her. He looked creepy, with a dark beard, hands stuffed in pockets and head buried in the fur-trimmed hood of his jacket. Summer told herself she was being paranoid, but just to be sure she stopped walking in the well-lit space by the off-licence at the end of the shopping parade and glanced at her watch, as if she was waiting for someone.

The man kept going towards the flats and Summer spent half a minute rubbing hands and stomping feet before resuming her walk home.

She was alone on the cracked path leading up to her block when something flickered, making her look back. It was the same beard, same hood, same hands buried in pockets. Maybe he'd just been pissing in the bushes, but it felt all wrong and now Summer was in no-man's-land between home and the shops.

She shuddered as she breathed. To get to the stairs leading up to the flats you were supposed to type 528 into a security gate, but people always left the gate open and presently it was wedged with a board, possibly by engineers working on the lifts, or someone moving house.

Either way, the gate offered no protection and the ground floor was a warren of corridors and disused storage units where a woman had been raped on Christmas Eve.

Summer doubted she could outrun a grown man over eight flights up to her flat, so she cut left across the grass. It had been raining and the ground squelched. She knew there was dog shit everywhere, but it was too dark to pick it out.

The man followed. There was no logical reason for him to walk this way, so now she knew he was after her. Summer upped her pace, hoping to find a group of lads – including Kevin from her class – who spent most nights hanging out at the side of the building.

Light from the flats above caught the shattered neck of a Newcastle Brown Ale bottle. Summer saw its potential and swept it off the muddy grass without breaking stride. But as she straightened up, the man broke into a run.

19. Lion's Mouth

Jay opened the window on the landing between the first and second floors of his flat. He stepped out on to a zinc ledge about the width of two shoes and scuffled along towards the pub next door. His mum and Aunt Rachel went potty if they caught anyone doing this, but Jay's family had been crossing between the adjoining buildings this way for years and nobody had fallen off yet.

The rooms above the White Horse pub had the same layout as those above the fish and chip shop, but Aunt Rachel had four daughters so there were high heels instead of football boots and the toilet seat stayed down.

Adam followed, closing the window as Jay headed upstairs and knocked on the door of a second-floor room, which Erin shared with one of her older sisters. It was the same room Jay and Kai had next door. Even the layout, with bunk beds and a desk just inside the door, was identical but the girls had fifty times more junk and the door snagged on jeans and towels as it opened.

Erin was alone at her desk, working through a World War Two question sheet, identical to one Jay had in his school pack. She was a good-looking girl, with dark eyes and shoulder-length black hair. She hadn't changed out of her school uniform, but had undone the buttons on her blouse so you could see a turquoise bra and a belly button.

'Never realised your class had Mrs Ambrose for history,' Jay said, as he studied the answers over his cousin's shoulder.

'Do your own,' Erin teased, as she turned the paper over, but then shrugged. 'Copy it if you like. I don't *really* give a toss.'

'Hitler invaded Poland in 1939, not 1940,' Jay said, smiling.

Erin tutted as she scrawled out 1940 with her Biro. 'I hate history *so* much. I mean, it already happened so who cares? What are you two after, anyway?'

Adam smiled charmingly. 'What makes you think we're after something?'

'You usually are if you come up here,' Erin smirked. 'And don't think I'm taking your shift in the shop. The smell down there gets in your hair. You have to shampoo about six times and it still stinks of chip fat.'

'Me and Adam are starting a band,' Jay explained. 'We need a singer and your guitar playing wouldn't do us any harm either.'

Erin smiled, and turned her chair around to face the

boys. She was barefoot with orange varnished toenails. They looked dead slutty and Jay was ashamed to find himself getting turned on by his cousin.

'I thought you were in Tristan's band,' Erin said.

'It's not *Tristan's* band,' Jay answered irritably. 'I started Brontobyte. Tristan just came up with the stupid name.'

Adam shook his head impatiently. 'Whoever's band it was, Jay's not in it now.'

'So what happens to Brontobyte?' Erin asked. 'Have they broken up completely?'

'How should I know?' Jay snapped.

Adam was baffled. 'Who cares about Tristan, anyway?' he asked.

Jay pointed at Erin. 'She's had a crush for years. She'd never play with me when we were little, but if Tristan was over you couldn't get shot of her.'

'I'm not gonna lie,' Erin said, as she turned a bit red. 'I've always liked him.'

'He's almost as big a loser as Jay,' Adam said incredulously.

'Thanks, bro,' Jay grumbled.

'So,' Erin said, deep in thought as she rocked her swivel chair from side to side. 'There's you two and who else in this new band?'

'There's a drummer we're looking at,' Jay said. 'I've got to speak with him, but I reckon he'll go for it.'

'And what are you called?' Erin asked.

Jay shrugged. 'That's still up for grabs.'

Erin bit a thumbnail before speaking again. 'I tell you

what,' she said uncertainly. 'Tell you what, tell you what, tell you what.'

'Come *on*, Erin,' Adam urged. 'Who doesn't want to be in a band? It'll rock!'

'Maybe,' Erin said, giving a cheeky smile. 'But my drama club's got a big production coming up after Easter holidays and if I land a good part in that . . . Can you just let me think it over for a day or two? I'm leaning towards yes, but I don't want to agree now and then mess you about later.'

'Can't say fairer,' Jay nodded.

'OK,' Erin said, as she gestured towards her homework. 'I've got mounds of this stuff to get through, so if you two don't mind.'

'Let us know before Monday, yeah?' Adam said, as the boys headed out.

As they started down the stairs Adam whispered awkwardly in Jay's ear. 'Is it just me, or is our little cousin looking *seriously* hot these days? Those legs!'

Adam blew a kiss to emphasise his point. Jay felt much less depraved knowing that his brother had been thinking the same way as him, but he wanted revenge on Adam for calling him a loser.

'I could *never* look at Erin that way,' Jay said indignantly. 'She's our cousin. You're a sick dude, Adam.'

*

Summer's breath curled through cold air as her legs strained and school books thumped against her back. She'd almost reached the two-storey houses at the end of her block. If the lads weren't around, she'd find a house with a light on and hammer on the front door.

But would she get that far?

The man was closing up. Summer heard his breath and the Toblerone flew from her coat pocket as he shoved her sideways. She stumbled, almost ploughing into the mud and only staying upright because her pack grated against the breeze block wall of her building.

Booze breath hit Summer's face as the man's eyes flickered, just centimetres away. The beard had made her think he was old, but close up he looked about twenty, with acne spattered across his forehead.

'Gotcha now, schoolgirl!'

He grabbed Summer and mauled her breast, while trying to get his other hand over her mouth.

Summer gripped the jagged bottle top and thrust upwards. The glass stuck in the man's wrist and made him let go. Summer squealed as she ducked under his other hand. Her back foot slipped and she overbalanced. Her bare knee touched down in mud, but she managed to scramble up and break loose as her attacker lunged, trying to grab her pack.

'Help me!' Summer yelled, as she started to run.

The man chased, with blood dripping off his arm and hunter's eyes. A dozen stumbling steps took her off the dirt, on to the pavement at the end of the building. There was street lighting here, and salvation.

The track-suited pair were fifteen or sixteen, jogging along searching for the source of the screams. They recoiled at Summer's bloody school shirt and muddy legs.

'You all right, love?' the smaller of the two asked.

She didn't know their names, but their faces were reassuringly familiar. Kevin and three other lads were also striding in from their regular hangout by the driveway that led down to underground garages.

'Bloke chased and groped me,' Summer blurted, trying not to imagine where she'd be right now if she hadn't spotted the broken bottle.

No more explanation was needed because the bleeding man emerged just behind her. He spun at the sight of six lads, but his Reeboks were muddy and he lost traction. The biggest lad caught hold and brought him down with a knee in the stomach.

Kevin comforted Summer, but the other lads waded in. As the biggest kicked the bearded man in the head and called him a pervert, a squashy-nosed brute stomped his ribs, while his near-identical brother rifled a Timberland boot into his balls.

'Paedo scum.'

Summer shook all over. The beating was turning into a frenzy and, much as she wanted her tormentor to suffer, she didn't want the lads getting done.

'You'll kill him,' she shouted, as she pulled away from Kevin. 'Hold him down and call the cops.'

Two men had emerged from one of the houses. They had no idea what had happened to Summer. All they saw was

Kevin's mates – who had a reputation for being a nuisance on the estate – laying into the bearded man on the ground.

'Come here, you little bastards!' one of the men shouted. He was a big bloke with grey hair, still wearing boots from a day on a building site. He looked like he could snap any of the teens in half and his mate was bigger.

The lads took one look and started running. Kevin yanked Summer by her coat. The others had already run past, while the guy who'd assaulted her grabbed a litter bin to haul himself up.

'Come on,' Kevin said, tugging at Summer's coat. 'Cops round here have our number. They'll do the lot of us for assault.'

'He could have raped me,' Summer said indignantly. She didn't want her attacker to get away, but the lads had saved her and she felt loyal to them.

As Kevin and Summer started running one way, the bearded man stumbled the other, across the mud. The giant builder shouted after him.

'You need a hand, pal? We've called the cops on 'em.'

Summer and the six lads turned down a driveway into the garage blocks. They were built underneath the eight-storey towers, but drivers had long abandoned them to graffiti artists, rats and skateboarders. The drains were half clogged and Summer sploshed through ankle-deep water in pitch darkness.

'Police can't do us for assault if the victim's run off,' the biggest lad said breathlessly. Then with his tone more like an order, 'If we get pulled, keep your gobs zipped and we should be all right. But say one word that puts us at the crime scene and the cops'll have us by the short and curlies.'

Summer didn't say anything, but it was clear the instructions were meant for her too.

'Scarpered cos he's a known pervert, I bet,' one boy said.

It was pitch black and, apart from Kevin, Summer didn't know any of them well enough to recognise voices.

'Heard the bastard's ribs crack when I stomped him,' another said. 'Wish we'd videoed it.'

Summer jumped as Kevin grabbed her wrist in the darkness. 'Stay this side,' he warned. 'There's a missing manhole cover over there. Skateboarder went down it once.'

'It were Max Hooker,' another lad laughed. 'Funniest thing ever.'

Kevin kept hold of Summer's hand as cop sirens whirred up above. Despite the blackness, the boys knew exactly where they were heading.

After fifty metres, they cut into a corridor with a sloped floor and a dizzying smell of aerosol left by graffiti artists. This led up to a flight of steps with chinks of light around the door at the top.

Summer was surprised to emerge through a doorway a few metres from the out-of-order lift up to her flat.

'I've lived here for years,' she said, as she looked back down the steps. 'I never knew you could get in that way.'

'VIP entrance, innit!' the squashy-nosed boy said, but Summer didn't laugh because she couldn't take her eyes off the blood spattered over his tan-coloured tracksuit bottoms. How far would the beating have gone if the builder hadn't run them off?

'Right, my boys,' the big lad said. 'Get yourselves home. If you're going to another block, leave one at a time so the cops don't see yous together. Remember, the golden rule is *keep your mouth shut* and that includes gobbing it to other kids round the estate.'

The lads all nodded and one went straight out the front gate. Kevin looked at Summer. 'I'll walk you up to your flat.'

She thought about saying no, but she was trembling and she liked the way Kevin was being all protective, saying *I'll take you*, rather than asking if she wanted him to.

'Sorry the boys got carried away like that,' Kevin said, as their shoes squelched up the stairs. 'Lee and Milo are headcases. They'll end up in the nick, hundred per cent. But they're good boys to cover your back.'

'Just be sure they don't drag you with them,' Summer warned. 'You're a nice guy, Kevin.'

When they got to the fourth floor Summer unlocked the metal gate over her front door.

'I'll be off then,' Kevin said, as he pointed at the floor. 'I'm only one below you.'

'Make sure you tell the other lads that I said thanks,' she said.

Summer wanted to do something for Kevin and felt she only had one thing to offer. She went up on tiptoes and kissed him quickly on the lips. Kevin looked startled as

Summer pulled closed the metal gate and shut her front door.

'Night then,' Kevin said through the door.

'That you, love?' Eileen asked.

'No, it's the burglars again,' Summer said, repeating a very old joke as she looked down at herself.

Her hands were grazed where she'd hit the wall, her knees muddy, and the pumps Lucy gave her the day before looked fit for the bin.

Summer breathed deep and expected to cry. But tears weren't in her. She thought about the band and her new friends. She thought about grabbing the bottle and fighting back, then surprised herself with the vengeful satisfaction she felt as her mind replayed the savage beating. She wasn't exactly happy, but not sad either and the buzz of everything going on gave her a strange sense of elation.

20. Dead Cat

People remember the results of battles rather than how they're won. Dylan might have stabbed Owen with a fork, made a cowardly run towards the teachers' tables and then caught his opponent with a lucky elbow in the face, but all anyone at Yellowcote school knew was that Dylan had been picked on by one of the hardest kids in his year, and the guy had ended up with a broken nose and eight stitches in his thigh.

Dylan expected his newly won status to go down badly with school's real hard men, so he spent the weekend in public places like the dining room and library, where vengeful rugby boys couldn't lay hands on him. Luckily the squad was on best behaviour after Sir Donald's ruling that any player getting in trouble faced a two-year ban.

By Monday lunch-time Dylan had received enough comments and slaps on the back to adopt a subconscious swagger as he came out of the dining room after lunch. He was dying for a piss and a smoke, and tried to think of someone he could bum cigarettes off as he cut into the toilet.

'Fancy seeing you here,' Owen said, coming out of a cubicle and stepping on to the plinth in front of the urinal trough as Dylan shook off.

Dylan shuddered as he glanced sideways at Owen's black eye and the protective mask taped over his nose. Owen wore a T-shirt and baggy shorts rather than school uniform, because the bandages around his enormous thigh made trousers impossible.

'Spent yesterday recovering at home with my 'rents,' Owen said, as he stared at the wall over the urinal. 'Dad's finding me a different school, seeing as I can't play rugby here.'

Dylan kept silent as he zipped up. He tried stepping off the plinth, but Owen put an arm out to block him. Dylan remembered how effortlessly Owen had banged his head against the curry plate three nights earlier and nobody seemed to be coming in or out, which probably meant Owen had a couple of pals blocking the door.

'I'd *love* to smash you up,' Owen said matter-of-factly, as he pulled down the elastic waistband of his shorts. 'But serious violence might create problems getting into another top rugby programme.'

Owen started pissing in the urinal, but swung his aim towards Dylan, pelting the leg of his trousers. Dylan scrambled back, but he was only two steps from a wall and Owen knocked him into the corner of the trough.

As Dylan's shoe sploshed into the lake of urine around the drain hole, Owen kept pissing until his trousers and shoes were drenched in the warm yellow liquid.

'Ooops,' Owen said, smirking as he pulled his shorts up. Then he made Dylan flinch with a punch that stopped two centimetres from his nose. 'Have a nice life, loser.'

Owen grunted with laughter as he strode out. Three boys who'd been held back at the door came in and saw Dylan dripping all over the tiles. A little lad shot into a cubicle to take a dump, but two year tens laughed out loud.

'Can't you control yourself, Wilton?'

'Dirty boy!'

'Screw you both,' Dylan spat, as he stormed towards the exit.

Dylan couldn't grass. Snitches were social lepers and it would be humiliating having to tell a teacher how he'd let another kid take a piss on him. All he could do was get up to his room, take a shower and put on fresh clothes before too many people saw what had happened.

Owen had fled, but all his year nine rugby mates were waiting in the hallway.

'Piss boy!' one of them shouted, as another fired off the camera on his phone.

Kids cleared space in the busy hallway as Dylan dripped towards the stairs up to his room. One of Owen's mates stuck his foot out, sending Dylan stumbling forwards into a prep school kid.

'Give us a smile, pal!' the photographer shouted, as Dylan

started up the stairs, trailing wet shoe prints as kids coming down scrambled out of his path.

Dylan hadn't cried over anything for a couple of years, but he was close as he kicked his bedroom door shut and ripped the belt out of his sodden trousers.

*

Half an hour later, Dylan walked through the side door of Yellowcote's main performance hall with freshly washed hair and clean uniform. He had his trombone case in hand and a small hunting knife in his trouser pocket, which he was angry enough to use.

The school orchestra was assembled on stage and several kids laughed and whispered when they saw Dylan. News had travelled fast, but not as far as the glowering Miss Hudson.

'Well, this is a good way to make a fresh start,' she said, glancing at her bare wrist, before turning behind to look at the giant clock on the back wall. 'Fifteen minutes late. Let's start with a chat in my office, shall we?'

Miss Hudson left a couple of sixth formers in charge of the orchestra.

'Sorry, miss,' Dylan said, still so angry about getting pissed on that he couldn't focus. 'I just got caught up with a few things.'

'Dylan, I *don't* care,' Miss Hudson said, as she led him into her office and opened a desk drawer. 'I suppose you're pretty pleased with yourself, hoodwinking Sir Donald into getting you out of rugby? I spoke to Mr Jurgens this morning.

He's not happy to have lost Owen, so I'd give him a wide berth if I were you.'

'I'm not the most popular kid in town,' Dylan noted dryly.

Miss Hudson produced a key attached to a large triangle of Perspex and jiggled it in Dylan's face.

'What's that?'

'Practice room one,' Miss Hudson explained. 'It's right up the far end. The acoustics aren't great, so we mainly use it for storage.'

Dylan looked baffled. 'What am I supposed to do in there?'

Miss Hudson gave a dramatic shrug that set the bangles up her arms jangling. 'Whatever you like,' she said forcefully. 'I have a year seven boy playing trombone now and I'm not kicking him out of the orchestra for your sake.'

'So I just sit there?'

'If you like, Dylan. Or you can practise music, send text messages to your girlfriend, do your homework. Two rules: you leave the room the way you found it and if anyone asks, you're practising for a trombone recital.'

Dylan looked a bit down as he took the key.

'Well, it's what you want, isn't it?' Miss Hudson asked. 'Two afternoons a week of bone idleness, while I concentrate on students who actually give a damn.'

'Yeah, I guess,' Dylan said.

Dylan had enjoyed the afternoons he'd spent bumming around in his room, but the appeal had lain in subterfuge and smoking. The idea of being stuck on his own in a music practice room for two hours was depressing and Dylan was offended that Miss Hudson held such a low opinion of him.

'Off you go then,' she said, shooing Dylan away as she hurried back to the orchestra.

Dylan heard groups and individuals inside the practice rooms as he turned right out of the office and down a narrow corridor towards room one. He put the key in the lock, only to realise it was already open. The room was six metres square, with three dirty windows along the farthest wall. Although it was daytime, the light was mostly blocked out by shelving units stacked with junk.

A flip of the light switch set off a bank of fluorescent tubes, two of which were dead. He grabbed a chair wedged under a desk, and a whole stack of hymn books and ancient cassette recorders clattered to the ground on the other side.

Then he sat down and made himself feel sick thinking about the knife. On the one hand he had to protect himself from Owen. On the other, the knife could land him in deep trouble. And not just school trouble, but police, judges and cells trouble.

He pulled the knife out of his pocket, unfolded it and studied his distorted reflection in the blade. There was satisfaction in imagining the blade sticking out of Owen's gut, or better still with his eyeball skewered on the end. But it mainly scared him. And someone as hard as Owen might just snatch the knife and stick it in him.

The big question was whether Owen would attack him

again? Dylan remembered his parting words *Have a nice life*. Hopefully that meant the score was settled and Owen wanted nothing to do with him. Or was he reading too much into four words spoken by a moron?

Dylan folded the blade and moved to pocket it, but at the last second he threw the knife into the far corner. It skimmed over piles of junk and clanked on a metal shelving unit before dropping down. He'd only get it back by pulling out stacks of boxes, crates and an old filing cabinet, and even then there was no guarantee he'd find where it went.

What the hell was I thinking, carrying a knife? But on the other hand, *Now what happens if Owen comes after me again?*

It was the kind of dilemma that doesn't go away and the worst thing to have on your mind when you've got two hours with nothing to do but dwell on it.

Dylan thought about listening to something on his iPhone, but he could never get into music when he was in a bad mood. If he'd brought some books he could have done some homework, but he couldn't be bothered to traipse all the way across the school to his room so he started looking at the stuff on the shelves.

Most of it was rubbish and the further back he reached the thicker the dust got. There was a box of leggings from a Christmas panto, a carrier bag filled with broken recorder pieces, stacks of ancient music books, skinless bongos, a giant drum turned on its side and filled with lost property and even a couple of the straw hats that Yellowcote boys once wore in summer term.

There was something oddly compelling about all this junk. Dylan pulled out a shoe box filled with photographs. Some were of theatre productions with the neighbouring Rustigan College. He lusted after the girls in a production of *Cats*, with shimmering leotards and whiskers drawn across their cheeks. When he finally found the date – 1986 – he realised that these hot teenagers probably now had kids older than himself.

At the end of the box were a couple of newspaper clippings, and a copy of the Rustigan school magazine with one of the whiskered girls on the cover: *Sarah Louise McFarland 1970–1990 – Former Rustigan student dies after a two-year battle with cancer.*

She'd been the happiest girl in all the pictures and Dylan felt sad, then felt very weird about having a bulge in his pants caused by a dead chick dressed as a cat.

21. Cold Sweat

Summer didn't tell anyone about getting assaulted. If her nan knew she'd get upset every time Summer left the house. She almost told Lucy, but her narrow escape might invite more pity and Summer wanted her new friends to think of her as an equal, not some charity case.

In her own head Summer swung from being the bottle-wielding hero who fought off grown men, to a girl who woke in an icy sweat and had to check every room because of a creepy feeling that someone had broken in.

But she was determined not to let fear win, and she walked from the bus stop to her flat in the dark after Sunday rehearsals, even though she almost puked with nerves.

On Monday she acted normal in morning lessons, but worried because Kevin wasn't in class. At lunch-time she deliberately lost Michelle and found the big lad who'd led the beating. He stood under a covered walkway with three other year elevens. She asked for a quiet word.

'I don't know your name,' Summer confessed, as the boy's mates looked on curiously.

'Have you got another one of your slags pregnant?' one lad shouted.

'Shut your face,' the big lad ordered, before looking back at Summer. 'Sorry, they're arseholes. My name's Joe.'

'Kevin's not in class today. Is everything OK?'

'As far as I know,' Joe nodded. 'Kev's dad's in the army. Got home from deployment yesterday and I think they all went into Brum for a fancy lunch.'

Summer gave a relieved smile. 'I've just been worried about Friday. Did the cops speak to anyone?'

Joe shook his head and put a reassuring hand on Summer's shoulder. 'The perv ran off, we ran off. So what have the cops got to go on? The worst that'll happen is the community support officer might hassle us over it next time she patrols the estate.'

'That's a relief,' Summer said. 'Though it creeps me out knowing that guy is still on the loose.'

'Doubt he'll show his face round our way after the kicking he got,' Joe said. 'Me and the lads are always about. Give me or Kev a call any time you're on a late bus and we'll walk you from the stop.'

'Thanks,' Summer said, gratefully. 'I might take you up on that.'

'It's no bother, we do it for sisters and girlfriends all the time. Give us your homework diary.'

Summer pulled her diary from a pocket on the front of

her rucksack. Joe leaned on a post and wrote his mobile number on the back cover. His two mates were just out of earshot and assumed Joe was fixing up a date.

'Don't go near him, babe,' one said. 'He's got crabs.'

'Raging cock rot, more likely,' his smaller friend added, holding inky hands over his mouth and sniggering like a five-year-old.

Joe lunged and chinned him. The kid stumbled backwards into a bunch of year eight girls. Then he reared up.

'I dare you,' Joe teased, as the kid backed off. 'Take a swing. See where you end up.'

Summer was appalled at how violent Joe was, but it was also kind of cool having him on her side.

*

Dylan spilled the box of photos as the door came open. His heart leaped, imagining that Owen had come to finish him off, but it was an oafish year ten kid called Leo Canterbury. His school shirt hung out and you could see man boobs through thin white fabric.

People assumed Leo was dumb because he was overweight and spoke slow, but – apart from a few rugby scholars – Yellowcote's entrance exam meant you didn't get through the gates unless you were brainy.

'You're Dylan,' Leo said, as Dylan stood amidst all the junk with dusty hands and one leg in a tea chest. 'Is it true that Owen—'

Dylan didn't let Leo finish. 'Yeah, I got pissed on,' he said irritably.

'Bitch,' Leo said sympathetically. 'At least he's leaving, eh?'

'Not soon enough for me,' Dylan said. 'How long till he finds another school?'

'No, no,' Leo said, smiling. 'Owen's played like twenty games for Scotland under-sixteen. His dad had a huge row with Sir Donald over the rugby ban. He only came back here to collect his things.'

Dylan's eyes opened wide. 'Are you certain?'

Leo nodded. 'He sleeps three pods down from me. When I went up to get my guitar, he was on the landing saying goodbyes. Good job as well.'

'Not a fan either?' Dylan asked.

'Always on my back. Giving me slaps, or calling me lard ass, Zeppelin, fat boy, dumbo, duckbill fattypus. You're far from the only one who'll be happy to see Owen go.'

'I was scared he was gonna keep coming at me,' Dylan explained.

'So why you in here?' Leo asked.

Dylan thought about telling the truth, but he didn't know Leo well so he stuck to his cover story. 'Trombone practice.'

'I need an XLR lead,' Leo said, as he looked around. 'Miss Hudson says there's a box of them in here somewhere.'

'Could take a while to find 'em,' Dylan laughed, as he looked around at all the mounds of stuff. 'I'll give you a hand.'

The two boys started rummaging. Dylan had seen a box of tangled wires near the door, but it turned out they were all power cables and computer leads. He turned over bags and boxes, while Leo did the same, only with an accompaniment of grunts and moans.

After a couple of minutes Leo gave up.

'We've got phono leads,' Leo said, talking to himself as much as to Dylan. 'I don't see why one is better than another. It's just wire, but my band mate Max says it's got to be XLR if we're recording.'

Dylan looked interested. 'XLR is balanced,' he explained. 'Any analogue signal picks up interference as it travels down a wire, which you hear as crackles or hiss. XLR uses two cables running parallel. The music goes down one, a dummy signal down the other. The interference picked up by the dummy signal is run through an inverter and then subtracted from the music, giving you a really clean signal.'

Leo paused, scratched his chin and finally nodded. 'I *think* I understood that.'

'All you need to remember is always use a balanced connection if you have the option. What are you recording, anyway?'

'Couple of demo tracks for our group.'

'What's your group?'

'Pandas of Doom,' Leo said.

'What kind of music?'

'Kind of rock,' Leo said. 'But not mainstream. It's more punk rock, low-fi kind of thing. You probably have no idea what I'm on about.'

Dylan smiled. 'You mean like The White Stripes, Velvet

Underground, Iggy and the Stooges, that sort of thing?'

'Exactly,' Leo laughed. 'You like that kind of stuff?'

'I grew up with it,' Dylan said, as he gave a shrug. 'My stepmum's really into that whole scene.'

'We've been trying to record Talking Heads' song "Psycho Killer", but we can't get the opening guitars to sound right. Max keeps moving the microphones around, but wherever they go our sound gets swamped by the drums.'

Dylan shook his head and laughed. 'I'm not surprised. If you've got drums in a little rehearsal room they're always gonna swamp everything. Even for a basic demo you should really multi-track it: record each instrument separately and then put the song together with a mixer. Multi-track gives you control over the volume of each instrument, plus you can add effects like echo on vocals, or reverb, double up guitars, alter pitch, or whatever.'

'None of us knows anything about that stuff,' Leo said. 'Max likes to think he does, but we've had about twenty goes and it all sounds horrible.'

Dylan looked around the room. He didn't fancy spending any more time here on his own. 'Well,' he said with a casual shrug. 'I'm no studio engineer, but I've put a couple of little recordings together in my time. You want me to come and take a look?'

22. Dressed for Comfort

Dylan thought the Pandas of Doom were a strange lot. Besides lumbering Leo, there was Max, tall and slim with shoulder-length hair. Dylan recognised Max as part of the cross-country team that shot past his window when he leaned outside for his morning smoke. The year ten wore a retro-style three-stripe Adidas T-shirt with custard and broccoli down the front and school trousers that ended way above his ankles.

Last of the trio was Max's twin, Eve. Stockier than her brother, she sat behind a drum kit in the Rustigan uniform of grey stockings, pleated skirt and pale pink blouse. She was chronically shy and always seemed to be looking down at her feet.

'How come you know so much about recording?' Max asked. He clearly thought of himself as the group's leader and his peevish tone made it obvious that Dylan undermined his authority.

Dylan was too chilled to get into personality clashes and turned towards the door. 'Screw it. If you don't want me, I'm gone.'

Leo blocked Dylan's way. 'It's not personal. Max just hasn't mastered all the social graces yet.'

Dylan sighed, like he didn't really want to explain himself. 'My dad worked in the music industry. I've hung out in recording studios a few times. I've mixed stuff for school concerts and even put a few of my own songs together, when I was bored in summer holidays.'

'What instruments do you play?' Leo asked.

'Bit of everything, though keyboards are my strongest,' Dylan said. 'When I did my demo I used a drum machine, then I laid down keyboards, bass and lead guitar.'

'You played *everything* yourself?' Max said suspiciously.

'Drum machine,' Dylan repeated. 'I played the rest.'

Max looked like he didn't believe a word. 'So what music have you been doing at Yellowcote?'

'Trombone in the orchestra,' Dylan said. 'But it was boring and I got axed for giving Miss Hudson lip.'

Max smiled triumphantly. 'Trombone! Can you walk on water too?'

'Max, stop being a dick,' Leo said. 'You've been trying to record this since Thursday and we've got sweet FA.'

'Anything for a quiet life, me,' Dylan explained. 'I joined the orchestra to get out of rugby and picked trombone because there was no competition for places. If I'd gone for piano I would have had fifty pages of music to learn for every recital.'

'Sounds pretty lazy to me,' Max said accusingly.

Dylan was through with Max's sniping and turned towards the door. 'That's all, folks!'

Leo didn't try to stop Dylan from walking out this time. But Eve shot up from her drummer's stool and screamed.

'Max, you egomaniacal pustule! You have no clue what you're doing. Let Dylan help us.'

It was the first thing Eve had said and Dylan turned back to look, only to see Eve settling back at her drum kit like nothing had happened.

Max made a loud sigh, followed by an *if you must* shrug.

Dylan enjoyed playing around with recording equipment and was keener to get involved than he'd let on. There was an upright piano against the side wall. As Dylan walked past he flipped up the lid and effortlessly banged off the opening bars of Scott Joplin's 'The Entertainer', just to show Max he was no bullshitter.

'Not bad!' Leo laughed, as Max bristled.

A sixteen-track digital mixer stood by the window, with two microphone leads plugged in the back. The console looked intimidating with its rows of buttons, sliders, control wheels and four-inch LCD screen, but Dylan had used the same machine to record crashes and pipe whistle effects for the prep school Christmas panto.

His fingers moved expertly, zeroing all the sliders and creating a new project folder on the console's hard drive. When this was done he looked at the microphone stand placed in front of the drum kit and tried not to make his contempt too obvious.

'If you're using a single microphone, you want it up high to capture the ambience of the whole kit,' Dylan explained. 'But a stereo mix is always useful.'

'So you'd use more than one microphone on the drums?' Leo asked.

Dylan smiled. It was a testament to Max's arrogance that they'd been trying to make a recording for hours without knowing basic info you could learn after a two-minute Google search.

'In a proper studio you'd have two microphones in the distance and extra spot mics over individual drums,' Dylan explained. 'Maybe as many as eight or ten microphones altogether. But I'm just gonna record with two.'

Max interrupted. 'Maybe we should use spot mics then.'

Dylan gritted his teeth. 'Max, mate, two seconds ago you didn't know what a spot mic was, now you're telling me how to do my job. A studio engineer might spend half a day tuning and miking up a drum kit, but we're recording a demo not the new Radiohead album. If we keep it simple we can probably cobble together a couple of half-reasonable demo tracks before teatime.'

'Which is exactly what we're after,' Leo said, before heading out to look for taller microphone stands.

'Fine,' Max said, folding his arms and pulling a face.

The school had quite a few microphones and things, but they were designed for stage performance rather than the more subtle kit used in recording studios. It took about ten minutes for Dylan and Leo to improvise a set-up with two regular microphone stands standing on school desks.

Miss Hudson dropped in briefly. Dylan worried that she'd send him back to room one, but she seemed glad that he'd made himself useful.

As Miss Hudson headed out, Dylan stood by the mixer and looked at Eve. 'Start playing this one, just to set the recording level, OK?'

He pressed the red record button on the first mixing channel and gave Eve a nod.

'Psycho Killer' opened with a sparse guitar intro, accompanied by some delicate cymbal work. To help her keep time, Eve wore headphones and listened to one of the full band recordings they'd made earlier. She closed her eyes and tapped her foot through the opening beats.

She looked fragile and serious, more like she should be plucking a harp than sitting behind a drum kit, but when the song picked up Eve exploded. She was short and had to raise herself up off the stool so that she could hit the full-size kit hard. Her face scrunched and her long black hair flew.

It looked unorthodox, but Dylan's ears told him otherwise. According to the mixer's display the recording levels were fine and when Eve opened her eyes to see if she was supposed to stop, Dylan made a circling gesture with his hands and silently mouthed *Carry on.*

'Not bad at all,' Dylan said, as he saved the track as *Drums:*

Take One and then played a snippet back for everyone to hear. 'We'll do a couple more takes, then we'll move the microphones around and start laying down guitars.'

23. Traitor in Midst

After school Adam and Jay waited for Babatunde by the back gate of Carleton Road School.

'How'd it go with your two little chums today?' Adam asked.

'Horrible,' Jay admitted, as he held his phone in his hand, texting his cousin Erin. 'Salman's fine, but Tristan won't speak to me and it's like he wants Salman to only be with him. Every time I say something Tristan butts in with some stupid comment or tries to cut me out. When we had to find partners in PE Tristan went off on one because Salman wouldn't go with him.'

'It's good he picked you though,' Adam said.

Jay shook his head. 'Salman was sick of being piggy in the middle. He partnered with one of the girls. Tristan was last to pair off and got freaky Peter Frink who stinks of piss and BO. The look on his face was actually *classic*.'

'And Erin still hasn't made her mind up?' Adam asked. 'Typical girl.'

Jay shrugged. 'I just texted her.'

The phone rang as Jay jiggled it. A picture of Erin with a satsuma wedged into her mouth flashed up on the display.

'Perfect timing,' Jay said, as he answered. 'We're just waiting for Babatunde.'

'I won't be joining you,' Erin said. 'Sorry.'

Then in the background someone said, 'Tell Jay he's a big cock.'

Jay almost dropped his phone. 'Are you with *Tristan*?'

'Yeah,' Erin admitted. 'Brontobyte had an opening for a lead guitar player.'

'You took my old spot!' Jay spluttered. 'We're flesh and blood. I can't *believe* you.'

Adam looked shocked as he overheard. 'Erin joined Brontobyte?'

'Sorry, guys,' Erin said. 'When I thought about playing in a band it sounded like a really cool idea. But I don't want to sing and Tristan offered me lead guitar.'

Jay was aghast as Tristan shouted in the background again. 'Your stupid new band hasn't got no singer, you skinny wanker!'

'Erin, how can you like Tristan?' Jay complained. 'I know you fancy him, but he's the biggest spoiled brat you're ever gonna meet. The only person he cares about is himself.'

Erin laughed. 'If he's so awful, why was he your best mate until three days ago?'

She had him stumped, and Jay realised he wasn't going to gain anything by arguing.

'Sod it then, enjoy yourself,' Jay said. He ended the call, then turned towards Adam, shaking his head. 'Can you believe her?'

'Kind of,' Adam said. 'We know she's always had the hots for Tristan.'

Jay shuddered. 'If Tristan gets off with Erin I'll never hear the end of it. It wouldn't be so bad if she was ugly.'

'Erin and Tristan would make an A-list couple,' Adam teased. 'They'll be invited to all the cool parties. Eating at the diner with the baseball team. Going to the Thanksgiving ball. Losing their virginities in a Cadillac parked up on Shaggers Peak . . .'

'Shut up, dick brain,' Jay spluttered. 'I don't care about Tristan. But what are *we* gonna do for a singer?'

Adam looked at his watch. 'Where the hell is Babatunde anyway? You think he might have gone to the wrong gate?'

'There's a front gate and a back gate,' Jay noted. 'How hard can it be?'

Babatunde took another couple of minutes to arrive and came with a surprise: Jay and Adam's sixteen-year-old brother Theo.

Theo looked a lot like Adam, only ten centimetres taller and with dark hair like Jay. He went for the good-looking-thug image, with four earrings, a Mohawk hairstyle and a scorpion tattooed on the back of his neck. His token effort at uniform was a school tie worn over a lumberjack shirt.

'I never realised you had two brothers,' Babatunde told Jay. 'I thought Theo was Adam.'

'Guy comes up and starts talking to me about some rehearsal,' Theo explained. 'I had no idea.'

Theo's train of thought was interrupted by a recently qualified and rather beautiful art teacher walking through the gate and crossing the road.

'Miss Tucker,' Theo shouted after her. 'You wanna come back to my place and see my nine-inch sausage?'

Miss Tucker stopped walking and made a limp-dick gesture with her little finger. 'That's not what I've heard, Theo.'

Adam, Babatunde and Jay laughed, along with a couple of little year sevens who were passing by. Theo scowled at the year sevens and they shot off like bullets.

'Her arse is a peach,' Adam said, as they watched Miss Tucker walking down the road towards the tube station.

'She's a sweet lady,' Babatunde agreed, as he watched her over the top of his mad sunglasses. 'I bet you she only goes for high-end dudes like me.'

Theo eyeballed Jay. 'So why wasn't I told about this band you're starting?'

But it was Adam who answered. 'Why would you care? I haven't seen you play a note since primary school days.'

'We're planning a serious band,' Jay added. 'That's why I quit Brontobyte.'

Adam put a hand over his mouth and did a fake cough. '*Quit?*'

'I can be serious,' Theo said. 'Remember when that magistrate called me respectable?'

'You're a headcase,' Adam said.

Adam got on well with Theo and was probably the only kid who could have used a line like that without getting his head thumped against the nearest brick wall.

Jay gave Babatunde a resigned look. 'Trouble is, our singer pulled out. We can still go back to our place and rehearse though.'

'I'm sure we'll find someone,' Adam added.

'I'm an *awesome* singer,' Theo said.

Jay covered his ears dramatically as his brother broke into song, but Theo's gravelly voice had quite a bit of range.

'Heard a lot worse,' Babatunde noted.

But Jay was filled with dread. Theo was a nutter and a band with him in wouldn't be the professional outfit he'd spent all weekend fantasising about.

'How about I try for a bit?' Theo said. 'If it doesn't work out, tell me to piss off and get someone else.'

The band was important to Jay, so he put his neck on the line. 'Do you mean get someone else, or get someone else *after* you've gone psycho and kicked all of our heads in?'

Jay imagined his own death as the words left his mouth, and shuddered as Theo's expression turned mean.

'Pardon me, Jayden?' Theo hissed. 'I don't *quite* think I heard you correctly.'

Adam stepped in to save Jay. 'Theo, what he's saying is, this is about the music. Jay's a better musician than you or me. If a band is going to work it has to be based on who knows what they're talking about, not on the fact that you're the hardest.'

Babatunde didn't like the way things were going. 'I've been in three bands,' he warned. 'The chemistry either works or it don't. If it's wrong now there's no point going any further.'

Theo pressed his palms together and did an oriental-style bow towards Jay. 'I solemnly promise to treat you with absolute respect. Unless you smoke my drugs or shag my bird, in which case I reserve the right to squish you like a bug.'

Jay spoke warily. 'OK, I'll give you a trial.'

'Besides, Mum would kick me out of the house if I actually hurt you,' Theo added.

Babatunde clapped his hands. 'So are us ladies gonna stand around talking, or do I get to hit some drums?'

Theo pointed as the four boys started to walk. 'My car's parked just down here.'

Jay gawped. 'Car?'

Theo looked back at Jay like he was stupid. 'Yeah, you know. Metal thingies, four wheels, doors, steering wheel.'

'But I seem to recall some laws,' Jay said. 'You need to be seventeen, have a driver's licence, buy insurance. And you're still on probation.'

Theo tutted and smiled. 'Jay, if you're gonna make a fuss over every *tiny* bureaucratic detail you can get the bus.'

Jay's main worry was his mum's reaction if they all got

busted in a stolen car. But Adam and Babatunde weren't fussing and he didn't want to look wimpish in front of his new band mates.

24. Time for Bed

Pandas of Doom laid down two songs before Eve had to go back to Rustigan College for hockey practice. By teatime Dylan had put together a rough mix. The first track was Talking Heads' 'Psycho Killer', the second a song written by Max and Eve called 'Time for Bed' on which Dylan had improvised some keyboards.

Dylan dined at his usual window side table, while Leo and Max sat opposite, sharing the ear buds from his iPhone.

'It's a little flat,' Max said, in his usual clipped tone, but at the same time he smiled with involuntary approval.

Leo had no reservations, and sat rocking his head with a big grin on his face. 'You did the business, Dylan,' he said, as his fork shovelled from a mound of potatoes like a stoker fuelling a steam engine. 'Your keyboard bits really make "Time for Bed".'

'I'm not sure about them,' Max said. 'Because it's *our* demo and we don't have a keyboard player.'

Leo held his hands out towards Dylan. 'I know where we can get one.'

Dylan was flattered. He couldn't help smiling as he waited for the inevitable barb from Max.

'A band is a serious commitment,' Max said. 'Not really your style, is it, Dylan?'

Dylan shrugged as he chewed on fish pie. He'd realised that he wanted to join the band when he was mixing the track, but he didn't want to show all his cards only for Max to shoot him down.

'I enjoyed this afternoon,' Dylan said, avoiding the question. 'Do either of you guys like Black Flag?'

Leo nodded. '"Damaged" is a great album.'

'Same here,' Dylan agreed. 'What about you, Max?'

Max changed the subject, rather than admit that he didn't know Black Flag from Beyoncé.

'Maybe we do need a keyboard player,' Max said. 'They'd give our sound more scope.'

Leo smiled. 'What do you say, Dylan?'

'It could work out,' Dylan said, still trying not to seem too enthusiastic. 'What if we rehearse together a few times and see how it goes? And what about Eve, will she be OK with it?'

'I think she liked you,' Leo said. 'She never says much, but you'll hear all about it if she doesn't.'

'I emailed her an MP3 of your tracks,' Dylan said.

Max seemed less keen now he'd wriggled out of admitting he didn't know who Black Flag were. 'I'll definitely have to discuss it with her,' he said importantly.

But Leo ignored this and reached across the table to shake Dylan's hand. 'Welcome to the Pandas, baby!'

*

Big Len came in the chip shop, ducked under the counter and gave Jay's mum a kiss. The shop was in the half-hour lull between kids after school and the teatime rush.

'How'd it go?' she asked.

Big Len answered by pulling a cloth bag filled with jangling coins out of his pocket. 'Sixty-two quid from bingo,' he explained. 'Lively bunch of grannies. Well worth driving south of the river.'

'I'll need a hand in a bit,' Heather said. 'The lads are all downstairs practising.'

Len looked excited. 'The new band? I've got to hear!'

There was a racket of guitars and shouting directly below as Len hooked up his coat and charged down. The basement smelled vaguely of damp, with bare brick walls, spider webs and crumbling lino. It went quiet as Len came in. June and Patsy rushed over to hug their dad, but Hank was crawling around helping Babatunde line a bass drum with aluminium foil to sharpen its sound.

After giving each daughter a squeeze and a kiss, Len acknowledged Jay, Adam and Theo before heading up to the drum kit at the back of the room and introducing himself to Babatunde.

'I'm told you're a bit special,' Len said. 'I'm afraid these old drums of mine are past their best.'

'They've got character,' Babatunde said warmly. 'Who cares if it looks a bit shabby?'

'Lining a bass drum with foil is the sign of a true madman,' Len noted. 'You know that's a thirty-incher? I rescued the whole set from a skip when Lovegroove Studios went bust, more than twenty years ago.'

'Jay mentioned that you used to be a studio musician,' Babatunde said. 'Do you still play?'

Big Len looked embarrassed, and Adam answered for him. 'He sings to pensioners in community centres and old folks' homes.'

'To my eternal shame,' Len laughed, as Hank crawled away from the drum and hugged his thigh. 'What I do is, play 'em a few songs, get 'em joining in having a good old singsong. Then you whip out the bingo cards and get them all to spend a few quid while they're jollied up. It's not glamorous, but there's money in it and it's all in the daytime, so I can be here when the chippy gets busy.'

'Everyone's gotta make a living,' Babatunde said, as he leaned over and inspected Hank's handiwork with the tinfoil. 'Little man's done me a good job. Shall we play "Christine" again?'

'This I have to hear,' Big Len said, as he sat on the bottom of the stairs, with Hank and Patsy on either side and June in his lap.

'Don't expect much,' Jay warned. 'We've only been at it half an hour. We haven't got to the third verse without breaking down yet.'

Theo cleared his throat and read through the lyric sheet. Jay and Adam picked up their guitars and the three little kids stuck fingers in their ears.

'Ready?' Babatunde asked. 'Set? Go!'

He started drumming and Len saw what Jay had been raving about. The sound didn't have the tightness of a band that had rehearsed together, but Jay was a good lead and Adam a solid bass player. Although Len had noticed that Erin wasn't there, it was only as the opening bars sped by that he started wondering if Theo could sing.

> Christine, Christine, I'm not being mean,
> Your body's not the best that I've ever seen,
> But I'm a desperate guy, never catch a girl's eye . . .

The answer was no. At least not in the sense that a great voice can send chills down your back. But in rock music your voice is often less important than your stage presence. Theo spat lines like he wanted to stab you with them. His posture was powerful, making swift muscular gestures straight out of a boxing ring. He was a good-looking badass, who every girl would want to tame.

Len knew he'd seen potential as 'Christine' disintegrated at the end of the third verse. This was the furthest they'd got and they hadn't yet worked on the final repeat chorus and wind down. The two little girls clapped, as Hank jammed two fingers in his mouth and made a loud whistle.

'I'm feeling vibes there,' Len said enthusiastically, as he

stood up.

Jay wore a huge grin. *Screw Tristan, screw Erin.* He felt like he'd abandoned a push-bike and climbed into a rocket-propelled Ferrari.

'A few rehearsals and we're gonna nail this shit down!' Adam shouted, as he gave Theo a high five.

Len pointed at the little kids. 'Language!'

'You've been in bands before,' Jay said, looking at Babatunde. 'What do you reckon?'

'Needs sharpening up,' he answered. 'But the ingredients are all here.'

'I had a Starbucks with my pal Steve earlier,' Len said. 'He runs the Old Beaumont in Camden Lock. When I told him about you lot, he mentioned that Terror FM have their junior battle of the bands there during your Easter holidays. He gave me a web address for you to look it up.'

Len rummaged in his leather jacket until he produced a folded napkin and handed it to Jay.

'I've heard of Rock the Lock,' Jay said. 'There are some pretty naff competitions around, but this is supposed to be one of the best. I say we should go for it if we can still register.'

'Is three weeks long enough though?' Adam asked.

'I reckon so,' Jay nodded. 'It's not like a gig where you've got to play a whole set. We'd just have to practise a couple of songs, three at most.'

Babatunde did a little drum roll and clanged his cymbal. 'I'm in.'

Theo nodded in agreement.

'It's good to have a target to focus on,' Adam said.

Jay looked at his brothers. 'Just don't let Erin know about it. I don't want Brontobyte turning up.'

Three Weeks Later

25. My Lovely Family

Summer had her alarm set for seven a.m., but she was excited about her first trip to London and had already showered and dried her hair when it started bleeping. Dressed in bra and knickers, she rushed in to shut off the noise, and the blast of air from the swinging door blew some of the fourteenth birthday cards off her bedside chest. She'd had eight altogether, which was seven more than the year before.

'Can I use the loo now?' Eileen asked, from the hallway. 'I didn't want to hold you up.'

'No problems, Nan,' Summer said cheerfully. 'I'll do scrambled egg for brekky in a minute, and I'll make your sandwich for lunch-time. I don't know what time I'll be home, but there's a Tesco lasagne to heat up if you get hungry.'

'Put on a dressing-gown or something,' Eileen said. 'You've not even dried off properly. You'll catch a cold.'

Summer looked at the sunlight blazing through her window. 'Nan, look at it out there! I had the radio on in the shower. Weatherman said it'll be lovely today.'

Summer picked an outfit off her bed and held it up: a shimmering black mini-dress and knee-high, black and red striped stockings. 'I've got a Clash T-shirt to go over the dress, so it looks more punky.'

'Very nice,' Eileen said. 'Are they from Lucy?'

'I borrowed the dress off her,' Summer admitted. 'But I got the tights from the market. Four fifty from my birthday money. Knocked the man down from a fiver.'

Summer didn't want to put her outfit on until she'd cooked breakfast, because she just knew she'd blob butter down it or something. To keep her nan happy, she slipped a white school blouse over her arms before hopping across the hallway to start the eggs.

The sun was on the kitchen window and the warmth on her back felt nice as Summer stirred the saucepan of eggs. Then she heard the wheeze of her nan's inhaler and rushed out into the hallway.

'You OK?' Summer asked.

'Don't you worry yourself,' Eileen said, as she rested against the wall. But her breathing was shallow and her face chalk white.

'Come on,' Summer said gently, as she grabbed her nan under the arm. 'Let's get you in the chair and put your oxygen on.'

To minimise the length of trips to the bathroom, Eileen's

armchair and oxygen supply were just inside the living room door. But the four steps took half a minute. As Eileen slumped unevenly on her cushions, Summer turned on the oxygen supply and stretched the elastic strap of her breathing mask around the back of her head.

'Slow breaths, as deep as you can,' Summer said, keeping her voice calm but fretting on the inside.

Her nan got attacks like this about once a month and it might be several hours before she felt strong enough to get to the toilet or kitchen unaided.

Eileen pulled her mask up and tried to smile. 'Don't you worry, love,' she gasped. 'I'll be fine in a jiffy. You'd better get dressed. What time is the car picking you up?'

'Eight,' Summer said. 'But they know I can't go if you're sick.'

'You go to school when I'm like this.'

'That's just up the road though,' Summer said. 'The longest I'm away is three hours between registration and lunch. If I go to London you might not be able to use the loo or get a drink until this evening.'

'I've just been,' Eileen said. 'I'll manage.'

Summer resented her nan a little. Of all the days this could happen, it had to be today.

'I'll give the Weis a call straight away,' she said, as she tried to remember where she'd left her mobile. But then she smelled burning. 'Oh tits. I've left the eggs on!'

*

Jay lay in bed with one eye peering out from his duvet. Kai

looked infuriatingly strong and handsome as he did knuckle push-ups on the carpet.

'What you staring at me for?' Kai asked, as he rolled on to his back to do crunches. 'Getting a stiffy?'

Jay smiled slightly. 'Kai, if I *was* gay I wouldn't go for someone who went to bed in his stinking boxing kit.'

Kai hooked his feet under the bottom of the radiator and started doing crunches. 'The birds hanging out around the gym last night didn't seem to mind,' he said boastfully. 'Haven't seen too many girls near *you* lately.'

This hit home because Kai had knocked around with a couple of girlfriends, while Jay had never had one. Fortunately, Jay's pride was saved because their mum came in, whacking Kai with the door as she flung it open.

'Bacon and eggs on the table in ten minutes, binned in eleven, so get your pimply bods downstairs. And Kai, you stink to high heaven. What kind of mother will people think I am?'

Jay grinned as his mum yanked Kai up by his boxing vest, dragged him into the hallway and shoved him towards the bathroom.

'Don't lock the door,' she shouted. 'The others might want the toilet.'

'I need a towel,' Kai protested.

'You'll get more than a towel off me in a minute,' Heather shouted. 'Use one of the ones on the floor.'

Jay laughed as he rolled out of bed, and he wandered into the hallway, scratching his nuts. His mum flung open the room next door. She might have seemed tough to an outsider, but she was a mother of eight, she had a business to run and that didn't leave much time for subtlety.

'Adam, Theo, breakfast in ten minutes, bin in . . . Adam, where the hell's your brother?'

Jay listened curiously as Adam spoke. 'Didn't come home last night.'

'What do you mean, didn't come home? What's he been up to?'

'I'm not his keeper,' Adam said. 'He never came home after boxing. Kai might know.'

'How should I know?' Kai shouted from the bathroom, as Hank and June raced past Jay in their nightclothes.

'You two, don't you dare set foot on those stairs until you're dressed!' Heather shouted down the hall, before turning back towards Adam. 'What am I supposed to do if Theo's parole officer rings up? He's supposed to be home under this roof by nine p.m.'

Jay was still smiling after what had happened to Kai, but cheeriness was a big mistake when his mum was riled up.

'I went down in that basement to get a can of frying oil yesterday,' she snapped. 'It's a disgrace: glasses, crisp packets, cans, toys, trainers. When you've had your breakfast, you can go down there and pick the lot up.'

'It's the battle of the bands today,' Jay said.

'And you won't be going to Rock the Lock until it's tidy down there, so get moving.'

Kai leaned out of the bathroom door. 'You tell him, Mum!' he shouted enthusiastically.

'Kai,' she roared. 'If you're not under that shower in ten seconds I'll come in there and scrub you with the toilet brush.'

Adam had crossed the hallway to the bathroom. Jay heard Kai protesting as he walked down to the kitchen.

'Adam, you dirty git! You can't sit and crap while I'm in the shower.'

*

Mr Wei picked up the phone and realised that Summer was close to tears. He stood in a spacious fitted kitchen, with Michelle on a stool at a breakfast bar, eating chocolate cereal and deliberately letting the brown milk dribble down her chin on to her nightshirt.

'Summer, I need you to calm down,' Mr Wei said. 'I'm sure we can work this out.'

As soon as Michelle heard Summer's name she rushed over, bare feet slapping on the tiles. Mr Wei pointed towards the stairs. 'Fetch your mum, *quickly*.'

'I'm really sorry,' Summer said miserably, on the other end of the line. 'I feel so bad. The others have practised so hard for this, but I can't leave my nan here in this state.'

Mr Wei spent half a minute calming Summer down before Mrs Wei strode into the kitchen in her bathrobe. She was broad-shouldered, with long black hair almost down to the base of her spine, and she looked grumpy.

'Summer, can you hold for a few minutes?' Mr Wei asked.

'Call me back,' Summer said desperately. 'I've only got sixty p credit. Have you got my number?'

'It's on the caller display,' Mr Wei said.

He put the cordless handset down as Lucy came into the room, combing damp hair.

'Summer's nan's having a bad morning,' he explained. 'She'll probably be fine, but it'll be evening before you all get back from London and we can't leave her alone for that long.'

Mrs Wei shrugged. 'And what do you expect me to do about it?'

'You said you were working from home today,' Mr Wei said. 'It's only a ten-minute drive so I was hoping you could drop by and check on her a couple of times.'

'I'm not going near those flats,' Mrs Wei said, as she shuddered theatrically. 'I don't even like *driving* around that area.'

'Mum, we can't play without Summer,' Lucy explained.

'You're such a cow,' Michelle added unhelpfully. 'You've always hated our music.'

Mrs Wei didn't deny the accusation as her husband rubbed his palm across his forehead, deep in thought.

'It's putrid noise,' Mrs Wei said acidly. 'I'd help if you played proper music. That's why I started you both with violin and piano.'

Lucy scowled as she slammed the fridge door and slugged orange juice from the carton. 'Two little Asian girls in flowery dresses at piano recitals. Could that be any more of a stereotype?'

'Well, I don't see good grades,' Mrs Wei said. 'What I see is hours sitting in the pit, making that awful noise, and with boys in and out.'

'What century are you from?' Lucy shouted with exasperation.

Mrs Wei turned towards her husband. 'I have a lecture tour to prepare and papers to grade. If I'd wanted to be a nurse I'd have trained as one.'

'I wish you'd just die, Mother,' Michelle screamed.

Mrs Wei gave Michelle a look of complete indifference. 'Your father's the one who said you can have a rock band.'

As Mrs Wei walked serenely upstairs, her husband gave a resigned sigh before picking the telephone off the counter top and dialling Summer's mobile.

'How's your grandmother?' he began soothingly.

'Gradually getting her colour back,' Summer said. 'She says she's OK, but there's no way I can leave her for ten hours.'

'I know,' Mr Wei said. 'If I drive over and pick your grandmother up, she can spend the day at my offices. There's a disabled bathroom. I'm sure we can dig out a DVD for her to watch and at lunch-time I can wheel Eileen over to the canteen for some proper cooked lunch. How does that sound?'

'The lifts are working so it should be fine,' Summer said.

'There's a full oxygen bottle in the hallway, and you'll have to take her breathing apparatus, but . . .'

Summer paused for a moment to see if she'd forgotten anything.

'No, that should be fine,' she confirmed.

'OK,' Mr Wei said, as he gave his daughters a thumbs-up gesture. 'I'll get in my car right now and help you get your nan and the oxygen downstairs. Coco's mum will pick you up at eight, as planned, then she'll drive over here to get Lucy, Michelle and your instruments from the pit. I'll leave as soon as I've put a shirt and shoes on.'

Summer laughed and choked back tears. 'Are you sure?' she sniffed. 'That's really kind. I'll just check with my nan, but I'm sure she'll be OK about it.'

Mr Wei ended the call and smiled as his daughters wrapped their arms around him.

'Best dad ever,' Michelle smiled, kissing Mr Wei on one cheek as Lucy kissed the other.

26. Flying Egg Sandwich

Jay came out of the kitchen with a bacon and fried egg sandwich, just as a pair of dirty boxers sailed down the hallway. They hit him in the face and landed on his plate. He looked up, seeing Kai on the staircase taking aim with balled-up socks.

'That's my breakfast, you dirty bastard!' Jay shouted, before violently flinging plate and sandwich up the stairs after his younger brother.

It hit Kai on the leg, leaving a big ketchup stain on his freshly laundered jeans.

'Jay and Kai are fighting again!' Patsy shouted, as Kai vaulted the bottom half of the stairs, grabbed Jay around the neck and flung him to the carpet.

'Get off me,' Jay yelled, as he tried to bend Kai's fingers back.

But Kai put his strength to good use. He flipped Jay on to his chest, pressed his kneecap hard against his back and twisted his arm into a painful lock. Adam heard the commotion from the living room and there was a sharp crack as he smacked Kai in the face before dragging him backwards.

'You want to fight someone, fight me!' Adam said, as he shoved Kai against the wall and faced him off.

Kai loved a scrap, even against a bigger opponent. He wriggled free and punched Adam in the side of the head.

Adam was two years older, but he lacked Kai's boxing experience and wondered if he'd bitten off more than he could chew as Kai threw a swift volley of punches, knocking him dangerously close to the stairs leading down to the shop.

Jay was back on his feet and ran up behind Kai, kicking him in the back.

'Ooof,' Kai groaned, catching a punch in the ribs from Adam as he collapsed to the floor.

Jay was about to stamp on Kai when Big Len plucked him off the ground and threw him towards the kitchen.

'Pack it in,' Len boomed. 'You're getting too old for this shite.'

Heather roared from the top of the stairs with devil slits for eyes. 'Can't I even sit on the loo for two minutes without you three kicking off?' she shouted, as she rushed down.

Adam was nearest the stairs, so he caught a whack across the back of the head.

'Look at this,' she shouted, as the little kids peeked nervously out of the living room. 'Food all up the stairs.

Clothes in a state for muggins here to wash, no doubt. Why can't you just leave each other alone?'

In the midst of all this, Kai was slumped against the wall of the narrow hallway, clutching his chest and groaning softly.

'You should know better at your age!' Heather told Adam.

'It was an accident, I caught him with my knee,' Adam said.

Jay felt bad, because Adam had stood up for him and was now copping the blame.

'He started on me as usual,' Jay said, pointing down at Kai. 'He *always* starts it.'

'You threw your breakfast at my head,' Kai snivelled. 'You're such a girl. You freaked out because I threw a little piece of cloth at you.'

Jay reared forwards to kick Kai, but Len yanked him back.

'I don't want your shitty pants in my face,' Jay shouted, close to crying at the frustration of having to share his life with Kai. 'I hate you.'

Heather wrung her hands furiously and sobbed as she looked at Len. 'I can't cope with this every morning,' she said. 'My nerves are in shreds.'

Jay and Adam felt guilty as their mum rushed upstairs in a state. Len glowered as he helped Kai to stand up.

'Nice work, boys,' Len said angrily. 'Your mother works seven days a week in the shop. She's got seven of you to look after and you older boys don't lift a bloody finger.'

'I'll pick the mess up,' Jay said guiltily. 'And stack the breakfast stuff in the dishwasher downstairs.'

'OK, then,' Len said. 'Adam, you make sure the little ones eat their breakfast and get their clothes on. Kai, you go tidy up the basement.'

Unlike his brothers, Kai felt defiant rather than guilty. 'I ain't had no breakfast yet.'

Len laughed. 'Got what you deserved for once, didn't you? Always dishing it out, but doesn't like taking it.'

'You're not my dad,' Kai spat. 'I'm not doing what you say.'

Len rarely even raised his voice, but Kai was winding him right up. He grabbed Kai and held him up so that his feet dangled a full metre off the ground.

'I knew your dad,' Len bellowed. 'If Chainsaw Richardson saw you upsetting your mum like that, he'd put you in hospital for a month.'

After Len let him down Kai sloped off downstairs. Jay knelt on the stairs going up, grabbing the bacon and brushing bits of egg on to his plate. He dumped it all in the kitchen bin, while Len stood at the counter making him a replacement sandwich.

'There you go,' Len said warmly. 'You hurled the last egg at your brother, so it's just bacon.'

Jay half smiled as he lifted the top off the sandwich and squirted on ketchup.

'I try not to upset Mum,' Jay explained, as he stood by the

sink and took a big bite. 'Kai just pisses me off and with us sharing a room there's no getting away from him.'

Len nodded in agreement as he made himself an instant coffee. 'He's a gobshite, that's for sure.'

'Mum's got a blind spot,' Jay said. 'Kai pushes me around but she'll always have a go at both of us. He's built like a tank. I'd have to be a complete *idiot* to start on him.'

Len smiled. 'Your mum knows Kai's a little idiot, but she loves all of you the same.'

'If the basement wasn't so damp, I'd sleep down there,' Jay sighed.

Outside a car horn beeped. Jay looked through the window behind the sink and was shocked to see Mrs Jopling's enormous Porsche Cayenne on the cobbled yard out back. Tristan and Alfie sat in the rear seats and there were guitars and drums piled up in the boot.

'Seems our little secret got blown,' Len smiled, as Erin ran out on to the cobbles.

'Good luck, you lot,' Jay's auntie Rachel shouted, from the back doorway of the pub.

Jay knocked the washing-up liquid in the sink as he leaned across to yell out of the window.

'Where are you losers going?' he shouted.

It was a sunny morning. Erin looked good in a tight T-shirt and dark green leggings as she turned back and flicked Jay off.

'Same place as you, I guess,' Erin shouted up.

'How'd you find out?' Jay asked.

Erin smiled knowingly. 'Little sisters have big mouths.'

Jay was annoyed that Brontobyte were going to Rock the Lock, but what really irritated him was the way Erin ignored the empty front passenger seat and got in the back of the big Porsche, snuggled up next to Tristan.

'I'm not worried,' Jay told Len as he closed the window. 'If we can't beat a band with Tristan drumming we should burn our instruments.'

'Not without a singer we won't,' Len said, as Mrs Jopling's Porsche pulled off into the alleyway. Then he called out, 'Adam, can I have a quick word, mate?'

Adam came in from the living room with Hank in tow. Hank had ketchup all over his face and he squirmed as Jay sat him on the counter top and wiped his lips with a damp kitchen towel.

'Where's our singer?' Len asked.

Adam always got irritated when people asked him about Theo. They got along OK, but socialised with completely different crowds.

'Kai reckons Theo was sniffing around some bird after boxing. He didn't come home, so I'd guess he got his end away.'

Len shuddered and laughed. 'Dear lord, the thought of *him* breeding. Not to mention your mother's reaction.'

'What's *getting your end away*?' Hank asked.

'As long as Theo's not been nicked again,' Jay said, ignoring Hank's tricky question.

'Theo's under eighteen,' Adam said, as he shook his head.

'Cops have to contact a parent or guardian straight away if they arrest a minor, so they can't have nicked him.'

Len looked at the wall clock. 'Well, we need to be at the Old Beaumont in an hour, so he'd better show his face soon.'

27. Darned Builders

Coco had the longest legs, so she sat up front with her mum, Lola, as Industrial Scale Slaughter headed down the M1 towards London. The traffic was heavy, but nothing compared to the morning log-jam heading the opposite way into Birmingham.

The car was a battered Peugeot people carrier, with Michelle, Lucy and Summer in the middle row, and the third row of seats folded flat to make space for drums and guitars.

'So I had this dream,' Michelle began.

Lucy moaned and covered her ears. 'I don't want any window into your warped psyche.'

Michelle folded her arms and sulked. 'Fine, I won't tell you then.'

'Van man dipshit!' Lola screamed.

She'd been forced on to the brake pedal as an open-topped truck overloaded with builder's waste cut into the lane ahead of them. She followed up with a double blast on the horn.

'Mum!' Coco rebuked, before looking around at her friends in the back. 'She gets *so* aggressive when she drives.'

Lola took a deep breath and deliberately steered the conversation away from her occasional road rages. 'I never remember my dreams anymore.'

Coco snorted. 'All the booze practically wiped out your brain.'

Lola laughed, then teased her daughter back. 'I'll remember that line next Friday when it's *Mum, my allowance ran out. I need going-out money for the weekend.*'

As the girls laughed, the truck in front of them hit a pothole. Its frame shuddered and the tailgate rattled as chunks of broken plasterboard dropped out of the back. Plumes of white dust spiralled as it hit the tarmac ahead of them.

Lola didn't want to be around when the next batch flew off and was already indicating to pull into the slow lane out of harm's way when another shower hit the tarmac. This second jolt was more violent and bricks, electrical cables and a bundle of wire coat hangers hit the carriageway.

As the debris passed under Lola's Peugeot, the front tyre hit a chunk of brick, throwing it up into the wheel arch and making an enormous metallic *thunk* that jolted the entire car.

Michelle recoiled instinctively, leaning across Summer. Lola glanced anxiously in her side mirror. The driver in the left-hand lane had seen the debris come off the truck and made a space for her by slowing down. But the steering wheel was vibrating and Lola's fears were confirmed as a piece of shredded rubber flew away from the side of the car.

'Brace yourselves,' Lola ordered, while using all her strength to hold the juddering steering wheel. 'We've lost the front tyre.'

Her foot was off the accelerator and the driver behind blasted a horn as the Peugeot slowed to less than fifty miles an hour. If Lola hit the brake she'd have a dozen cars smacking into her, so she aimed for the hard shoulder by steering gently towards the slow lane.

The sideways movement caused the last piece of the tyre to break free and it thumped against the underside of the car. The driver behind had finally realised they were in trouble and slowed up as much as he dared.

Summer was glued in the middle seat with Lucy's nails clawing anxiously into her wrist. Lola was desperate to stop, but feared that the high-sided people carrier would roll if she made any dramatic moves with only one front wheel.

They were down to forty miles an hour as they drifted gently into the hard shoulder. It felt slow after travelling at motorway speed, but Lola was still battling the steering wheel. She wanted to stop as quickly as possible, so she gave a tiny dab on the foot brake.

The car lurched violently back towards the traffic, but the anti-lock brakes detected that something was wrong and took the brakes off before the swerve could turn truly nasty.

Lola straightened up as traffic steamed past at almost double their speed. After being bitten once she was afraid to touch the brake pedal a second time. She cruised on along the hard shoulder with the clutch down until she finally eased to a stop almost two miles from where they'd hit the debris.

Everyone gasped with relief as Lola took the key out of the ignition. 'I feel sick,' she confessed, allowing herself one deep breath to get a grip before going back to being a mum. 'Everyone get out on the passenger side and stand on the grass.'

Lucy and Coco were first out. As Lucy called the police on her mobile, Summer inspected the damage. Besides the absence of a front tyre there was a tennis ball-sized dent where the rubble had hit the bonnet. The front bumper hung loose, the wing on the driver's side had buckled, there were scratches and dents all along the side and a slow puncture from the rear tyre.

'That could have been a lot worse,' Summer said, as Coco hugged her trembling mother.

'You're bleeding,' Michelle noted.

Summer looked down and saw four red crescents where Lucy's anxious fingernails had dug into her arm.

*

Theo was always full of himself, but never more so than when he'd spent the night with a girl. He lay naked on a single bed, while cartoon penguins had a snowball fight on the duvet cover. His clothes were strewn across the carpet and the bottle-green blazer of a public girls' school hung on the wardrobe door.

Theo's conquest was showering in the en suite. He'd tried to get in and join her, but she'd put the bolt across the door. She came out in the inevitable pink dressing-gown. Long black hair and big eyes.

'You look hot,' Theo said, before smiling.

She gave Theo's well-muscled torso an admiring glance, but her tone was functional. 'Do you want a quick shower before you go?'

'Good idea,' Theo said, pouting because he knew girls like having enough of a hold to hurt your feelings. 'But don't I get a cup of tea and a bacon sarnie?'

'You should be happy with what you've had already,' she teased.

She opened a drawer and pulled out a clean bra and knickers as Theo tried to remember her name. Felicity? Fiona? Ffion? It was a proper posh-girl name and it definitely began with an F.

'So you just pick up a bit of muscle at the boxing club, take him home and dump him in the morning?' Theo asked.

The girl sounded irritated. 'Theo, I'll text you, OK? But my parents are home. I've got to stay in their good books. I've got my test next month and Daddy promised a Honda Jazz if I pass.'

The girl pushed her toes into one of Theo's trainers and flicked it up into his lap.

'Ten minutes,' she said firmly, as she gathered a bunch of

Theo's stuff off the carpet and threw it into the shower room.

Theo kept up the wounded puppy act as he strode towards the bathroom. He was compensated with a sweet smile, a kiss and toes tickling the back of his leg.

'You smell all soapy,' Theo said.

'You don't,' the girl said, then slapped him cheekily on the arse as he sauntered towards the shower. As Theo reached the bathroom, they both heard feet racing up the narrow staircase leading to the attic room.

'Sounds like my brother!' the girl gasped. 'Get in there. Close the door!'

As Theo shut the bathroom door the girl glanced around, quickly burying Theo's jeans under bedclothes and kicking his bag of boxing kit under the bed. A boy of twelve stepped in, dressed in a T-shirt and pyjama bottoms. His hair stuck out in all directions like he'd just rolled out of bed.

'Phoebe—'

'Haven't you heard of knocking, Marcus?' she interrupted.

Phoebe, Theo thought, as he stood behind the shower door. He knew it began with an F.

Marcus continued. 'Mum says breakfast is ready and we've got to pack the car for the drive down to Granny's.'

'I could have been stark naked,' Phoebe said.

'Bonus,' her brother laughed. 'Especially if I'd made you scream.'

'Tell Mum I'll be down as soon as I'm dressed.'

As Marcus turned to head out a phone rang under

Phoebe's duvet. Marcus turned back and noted that his sister's phone was charging on her desk.

'Whose is that?' he asked.

Phoebe thought quickly. 'Naomi left hers at school on the last day of term. I've got to give it back after the holidays.'

'So why don't you answer it?' Marcus asked.

Phoebe gave her brother a shove towards the door. 'Why don't *you* keep your nose out?'

This was a horrible error, because it's a law of the universe that little brothers will do the opposite of what you want if you try bossing them around.

Marcus gave Phoebe a shove and lunged forwards, reaching his sister's bed. His jaw practically hit the floor as he saw that the ringing came from the front pocket of a pair of boy's jeans. When Marcus looked up he saw Theo peeking at him through a gap in the bathroom doorway.

Marcus cracked a huge smile. 'You are *so* dead.'

Phoebe grabbed her brother around the waist. 'Fifty quid to keep your mouth shut.'

'Don't trust you,' Marcus squirmed, as he dragged his sister closer to the door. 'Besides, this is too good. You've *always* been Daddy's golden girl.'

Theo stepped out of the bathroom. 'Do you want me to shut him up?'

As much as Phoebe hated Marcus at that moment, she didn't want him to get hurt.

'Don't be bloody stupid,' she told Theo, as she let Marcus go.

The twelve-year-old bolted out of the room and shouted full volume as he raced down the stairs. 'Mum, Dad! Phoebe's got a bloke in her room. He's got no clothes on!'

'Get dressed,' Phoebe steamed, as she tugged Theo's stuff out from under the bed.

Theo's mobile stopped ringing as he scrambled into his jeans. Downstairs, Marcus was having difficulty getting his parents to believe him.

'Dad, I swear on my life. She's been doing it!'

Theo didn't bother with socks and slid bare feet into trainers as Phoebe's dad spoke in a crusty and slightly alarmed voice from the bottom of the stairs.

'Phoebe, darling. Is everything OK up there?'

Phoebe gawped mindlessly at Theo as her dad walked in. He was an average sort of posh bloke, dressed in chinos and deck shoes.

'Who the devil are you?' he shouted. 'What's going on here?'

The state of the bed, clothes strewn over the floor and the fact Phoebe had nothing on under her dressing-gown made things pretty obvious.

'Oh, isn't this just *great*?' Phoebe's dad shouted.

'I'm seventeen,' Phoebe said defensively, as tears welled in her eyes. 'I can do what I like.'

'Not while you're living under this roof you can't.'

Phoebe's mum came in and scowled at her husband. 'Donald, she's a big girl. Stop making such a scene.'

But Donald was having none of that and stepped up to

Theo. 'Well, what have you got to say for yourself?'

Theo smirked. 'You have a very nice home here, sir. But your daughter could really do with a bigger bed.'

'A bloody comedian,' Donald said, as he shook with anger. 'Gather your things and get out of my house.'

Phoebe interrupted. 'Daddy, you're acting like it's 1950.'

Donald jabbed Theo in the chest. 'I was in the RAF you know. If I see you here again, I'll thump you one.'

Theo smiled as he pulled his head through a sweaty training vest. 'Don't go giving yourself a heart attack, *Donald*. I'm far from the first guy to sleep with your little princess.'

Phoebe slapped Theo across the back. 'Don't talk about me like that.'

'Cocky little bastard!' Donald roared. 'I'll show you.'

Donald was average height and quite heavily built. His punch would have knocked back most sixteen-year-olds, but Theo had a cabinet full of boxing trophies. He ducked Donald's blow, then bobbed up and slugged him in the gut.

Theo could have hit Donald in the head and knocked him cold, but he just gave him a two-handed shove across Phoebe's bed.

'Lovely to meet you all,' Theo said.

As Donald lay across his daughter's bed, severely winded, Theo checked that he had his phone, wallet and keys before grabbing his boxing bag off the floor. Then he looked briefly at Phoebe and her mum, who were both tearful.

'He threw the first punch,' Theo said. 'What was I supposed to do?'

Phoebe's brother bolted when he saw Theo storming downstairs. Theo was tempted to give him a slap, but he was only a kid so he went straight out the front door.

Theo smiled to himself as he passed mock-Tudor semis owned by bankers and doctors. He reckoned he'd blown his chances with Phoebe, but he had a great story to tell Adam and the lads at boxing club.

A six-year-old Nissan Pathfinder stood at the end of the road by a postbox. Theo had stolen it four months earlier and a man in the motor trade had given him a fake tax disc and cloned number plates as payment for stealing a Golf GTI.

It stank inside from the kebab he'd eaten with Phoebe the night before and he kicked the greasy polystyrene boxes into the gutter before starting the engine. He was about to head home when he remembered the missed call that had set off the whole chain of events. Adam's name was on the display and Theo called him back.

'Heya, mate,' Adam said. 'I didn't call at a bad time, did I?'

28. Old Beaumont

The Old Beaumont would open its doors for Rock the Lock at 9:30 a.m. Babatunde hadn't lived in London long enough to know how long it took to get places and ended up standing outside its locked doors with his hands in his pockets at 8:55.

The blackened brick concert hall stood by the Grand Union Canal. It had been built as a cinema, bombed in the war, reopened, burned out and derelict for sixteen years before re-emerging as a hip venue for punk and new wave bands in the late seventies and eighties.

Babatunde didn't know Camden Town, but he got bored just standing around looking at Chinese food stalls with their shutters down and decided to kill time with a stroll. Hardly anywhere was open this early, but he found a Pret A Manger on the main road and bought coffee and a mozzarella croissant, before heading into the seating area at the back.

'Babatunde!' Mr Currie shouted enthusiastically.

He was surprised by the sight of his school music teacher, sitting with Erin, Tristan, Alfie, Salman and a woman in a brown leather cowboy hat and sunglasses who had to be Mrs Jopling.

Babatunde dragged a leather stool across from the next table and squeezed between Erin and Mr Currie.

'What are you doing here, sir?' Babatunde asked.

Mr Currie smiled guiltily. 'Mrs Jopling has been paying me to do some private tutoring with Brontobyte these past few weeks.'

Babatunde laughed. 'Sounds like bias to me,' he said, as he bit his croissant, sending a shower of crumbs down the front of his hoodie.

'Absolutely not,' Mr Currie said. 'I'm proud to have two bands from Carleton Road School in the competition. I'd be very happy if either of them won.'

Mrs Jopling looked like she was sucking on a lemon as he said that. Tristan didn't look too happy either, because Erin was sweeping pastry flakes off Babatunde's hoodie.

'And you've got a blob of tomato on your nose,' Erin said.

Although he looked eccentric with his deep voice, giant retro sunglasses and hoodie, Babatunde was very well-mannered.

'You must be Tristan and Alfie's mother,' Babatunde said, as he looked at Mrs Jopling.

'That's right,' she nodded, still not looking happy. 'And you're a drummer like my Tristan.'

'He's better than me,' Tristan admitted.

'Well he would be,' Mrs Jopling said defensively. 'He's older than you.'

Tristan looked slightly embarrassed.

'So why did your family move down to London?' Mr Currie asked.

'Dad got a job at the Royal Free hospital.'

Mrs Jopling nodded. 'Unemployment's dreadful up north, isn't it? What is he, a porter or something?'

Babatunde smiled slightly. 'My dad's a surgeon. He's chief consultant at the new cancer unit. My mum's a GP, but she's working back in Nottingham until she relocates in a few months.'

'Two doctors,' Erin smiled. 'Your family must be minted.'

'Have you thought about becoming a doctor when you're older?' Mr Currie asked.

Babatunde shrugged and looked a bit sheepish. 'My two little brothers scooped all the brains.'

'I think I saw your dad on telly,' Alfie said. 'He's a black guy, isn't he?'

Everyone cracked up laughing and Alfie turned bright red.

'Let me finish,' Alfie protested. 'I mean, he was on the local news a while back, with the Mayor and Prince Andrew when the cancer unit opened.'

'Oh well,' Mrs Jopling said stiffly. 'It's good to hear that some of your people are doing well.'

Babatunde had heard stories about Mrs Jopling from Jay

and he had to mask his smile with the last third of his croissant. She was *exactly* how he'd imagined her.

'So what's the name of your new band?' Salman asked.

Babatunde laughed. 'That's the subject of hot debate. We rehearsed for three hours yesterday and the three brothers – Jay, Adam and Theo – were arguing the whole time. I kind of like Pony Baloney. Adam wanted it to be called It's Too Loud And I Can't Understand The Words, but that's way too much of a mouthful.

'We even thought about each putting a favourite name down and drawing them out of a hat. But we can't because Theo's nuts and keeps coming up with outrageous names like Seriously Stained Panties and The Vagina Miners.'

'That's our Theo,' Erin said, swelling with mock family pride.

Tristan sneered. 'I could just about live with Pony Baloney, but they're all fairly awful.'

'We can talk,' Erin scoffed. 'Brontobyte is like the geekiest band name *ever*. I told my mates I'd joined a band and they were all like *that's so cool*. Then they heard the name and it was like *or maybe not*.'

'Well, the band name was fixed long before you rode in,' Mrs Jopling said acidly.

Babatunde sensed friction between Erin and Mrs Jopling, and Erin's reply confirmed it.

'Well let's face it, mums are always biased,' Erin said. 'Tristan could write his name on the wall with a turd and you'd declare it a masterpiece.'

Alfie, Salman and Babatunde started laughing, but Mrs Jopling was outraged. 'Don't you *dare* take that tone with me,' she gasped. 'Maybe your family speaks like that, but I happen not to like it.'

'And what do *you* know about my family?' Erin said indignantly.

'Hey, hey!' Mr Currie said smoothly. 'We're not going to win with this sort of attitude. Let's all take a deep breath and count to ten, eh?'

*

Michelle was one of the least patient people on the planet and the wait for the tow truck made her crazy. She stood on the overgrown embankment beside the motorway, tearing weeds out of the ground and throwing them high into the air, showering everything around her with dry earth.

'If any more of that hits me I'm kicking you up the arse,' Lucy warned, as she shook black clumps out of her hair.

Summer stood by Coco's mum Lola, who was speaking to the recovery service on her mobile. It didn't sound good.

'We've been here nearly an hour,' Lola said. 'The police have been and gone ... Well, how much longer? ... But how can that be, it's exactly what you told me thirty-five minutes ago? ... Of course I'll wait. I'm standing on the edge of a motorway, where do you expect me to go?'

Lola snapped her phone shut furiously and shook her head. 'Our recovery truck is stuck in traffic jams heading into Birmingham. They're seven miles away, but they've got no idea when they'll get here.'

Summer looked disappointed. Michelle's reaction was to run to the top of the embankment and scream out. Then she turned around and saw that they were less than a hundred metres from a depressing-looking estate of recently built houses.

'Lucy, take a look up here,' Michelle shouted, as she pulled out her iPhone and hit the pinpoint icon.

The motorway and the layout of the housing estate emerged on to the phone's screen. Michelle zoomed the map out to get a better idea of their location.

'What's the matter now?' Lucy asked impatiently as she arrived alongside.

Michelle pointed at her phone screen. 'Rugby,' she said. 'The town centre is less than five kilometres away. How about we grab our guitars, get a taxi to pick us up and head for the station? Remember when we got the train to London that time Mum dragged us to see that bloody musical? Rugby was only an hour from London. We could still make it to Camden by eleven o'clock.'

'If we got a cab quickly from somewhere round here and didn't have to wait too long for a train to London . . .' Lucy thought aloud. 'But I've got no idea how long it would take to get to the Old Beaumont. Even if we get there with the guitars, I won't have any drums.'

'There'll be boys with drums,' Michelle said, as she found a London Underground map on her phone. 'Flirt and ye shall have them. The train comes in to London Euston. It's one stop on the Northern Line to Camden Town. Easy peasy, lemon squeezy.'

Lucy still looked uncertain. 'You try and find a number for a local taxi firm,' she said. 'I'll go speak to Coco's mum.'

29. Grassy Knoll

The two-coach sprinter train had left Edinburgh Waverley fifty minutes earlier. It now trundled down a single track, with barren Scottish countryside spread out on either side. Being school holidays, and one of the first warm days of the year, the train was busy with cyclists and families dressed in cagoules and walking boots.

Fifteen-year-old twins Max and Eve Fraser were pinned at opposite ends of a three-seat bench, with a huge bare-kneed fellow reading an Ian Rankin paperback wedged between them. Their overnight packs were in the rack above, while their guitars stood precariously in the luggage bay and had to be grabbed every time the little train stopped, started or went uphill. Leo was squeezed in two rows behind, next to a toddler with pop-up froggy eyes on the toes of her wellies.

Their stop was an unsheltered platform in the middle of nowhere and the trio felt a vague sense of being in the wrong place as the train guard helped them with their stuff.

'Where is he?' Eve asked, as the only other passenger to leave the train moved quickly towards one of three vehicles in the car park.

They grew increasingly nervous as the train pulled off in a plume of diesel fumes, only for Dylan to reveal himself across the tracks behind the train.

'You made it!' he said cheerfully, as he jumped down off a tractor and stepped across the rails.

This seemed wrong to the other three quarters of the Pandas of Doom.

'Don't worry,' Dylan said. 'Next train will be coming in the other direction in about forty minutes. And they daren't go too fast up here, cos you get cows on the line and it makes a right mess if they splat one of them.'

'You're a proper country gent!' Leo laughed, as he crossed the line with his backpack in one hand and his guitar case in the other, studying Dylan's black rubber boots and waxed jacket.

The ground beyond the tracks was muddy and Dylan gave a nervous-looking Eve a lift over a ditch.

'Luxury transportation,' Dylan said, pointing towards the open trailer on the back of his tractor. 'One in the front with me. Two and luggage in the back.'

'Is it safe?' Max asked, with characteristic suspicion.

'Shotgun,' Leo shouted, as he stormed the cab.

'I've been driving on private land since I was twelve and I've never killed anyone yet,' Dylan said.

Leo looked awed as he sat next to Dylan in the cab. 'Does your family own all this land?' he asked.

'Everything on this side of the railway tracks, out about as far as the third hill with the electricity pylons.'

As the tractor engine clattered to life, Dylan leaned out the side window and yelled a warning to Max and Eve in the back. 'It gets bumpy!'

He floored the accelerator and aimed the tractor across a field. It was picturesque, with old stone walls criss-crossing the land and sheep dotted about. After a stop to open and close a metal gate, Dylan drove on up a private road towards his home.

Four centuries earlier it had been a castle with turrets at each corner, but only one turret and a long section of castle wall remained. These now formed one side of a vast manor house, with sweeping lawns and a lake. Its central island had a grand hexagonal pagoda and a bare-breasted mermaid rising up from its centre.

'That's what I call a house,' Leo said. 'You never struck me as such a country boy though.'

Dylan laughed. 'I went through my Rambo stage between eight and ten. Charging around with a couple of local lads dressed in camouflage, trapping bunnies, sticking fireworks in cowpats, that sort of thing. Then I turned eleven and I just decided that I couldn't be arsed with anything cold and muddy.'

'So what do your parents do exactly?'

'Sorry,' Dylan said, as the tractor drove over a deep rut

and shuddered violently. It was worse for the passengers in the back and Eve yelped.

'My mum's American,' Dylan explained. 'She lives in California with my two half-brothers. But I haven't seen them for about four years. My stepmum is an artist. She's quite famous if you're the kind of person who's knowledgeable about seven-metre-high rubber foetuses, and my dad owns a music publishing company.'

'I'm officially jealous,' Leo said when they got near the huge house.

Dylan used a plipper to open the door of a stable block that had been converted into garages.

To Leo's surprise the tractor rolled down a steep ramp, cutting from the rustic barn into a cavernous underground garage, hidden away like the lair of some James Bond villain. The brightly lit space was filled with Ferraris, Porsches and Lamborghinis, along with crazy stuff like a bullet-proof Russian limousine and a car shaped like a giant golf ball. Along the back wall were more than sixty motorbikes, from pre-war Triumphs to exotically customised Harley-Davidsons.

A Norton racing bike was up on a hydraulic plinth and Dylan's dad worked beneath it, dressed in blue overalls. He strode over as Dylan cut the tractor engine. He was tall and had lost most of the hair on top of his head, but compensated with a shaggy moustache and curly grey locks that were currently confined inside a hairnet.

'Get the pressure washer and hose them tyres off,' Dylan's dad ordered, as Max and Eve stepped off the trailer and grabbed their gear. 'Don't leave my garage stinking like a cow's arse.'

'Dad, these are the mates I was telling you about,' Dylan explained. 'Eve, Max and Leo. We're gonna be rehearsing and stuff. Maybe watch a couple of films in the cinema and generally chill out.'

Dylan's dad held up palms covered in bike grease. 'I'd offer to shake, but you might not like the consequences.'

Eve stared down as usual, but Leo and Max both found something oddly familiar about Dylan's dad, though the hairnet threw them off the scent.

Max got it first. 'Terraplane,' he blurted.

'Jake Blade,' Leo gasped, before looking at Max and bursting out laughing. 'Bloody hell, Dylan, you didn't tell me your dad was Jake Blade.'

Eve didn't know the face, but she'd heard the name Jake Blade. Lead guitarist and founder-member of legendary rock band Terraplane.

Formed in 1981, Terraplane were one of the biggest rock acts in the world by 1985. They'd recorded three of *Rolling Stone* magazine's twenty-five greatest heavy metal albums of all time, sold almost two hundred million albums, and released an animated movie that knocked Steven Spielberg off the top of the box office charts.

When they broke up in 1997, their press release said that they'd done it all and wanted to quit while they were at the top. They'd been turning down hundred-million-dollar offers to go on tour every year since.

'Why didn't you tell us?' Max asked, as Dylan walked towards the tractor holding the nozzle of a high-pressure hose.

'Because I'm me, not Jake Blade's son,' Dylan said, matter-of-factly. 'I don't want people going on about my dad, or asking me to get autographs, or being my friend because we're rich. So don't tell anyone when you get back to Yellowcote, OK? Now stand back, and get those guitars out of the way unless you want 'em spattered with mud.'

*

'Taxi's here,' Michelle shouted, from the grassy knoll overlooking six lanes of speeding traffic and the stranded Peugeot.

Lucy ran up the hill with a guitar in each hand, while Coco stood by the road with her mum.

'Are you sure you'll be all right on your own?' Coco asked.

'It's broad daylight,' Lola said. 'The tow truck must be due any minute now.'

Coco gave her mum a quick kiss, then charged up the embankment behind Summer.

'Good luck!' Lola shouted.

Michelle led the way down the opposite side of the embankment and across a little swing park towards the waiting Toyota taxi. It was a tight squeeze, with four girls, plus bags and guitars.

Lucy glanced at her watch and spoke to the driver as he pulled away. It was 9:41.

'Do you think we can make it to the station in time for the 10:03 to London?'

'I'll try my best,' the man nodded. 'But there's a few roadworks in the centre of town, so I can't promise.'

As they drove through the estate and made reasonable speed on the main road into Rugby, Lucy rummaged through her bag looking for the form she'd printed when they registered for Rock the Lock. She found it under her make-up bag, but there was no phone number, only an email address and an ominous warning that the bands all had to arrive at the Old Beaumont by 10:30.

'Michelle, look up a number for the Old Beaumont,' Lucy ordered, as she scanned the forms carefully, looking to see if she'd missed anything the first time.

Michelle got a number, but it just put them through to a recorded information line telling them another number that you could use to book concert tickets, along with some web addresses. At the same time, Coco had used her phone to get another number. She had a printout saying that the Old Beaumont was owned by a company called Regal Entertainment Ventures and she'd found a number for their head office.

After dialling, she gave a convoluted explanation to a secretary, who said she knew who was organising the battle, but had to check with her boss to see if she was allowed to give his number out. After listening to Bach for seven minutes, the secretary came back on and gave Coco a mobile number for a man named Steve Carr.

By this time it was 9:54. They were in the centre of Rugby and the driver was pointing towards a shopping centre.

'It's a mass of roadworks around the front of the station,' he explained. 'But if you hop out here you can run straight across the precinct. Go down the alleyway between Debenhams and Shoeland, which'll take you to the side of the station. It's barely two hundred metres.'

Lucy threw a tenner at the driver as Summer and Coco grabbed the guitars out of the boot. Michelle ran ahead, vaulting the outstretched legs of a homeless man and entering Rugby station through a side door with sticky tape holding the glass in.

A glance up at the board told her it was 9:59 and the 10:03 was on time, rolling in at platform two. There were several people queuing at the ticket desk and Michelle rushed up to the barrier.

'Can we buy tickets to London on the train?' she asked urgently.

The fluorescent-jacketed guard nodded. 'You have to pay full single fare though. It's pricy.'

Lucy, Coco and Summer all piled up behind Michelle as the guard opened the gate to let them through without tickets.

'It's just coming in,' the guard warned. 'Up over the bridge and on to platform two. Get your skates on.'

The four girls raced up the stairs and ran across the bridge as the red and silver train opened its doors on the platform below them. When they got to the stairs down to platform two there were people who'd just left the train blocking their path.

'Out my way!' Michelle demanded, as she shoved her way to the bottom of the staircase and charged at the door of the train as the platform guard blew his whistle. Summer and Coco shot through a door into the next coach as the doors started to bleep.

Michelle tried holding the door open for Lucy, but she couldn't get a grip on the rubber edge. The metal step was folding back into the side of the train as Lucy smacked into the closing door. She saved herself from falling by grabbing a handle, but Michelle was gaping at her through the tinted glass with a look of open-mouthed horror.

'Stand back from the train!' the platform guard shouted. 'It's about to shift.'

As the train juddered forwards, Michelle looked about frantically before eyeing the passenger emergency alarm and reaching up to give it a tug.

30. Quiet Carriage

Big Len was one of a dozen drivers charged a tenner to park in a gravel lot overlooking the Grand Union Canal, beside the Old Beaumont. It came on top of the forty-pound entry fee for each band, three-pound tickets for spectators, plus the bar was open inside doing bacon butties, tea and coffee and a bunch of kids were feeding arcade machines and pinball tables while they waited for their band to play.

Len had been in the music business his whole life and added numbers in his head as he carried Babatunde's bass drum through the enormous side doors of the Old Beaumont. He looked back at Jay, who was just behind carrying a cymbal stand.

'I reckon they can make a grand, perhaps even a grand and a half out of this competition,' Len told Jay. 'It's not bad going for a venue that just sits empty every day. I bet I could set one of these battle of the band thingies up and make a few extra quid myself.'

Len didn't understand Jay's expression until they reached the centre of the room and Jay spun around in awe. The Old Beaumont's capacity was three thousand, with steeply sloped seats up in the royal circle and a large standing area in front of the stage. There were five-metre speaker stacks, spotlights rigged up on a gantry overhead and an authentic rock venue smell of old sweat and spilled beer.

'Cool,' Jay grinned. 'It's *massive*.'

Len's business brain saw a way of making money out of an empty concert hall, but for Jay and all the other kids Rock the Lock was a chance to plug their guitars into a 25,000-watt PA system and indulge their fantasies of being real life rock stars.

'Nice place,' Babatunde laughed, as he did a full three-sixty-degree twirl. 'I might go out back and see if there's any groupies waiting.'

The scene around the stage was chaotic. Parents and band members had brought in drums, guitars and equipment and had no clear idea where to go with them. On one side a pair of women in Terror FM T-shirts were figuring out how to put the radio station's metal display stand together. The next table along was better organised. It was selling Rock the Lock T-shirts, beanies and guitar plectrums and had already attracted a girl clutching a ten-pound note.

'Are we ready to rock!' a beanpole on stage shouted, demanding attention because his voice was amplified through the giant loudspeaker stacks. He was geeky-looking, wearing tight-fitting tartan trousers and a white leather jacket with *Country Sucks* written across the back in rhinestones. 'Can I have all the contestants gathered around the stage please?'

It took about a minute for a crowd to gather. Jay ended up standing near Salman and Alfie, who both acted friendly.

The Country Sucks man didn't use the PA once the crowd was gathered front of stage. 'Good morning, everyone,' he said. 'I'm Steve Carr, welcome to Rock the Lock, which is the London leg of the Terror FM battle of the bands 2014. We've got eighteen bands lined up today. If you're due to play after lunch, you should *not* be bringing equipment into the building now.

'Each band can be accompanied by a maximum of two adults. Any extra bodies need to leave *now*, then go around to the front and buy a ticket when the main doors open. In order to let eighteen bands play in one day, we've split the stage down the middle. If you're playing first, third, fifth, seventh or ninth, you set up in Zone A to my left. If you're playing second, fourth, sixth or eighth, you need to use Zone B to my right.

'Each band has fifteen minutes to set up and sound-check with the engineer, followed by your ten-minute set. As soon as you've played, clear off your equipment quickly. If your set goes over ten minutes the PA will be switched off. If you take too long to set up, you'll lose playing time.

'The first band from the morning group will play at 10:45. The next band at 11:00, 11:15 and so on. The last morning band will finish playing at 1:00. The afternoon session runs from 1:45 to 4 p.m. and final results and award ceremony will take place shortly afterwards. Any questions?'

A few parents asked questions and a mum complained about the parking being a rip-off.

'Bands play in alphabetical order,' Steve said finally. 'First up are The Albinos in Zone A. Followed by Brontobyte in Zone B.'

Jay gave Alfie and Salman a smile. 'Good luck. You might finish second behind us if you play *really* well.'

Salman gave Jay a friendly up-yours gesture as he headed up towards the stage. Tristan was moodier and gave Jay a dig in the ribs as he walked past. Adam dug Tristan back and growled.

'You starting on my baby brother?'

Tristan looked scared, but Mrs Jopling saw what was going on and stormed over.

'Go and get set up, Trissie,' she said acidly. 'He's just trying to rile you.'

Adam laughed and adopted a high voice. 'Kissy, kiss, Trissie Poos! Mommy loves you!'

Mrs Jopling eyeballed Jay and wagged her finger. 'Stay away from my boys. You've already caused enough trouble.'

Her boots clacked across the wooden floor as Adam and Theo noticed their mum coming in the back of the hall with Hank dragging her by the hand. As the boys walked across to say hello, Len pulled Jay aside and introduced him to Steve Carr.

'Steve runs the Old Beaumont now,' Len explained. 'But

we worked together at Lovegroove Studios back in the day.'

'Good to meet you, Jay,' Steve said. 'We've got a tiny problem with your registration. I can't put your band in alphabetical order when you haven't got a name.'

'Oh,' Jay said, as he glanced around looking for his band mates.

'It doesn't really matter,' Len said. 'It's just for today.'

'And it has to start with a letter between C and N, because A and B are already setting up and N through Z play after lunch,' Steve added.

Jay thought of all the names they'd fought over the day before. Pony Baloney was his favourite, but P was too far down the alphabet, so on the spur of the moment he blurted, 'Jet.'

'Nice and short,' Steve laughed. 'That should put you on eighth. You'll need to be ready to set up in Zone B at 12:15.'

*

The train stopped after moving a few metres down the platform but the doors remained closed. A siren squealed, interrupted after every third whoop by a well-spoken lady.

The passenger alarm has been activated in coach C. Please remain seated and await instructions from the guard or driver.

Michelle felt uneasy as she read the sign below the door: *Fine up to £1000 for improper use.* Her dad would fork out, but her Christmas list would be severely endangered.

Summer and Coco came through from the next carriage. A train guard ran from the opposite direction, his grey uniform bulging with change and a ticket machine straining around his clammy neck.

'What's gone off here then?' he asked, breathlessly.

Michelle had a plan and made a discreet go-away signal to Summer and Coco. 'My sister's out there,' she wailed, in an extraordinarily high pitch. 'I'm sorry, I got really scared.'

The noise was like scraping chalk and the guard recoiled. 'All right, love, calm down, eh?'

He grabbed his walkie-talkie and told the driver to open the doors.

As Lucy hopped aboard, the platform guard rushed over.

'You shouldn't let her on,' he moaned. 'They ran at the door. She almost went down between the train and the platform. They would have had my job if she did.'

'We're visiting our mum in hospital,' Michelle yelled dramatically. 'She's got breast cancer. She might die!'

Summer and Coco stood in the end vestibule of the next carriage. They looked at one another, unsure if Michelle had pushed her story beyond credibility. But Michelle was as smart as she was crazy and the mention of breasts and cancer were perfectly calculated to make the male guard uneasy.

'I'm not standing here arguing, we're losing time,' the train guard told his colleague, though he wondered if he'd been conned when he saw Lucy smile at Summer and Coco with their guitar cases.

The train left Rugby nine minutes late, and the four girls got scowled at by irritated passengers as they moved down a crowded carriage. They traipsed the full carriage and halfway down the next one before finding an empty table with four seats around it. By this time, the train was almost up to full speed.

As Lucy and Summer stashed the guitars in the overhead rack, Coco pulled her mobile from her pocket and dialled. Steve Carr answered quickly, but it was hard to hear with the combo of train noise at this end and guitars tuning up at the other.

'Is that Steve?' Coco shouted, as she noticed the *Quiet Carriage* sticker on the train window.

The other three listened anxiously as Coco explained about the car accident, then gasped with relief when Steve said that they could move into the last morning slot and wouldn't be scheduled to set up until 12.30.

If the train arrived on time they'd have an hour to go one stop on the tube and find the Old Beaumont. Steve even spoke to someone called Big Len, who said he'd be happy for the girls to use his drums.

Coco had a huge smile on her face as she ended the call. 'Steve said that he always waives the thing about being at the concert early if it's a genuine emergency. We've got time, we've got drums.'

'I may not be able to play my best on a strange kit, but apart from that it's all good,' Lucy said.

A man in a suit leaned over from the seats behind and aimed a finger at the *Quiet Carriage* sticker. 'Excuse me, I'm trying to read here.'

Summer looked apologetic. 'We've just had a bit of an emergency, sorry.'

'There's a sign on *every* window,' the man huffed.

Michelle looked at the sticker and spoke with a dumbo voice. 'Qui-et car-riage,' she read. 'So does that mean I can't do this?'

Michelle stood up on her seat, flapped her arms like a chicken and howled at the top of her voice. 'SQUAWWWWK! SQUAWWWWK! SQUAWWWWWWWWWK! Who's a pretty birdie? SQUAWWWWWWWWWWWK! Don't make noise. SQUAWWWWWWWWWWWK! Quiet carriage. SQUAWWWWWWWWK! SQUAWWWWWK! SQUAWWWWWWWWWWWK! Be quiet and let the slap-head sitting behind read his Kindle.'

Half the carriage was looking their way as Lucy grabbed Michelle's legs and swept her feet off the seat. Summer and Coco were in an uneasy spot, halfway between laughter and fury.

'Stop pissing about,' Lucy ordered, as she tried clamping her hand over Michelle's mouth.

'SQUAWWWWWWWWWWWWK!'

Michelle finally quietened down when the guard who'd opened the door for Lucy came storming down the aisle. He already felt conned after seeing the guitars and he wasn't happy.

'If I get any more aggro from you lot I'll kick you off at the next stop,' he shouted. 'Now, where's your tickets?'

'We haven't got any,' Lucy said, as she reached into her

bag for a purse. 'The guy on the ticket barrier said we could buy on the train.'

The guard nodded, and pressed a couple of buttons on the ticket machine around his neck. 'How old are you?'

Lucy pointed at Coco. 'We're sixteen, these two are fourteen.'

'So that's two adults and two children, Rugby to London Euston. Comes to one hundred and seventy-six pounds eighty.'

All four girls gawped.

'Eh?' Lucy said, before looking at Coco. 'Have you got money?'

'Mum gave me fifty quid,' Coco said. 'But I had no idea it was *that* expensive.'

'It would have been about seventy pounds if you'd queued up in the station,' the guard explained. 'We can only sell the most expensive single tickets on the train.'

'We were late,' Michelle said. 'We had to run.'

Lucy looked in her purse. She had the forty pounds her dad had given her and about ten pounds more. Michelle about the same, Coco had thirty pounds.

'I've only got money for my lunch,' Summer said guiltily, as she pulled a crumpled fiver out of her bag.

When all their money was pooled in the middle of the table, Lucy counted and it only came to £152.

'And we'll need money to get back to Birmingham this evening,' Summer said warily.

The guard grunted as he raised his radio to his lips.

'George here. Can I get the train manager down to coach B, urgently please?'

Coco looked pleadingly at the guard. 'So what happens now?'

'Train manager's decision,' he explained. 'If you've no way of paying she'll probably arrange for the BTP to pick you up at Milton Keynes.'

'What's BTP?' Summer asked.

The guard smiled at her naivety. 'British Transport Police.'

31. Giant Bluebottle

Dylan was too modest to take his band mates on a tour of the house, but they got a decent idea of its vastness as their footsteps echoed along a broad, oak-beamed hallway more than a hundred metres long. Bizarre conceptual art adorned the walls, from a giant mirror-finished Jeff Koons balloon dog to a two-metre-high bluebottle with all the legs on one side snapped off.

'The courtyard goes around in a square,' Dylan explained, as the others looked about in awe. 'It was originally built so that the owner could exercise his horses indoors in the winter.'

For once Eve was looking up at the ceiling instead of down at the floor. 'Does your dad have horses?' she asked.

'Nah,' Dylan said. 'But he's been known to have motorbike races around here when he's pissed. That's how Dave Ingram smashed up the bluebottle last Christmas. Boy, was my stepmum pissed off about that.'

Leo laughed at the mention of Dave Ingram. 'I don't care what anyone says, Ingram's the best guitarist ever. Hendrix and Clapton are nothing in comparison. Do you know him?'

'He's my godfather,' Dylan said. 'And he's married to my auntie.'

Max looked his usual irritated self as he studied a sculpture made from hundreds of toilet seats.

'It's obscene really, isn't it?' Max said. 'That you can get all this material wealth by playing a few rock songs, while other people slave all their lives and make next to nothing.'

Leo laughed. 'Oh, you can talk, Max. Your dad's a divorce lawyer. At least Terraplane's records made people *happy*.'

'This is the studio and rehearsal wing,' Dylan said, as he pushed open a huge walnut door. 'It used to be the ballroom, but there's not much call for balls these days.'

'Nice,' Leo said, as he entered a long, narrow balcony area lined with huge leather sofas and a bar at one end.

There were posters for obscure movies all along the walls, most of them Scottish. Down below was a large rehearsal space, with a huge collection of exotic guitars along the back wall.

'I've seen this movie,' Max said, as he studied a poster depicting a drugged-out student standing by a crashed car. 'It's bizarre. It makes absolutely no sense.'

'Cinema's my dad's main thing now,' Dylan explained. 'He puts money into low budget movies, and does the soundtracks. He reckons soundtracks are more creative than four minutes of heavy rock.'

'So do you think your old man will ever get back with Terraplane?' Leo asked.

Dylan shrugged. 'The five band members get on pretty well, but my dad says that's as good a reason to stay apart as it is to get back together. And don't ask my dad about that. He'll happily spend all night talking about wild parties, trashed hotels and all the crazy rock star stuff, but he gets sick of people asking about Terraplane re-forming.'

Dylan walked down a few stairs and opened another door into a large sky-lit room lined with dark soundproof tiles. There were smaller rooms off three sides, visible through narrow windows.

'This is the main recording space,' Dylan explained. 'Off the back you've got two sound booths for recording drums, vocals and stuff. On that side you've got the main digital mixing desk. Opposite you've got another mixing desk that came out of Lovegroove. Have you ever heard of that?'

'Most famous recording studio in the country, apart from Abbey Road,' Leo nodded.

'Terraplane recorded all their stuff at Lovegroove,' Dylan explained. 'This room is closely modelled on Lovegroove's main studio and when they went broke, my dad bought the old mixing desk and anything else that's worth having and set it up here.'

'So it's just historic?' Leo asked.

Dylan shook his head. 'It's all in working order and it gives you a *beautiful* atmospheric sound, completely different to modern digital recordings. But it's fifty-year-old equipment, most of it hand built, so it's not very reliable and it has a horrible habit of going wrong. When my dad uses it, he has a couple of engineers flown up specially.'

Max laughed. 'So if we do any recording, we'll use the modern one?'

'Exactly,' Dylan nodded. 'So do you guys want a drink or something to eat first, or shall we start setting our gear up?'

'I had three McMuffins at Edinburgh station,' Leo said, as he rubbed his large stomach proudly. 'I say we get down to some music.'

Dylan stepped across to Eve, who was inspecting a set of drums. 'I set this kit up for you last night,' he explained. 'It's more or less identical to what you've been using at Yellowcote, but there's heaps of other equipment down in the ballroom if you want to take a look.'

Eve gave her approval with a nod and a smile, then she took off her backpack and unzipped the side pocket. She'd been using the same pair of Zildjian double-ended sticks for years. She chewed them habitually, like some people chew pencils, and the result was thousands of tiny teeth marks.

'There's about a hundred pairs of new sticks out back,' Dylan offered.

Eve shook her head, pulled the sticks close to her chest and rocked them like babies. Being shy around new people was one thing, but Dylan had been in the band for three weeks now and the more time he spent with Eve, the odder she seemed.

Max asserted himself as he took his guitar from its case. 'I've written two new songs,' he stated importantly. 'I think they're rather good and we should start by working on them.'

The studio was quite chilly and Leo laughed as he burrowed inside his overnight bag looking for a sweatshirt. 'Modest as ever, eh Max?'

As Leo pulled out his top, a black and gold can fell out of the bag and rolled across the studio floor towards Dylan.

'Rage Cola,' Dylan said, as he picked the can up and read the blurb. '*Warning – This Cola may be dangerously refreshing.* What kind of morons do they employ to come up with these awful slogans?'

'I've never tried it,' Leo said, as his head popped through his sweatshirt. 'They were handing out freebies at the station.'

Dylan was about to pass the can back to Leo when he saw the blurb on the back. '*Rock War – Do you know how to rock?*' he read aloud. '*We're searching for the twelve best young rock bands in Britain, to take part in a major televised competition. Visit ragecola.com now to upload your band profile, vote for your favourite band and get coupons for free music downloads for your mobile.*'

'Sounds tackier than a bucket of wallpaper paste,' Max sneered. 'Like X *Factor*, or *The Voice*. Your chances of getting in will be about a million to one. It's all based on looks rather than talent and even if you won you'd be permanently typecast as some cheesy act from a TV show.'

Dylan studied the can more carefully, reserving his

judgement. 'My uncle Teddy says there's no such thing as bad publicity.'

'And what would Uncle Teddy know?' Max asked.

Dylan mocked Max's sniffy tone. 'Uncle Teddy is the manager of Terraplane and about twenty other bands. He sold his record label to a major for thirty million pounds. So Max, it's *just* possible that he's one of the *tiny* number of people in the world who knows a *little* bit more about the music industry than you do.'

Eve gave a rare laugh.

'I say we should at least check out the website,' Leo said. 'There's thousands of kids like us in bands all over the country. You need to grasp every opportunity.'

'Perhaps later,' Max said reluctantly, as he pulled out the notepad he used to write songs. 'But I came out here for some serious rehearsals and that's what we should concentrate on.'

Leo clicked his heels, gave a military salute and barked, 'Sir, yes, sir.'

32. Late Arrival

Theo was full of himself as he rolled through Camden High Street's bumper-to-bumper traffic in the big Nissan. The sun was out, he had a Foo Fighters CD going full blast, drumming on the steering wheel. He had a decent car, money in his pocket and he'd spent the night with a hot girl who'd practically thrown herself at him. Now he was off to muck about at being a rock musician with his brothers and even the cute chick at the bus stop seemed to be smiling at him.

Did life get any better than this?

A lazy turn took the 4x4 up on to the kerb in front of the Old Beaumont. Theo thought about being cautious and parking his stolen car somewhere a few minutes' walk away, but he felt invincible so he rolled into the car park. The bays were all full, so he parked up near the fire exit alongside the building.

He'd been to a couple of gigs at the Old Beaumont, so he knew his way around and headed straight for the toilets. He hadn't showered or eaten breakfast and he stood in front of the mirrors, popping a zit on his chin.

'Who's a pretty boy then?' Adam laughed, as he stepped on to the tiles and slapped his brother on the back. 'I hope last night was worth it, because Mum's in there and she ain't happy with you.'

Theo tutted. 'You could have covered for me.'

'You know what Mum's like,' Adam said, with another laugh. 'Comes bursting into our room this morning. What could I do, pretend you were under the bed?'

Theo smiled as he led Adam out of the bathroom. 'It *was* worth it, anyway. I took some nude pictures of her on my mobile while she was sleeping. I'll Facebook them later.'

'You're not even human, are you?' Adam grinned.

As the brothers headed up a short corridor which opened out to the right of the stage, The Albinos were nearing the end of their set. The group comprised four clean-cut lads dressed in hoodies. They all played well enough and the singer had a decent voice, but the overall effect was bland.

There were roughly a hundred band members and spectators spread across the hall. Out of respect for little kids and parents in the audience, the PA was set somewhat below the ear-splitting level you'd expect at a full-on concert. You could hold a conversation without raising your voice too much.

Theo caught the smell of bacon as he reached the middle of the dance floor. 'I'm starved. Can you lend us a couple of quid, mate?'

Adam had a tenner, but lending money to Theo was no different to giving it away.

'Completely broke, mate,' Adam said. 'Sorry.'

Theo rummaged in his pockets and pulled out a crumpled fiver. As he waited in the sandwich queue with Adam, a tall blonde with a drinks cooler hanging off one arm and *Rage Cola* written in gold across her T-shirt approached. She pulled out black and gold cans and glossy leaflets.

'There you go, boys,' she said, as she smiled with big glossy teeth.

'Has it got your phone number on it, babe?' Theo said, raising one eyebrow cheekily as he inspected the leaflet with mild contempt.

The girl kept smiling through gritted teeth. 'It's all about *Rock War*,' she explained. 'It's going to be *huge*. Twelve under-eighteen bands get picked for a competition. The winners get a recording contract and then they spend Christmas in the Caribbean recording their first album. The show's going to be on Channel 3, starting in the summer holidays.'

Adam nodded and waggled the leaflet, as Theo reached the front of the queue and ordered his bacon roll. 'I'll show it to my little brother,' Adam said. 'Cheers for the freebies.'

Theo tore a huge mouthful out of his roll as the boys turned back towards the stage. Their mum Heather, plus Jay, Babatunde, Len and Hank, were all gathered together at the bottom of the stairs leading up to the seated area.

'Got to fight the dragon some time,' Theo nervously

whispered to Adam, then spoke enthusiastically to his mum. 'Really good of you to come and support the band, Ma.'

Heather wagged her finger in Theo's face. 'Don't you try soft-talking me, Theodore. I signed parole forms, agreeing to take care of you and help enforce your curfew when you got out of lock-up. What was I supposed to do if someone rang to check on you? Or if your parole officer knocked on the door?'

'I just forgot,' Theo said dopily.

'You're a bloody idiot,' Heather said, as she cuffed Theo around the head. 'You're grounded for the rest of school holidays.'

Theo looked aghast. 'You can't ground me. I'm sixteen!'

'If you want to live under my roof, you live by my rules,' Heather shouted.

'I'll move out then,' Theo said defiantly.

Heather laughed. 'Who'd have you? You've got no job, no money. And that's another thing. Your contract says you're supposed to go to school. You're going to end up doing a long stretch, like your dad and your older brother.'

The Albinos climaxed in the middle of Heather's rant and *You're going to end up doing a long stretch, like your dad and your older brother* echoed over a burst of applause. Loads of people looked around, including Mrs Jopling and Mr Currie who all stood less than ten metres away watching Brontobyte's final sound check.

'I met some bird who was up for it,' Theo shouted,

knowing everyone would hear. 'What sane man would turn that down?'

Jay was getting uneasy. They'd already reduced their mum to tears once that morning and she didn't look happy with Theo defiant and the entire hall gawping at them.

'Why don't we all calm down, eh?' Len suggested.

Mrs Jopling couldn't resist making a comment. 'Some families give the gutter a bad name.'

Len shouted back at her. 'Why not keep your beak out, princess?'

Jay was relieved. The one thing guaranteed to unite his family was an outsider having a dig at them.

Heather charged across the dance floor. 'How's your husband?' she asked Mrs Jopling. 'Is it the secretary or the squash coach he's having an affair with this month?'

Mrs Jopling looked like she'd been punched, but the clock was ticking on Brontobyte's set and the row got swamped out by Salman's voice coming through the 25,000-watt PA.

'We're Brontobyte,' Salman shouted. 'This is our first song.'

And he started to sing:

> Christine, Christine, I'm not being mean,
> Your body's not the best that I've ever seen,
> But I'm a desperate guy, never catch a girl's eye,
> And I can't deny, that you've got nice thighs.

Jay turned towards Len in a state of complete outrage. 'That's my song!' he shouted over the noise. 'They can't play that. I wrote the lyrics and I did all the arrangements.'

'Life's too short,' Len said, as he pressed his giant hands down on Jay's shoulders. 'Don't get yourself wound up.'

Mr Currie's tuition of Brontobyte had paid off with a tighter sound. At first Jay thought it was something to do with Erin being a better lead guitarist than him, but she needed practice after a long lay-off and sounded quite rusty.

Mr Currie's stroke of genius was to make Tristan play within his limited abilities. He sat behind a smaller drum kit, with no floor tom and a single cymbal. The tempo of 'Christine' had been slowed slightly and a complex section in the chorus removed.

All Tristan had to do was keep banging the same rhythm for two and a half minutes. It didn't sound great, but the four members kept time and Salman's powerful and quirky singing distracted the listener from the fact that the music was pretty basic.

'They sound a lot better than three weeks ago,' Jay told Adam warily.

But his brother dismissed the threat. 'Don't you worry, kiddo. We'll wipe the floor with 'em.'

33. Tiny Tina

Tina the train manager was a petite woman with a bulbous arse, dark glasses and the titchiest nose Summer had ever seen. She collected the four girls from coach B and led them and their guitars through six cars to an empty first class carriage.

'Right,' she growled, as the girls sat nervously around a table that was larger and more luxurious than the one they'd stood up from a few minutes earlier.

The ticket inspector stood behind his boss, eyeing the girls suspiciously. 'Watch out for 'em,' he warned. 'I've already heard some cock-and-bull story about a sick mother.'

'Daft business, running at trains,' Tina said, matter-of-factly. 'A twenty-two-tonne coach'll hack your legs like a knife through Cheddar cheese. Had one a few years back. Feet ended up three miles from his head. Bits of him all along the tracks and some poor bugger's job to clean it all up.'

This image made Summer queasy as the high-speed train blasted through a station.

'There's two ways this can go,' Tina explained. 'If you can give me some identity, or a phone number for someone who can pay by card, I'll give you a pass for travel to London. If you haven't got either of those, I'll have to hand you across to the cops at Milton Keynes or Euston.'

'We're not far from Milton Keynes now,' the ticket inspector noted. 'I expect it'll be Euston.'

Michelle looked at Lucy. 'Call our dad,' she ordered.

Lucy was wary, because while she got on with her dad, he was dead strict about his girls going out alone. 'He'll flip if he knows we're going to London without Lola.'

Michelle pulled out her phone. 'I'll call if you're too chicken.'

Lucy grabbed Michelle's wrist across the table. '*You're* not speaking to Dad. You've got all the tact of an angry bull and I'll end up grounded for life.'

Tina looked irritated and tapped her wedding ring on the table to get everyone's attention. 'OK, let's start with some identification, shall we?' She pointed at Summer first. 'What's your name?'

Before Summer could answer, Lucy screamed out as Michelle kicked her under the table.

'Let my arm go,' Michelle demanded.

'I'll call *my* mum,' Coco told Tina. 'She knows where we are and she won't mind paying as long as she gets the money back.'

But Lucy and Michelle were beyond the point of reasoning. Michelle kicked her sister under the table again, forcing Lucy to jump out of her seat.

'Sit down!' Tina ordered.

'Quit or they'll get the cops on us!' Summer said nervously.

Michelle followed Lucy up from the table, leaving Tina sandwiched between the sisters. Tina tried pushing Michelle back into the seat, but Michelle wouldn't budge.

The ticket inspector closed up behind Michelle. 'Pack it in,' he ordered.

'Don't kick me,' Michelle shouted to Lucy.

'OK, you lot have had it,' Tina roared. 'The cops can sort you out.'

The train was beginning to slow down for Milton Keynes as the train manager pulled out her radio. Lucy panicked and tried grabbing it.

'Oh no you don't,' the ticket inspector shouted, as he moved in to protect his boss.

'Why don't we all calm down?' Summer shouted desperately.

Tina keyed up her radio as the ticket inspector grabbed Michelle.

'Code three, code three,' Tina shouted. 'I need all train crew in coach . . .'

The decelerating train juddered before Tina finished her sentence. It wasn't much, but it was enough for Lucy to lose her tussle for Tina's radio. The train manager stumbled backwards and caught the side of her dark glasses on the hard edge of a headrest.

Summer and Coco screamed in horror as Tina's eyeball came out of its socket and bounced off the tabletop before rolling towards the window.

'Her eye!' Coco squealed, as she covered her mouth with her hands.

But as Coco spoke, both girls realised that they weren't looking at flesh. Tina's dark glasses had been hiding a false eye, which had been dislodged when her face hit the headrest.

'This is *so* bad!' Summer blurted.

Tina had broken free and was running towards the front of the train to get help.

'Run for it!' Michelle shouted, as she grabbed her guitar case and aimed it at the ticket inspector.

He raised his arms to defend himself, but the case painfully caught his elbow, knocking him back into a row of seats as Michelle forced her way past.

'Run where?' Coco asked.

Summer was torn: part of her was disgusted and didn't want to be involved, but who'd believe her innocence? And her nan would die from shock if she got arrested.

'Come on,' Coco shouted, as she grabbed the other guitar case and straddled the fallen ticket inspector.

Michelle and Lucy seemed to have forgotten their differences as they bolted back down the train towards standard class. The quartet only got through one carriage before finding themselves trapped in a queue of people waiting to get off. On the upside, anyone chasing after them would face the same obstacle.

'These doors had better open,' Lucy said, as she crouched slightly and watched the platform and a coffee bar passing slowly by the windows.

Five horrible seconds elapsed between the train stopping and the reassuring *bing-bong*, followed by the train doors opening.

The girls pushed their way off the train and raced up the stairs away from the platform. There were a couple of shouts down below, one of which sounded a lot like one-eyed Tina.

At the top of the stairs, the girls found themselves in a broad hallway, built above the platforms. There were electronic barriers up ahead, but they had no tickets to get through, so they backed up to the wall as the other passengers swarmed by.

'I say we storm the barriers,' Michelle said. 'I'll jump over first and grab the guitars.'

'And then what?' Summer asked anxiously.

'Jump on a bus, grab a taxi,' Lucy gasped. 'Anything that gets us out of here.'

But Coco looked up at the platform boards. 'Ten thirty-eight London Euston, platform three,' she read. 'Let's go for that, it's only six minutes.'

'But what if they see us?' Summer gasped. 'Even if we get away they could spot it on CCTV and pick us up further down the line.'

But the crowds leaving their train were thinning out and the die was cast as tiny Tina emerged at the top of the stairs. Before much longer there would be four easily identifiable girls in an empty hallway.

Lucy gave Michelle a shove. 'Platform three, shift!'

As Coco led the scramble down to platform three, her phone started to ring. She saw that it was her mum, Lola.

'We're just changing trains at Milton Keynes,' Coco said breathlessly. 'Can I call you back in a minute?'

'Sure,' Lola said. 'I just wanted to say that I'm in the recovery truck and everything's fine. How about you?'

'Yeah, we're great,' Coco lied, as she reached the platform. 'Love you, Mum, speak later.'

The information display over the platform said that it was 10:34 and that the 10:38 train to Euston was still on time.

'Could we still make the gig?' Michelle asked.

Lucy scowled at her. 'I doubt it. This train's making about six stops.'

'Who cares about Rock the Lock?' Summer said, as her hands trembled. 'I just want to get out of here without getting busted.'

'Four girls, two guitar cases,' Lucy said, as they moved further along the platform. 'We stick out a bloody mile.'

They all looked scared as a speaker announcement went across the station. 'Ladies and gentlemen, I'm sorry to announce that due to an assault on train staff, the service now waiting on platform one will be terminating here. Passengers for London are advised to cross over to platform three, where they will be able to board a London-bound service in approximately four minutes.'

Summer felt like she was going to hurl on the platform. 'If we get caught we're in so much trouble,' she said.

'State the obvious, why don't you?' Michelle said unsympathetically.

'It's coming,' Coco said, as she spotted a commuter train trundling towards the platform. 'We're less conspicuous if we split up.'

'We'd be much harder to pick out if we threw the guitars away,' Lucy suggested.

Coco shook her head. 'This guitar cost six hundred quid. We're not all rich girls, you know.'

'And what do we do?' Summer asked. 'Get off in a couple of stops, or what?'

The announcer spoke again. 'All tickets for the London express will be validated for the Midland Trains service now arriving at platform three. Unfortunately, we can't hold this service, so can passengers please hurry to platform three as quickly as possible. This service is due to arrive into London Euston at approximately 11:22.'

The four girls all looked at each other. 'That's only twenty minutes late,' Lucy said. 'It's tight, but we could still make it to the Old Beaumont.'

A great crowd now spilled off the steps on to platform three, as the shabby commuter train rolled in.

'We've come this far,' Lucy said. 'I'm not giving up now.'

34. Huge Brass Acorn

After playing 'Christine', Brontobyte clattered through a workmanlike version of The Rolling Stones' 'Start Me Up', and finished their ten-minute set with Erin joining Salman on vocals for a duet of 'Stan' by Eminem. The money Mrs Jopling had paid Mr Currie had been well spent, because they sounded ten times better than at the Camden schools competition four weeks earlier.

Erin gave Tristan a quick kiss, before helping him carry his drums off the back of the stage. Alfie and Salman both wore crazy grins as Mr Currie came out of the wings and slapped them on the back.

Jay had wanted Brontobyte to crash and burn and he seethed as the stage lights flicked to the band on the opposite side of the stage.

'We're the Free Rangers and this is gonna be loud!' a shaggy-haired boy shouted into the microphone.

'"Christine" is my song,' Jay shouted, when Tristan

emerged through a door at the side of the stage, next to the speaker stacks.

Tristan was buzzing after Brontobyte's performance and the kiss from Erin. He gave Jay the finger and a confident smile. 'We nailed it, Jay, you scrawny streak of piss.'

Mr Currie, Salman and Alfie had emerged through the door behind and Mrs Jopling was coming over to congratulate her boys. Feeling outnumbered, Jay retreated towards his family at the rear of the dance floor, but Tristan sidestepped his mum and went after him.

'Yeah, back off, you little chicken shit,' Tristan taunted, as the Free Rangers murdered a Red Hot Chili Peppers song up on stage. 'You really think you're the dogs, don't you? You thought we'd be nothing without the mighty Jay, but we play better without you.'

Jay stopped walking a few metres from his family. He spun around and pointed at Mr Currie and Mrs Jopling.

'Tristan, your rich mummy paid for a tutor. And all *he* did was scale back the drums to make them so simple that even a goon like you can play 'em.'

'Whatever,' Tristan scoffed, as he pointed at Heather. 'At least my mum can keep her legs together. *She*'ll probably have another three babies by the end of the day.'

Theo was too far away to hear what Tristan had said, but the pointing and the expression set off his thug radar and he stormed across the dance floor.

'Are you talking about my mum?' Theo demanded.

Tristan backed away, but he had no protection from Mr

Currie or his mum, because they were taking Brontobyte's equipment out to the Porsche.

'What did you say?' Theo repeated, approaching Tristan with both fists bunched.

Jay was conflicted: he wouldn't mind seeing Tristan get thumped, but his mum would get upset and they'd definitely get kicked out of the competition for fighting.

'Theo, he's not worth it,' Jay said, as he stepped in front of Tristan.

'Who asked you?' Theo growled, sweeping his arm across, knocking Jay out of the way.

It wasn't a hard blow, but the polished floor was slippery. Jay stumbled back and ended up on his bum. But his intervention had bought Tristan a couple of seconds in which to turn and run.

The hall wasn't packed out, but nor was there room for teenagers to run at full pelt without hitting people. Tristan sprinted towards the side door, hoping to find protection from Mr Currie and his mum in the car park. But it was a thirty-metre dash over the open floor and Theo got a hand on his shoulder after less than fifteen.

Fearing a beating from the sixteen-year-old champion boxer, Tristan ducked and spun. Theo was heavier and his momentum carried him on across the slippery floor. As Theo slid, Tristan began running the opposite way. Bodies blocked his path, so his only escape route was upstairs to the balcony.

By the time he'd reached the bottom step, Theo was

charging again. Adam saw what was happening and tried to get in his brother's way.

'He's just a little sprat,' Adam shouted. 'You'll get us kicked out.'

But Adam was a couple of paces too slow and Theo powered on, springing up three stairs at a time. Jay looked up from the dance floor as Tristan ran across the balcony in front of the cinema-style seats. He looked terrified and with good cause: Theo's muscular frame was closing fast and Jay suspected he was just crazy enough to throw Tristan over the balcony.

Erin had run out to get Mr Currie, who now dashed across the dance floor, with Mrs Jopling trotting after him.

Len had also sniffed trouble and was racing up the stairs behind Adam, but nobody would reach Theo before he got hold of Tristan.

Theo was within touching distance as Tristan reached a staircase at the opposite end of the balcony. Jay gasped as Tristan threw his leg over the brass stair rail. He almost overbalanced, which would have led to a fifteen-metre plunge and brains splattered over the dance floor, but he kept his balance and began to slide down.

Theo decided that he didn't fancy the slide and began running down the steps. After cutting across the landing halfway down, Tristan began a second slide to the bottom. Theo had lost ground, but Tristan was moving fast with legs astride the railing and the huge brass acorn at the end of the handrail about to hit him between the legs.

Tristan clamped his thighs tightly, trying to slow down, but as he squeezed the banister, his trainer caught between two stair rods, tilting him violently across the stairs. He landed hard on his shoulder and rolled down the last four steps.

Tristan was dazed, but as he hit the dance floor he could see Theo charging down the steps towards him. Fearing a boot in the guts, Tristan brought his knees up to protect his chest. As he rolled he hit a man striding out of the lounge area.

He was tall and slim, dressed in boots and black trousers and holding a large paper shopping bag. Further up he had a black blazer with three stripes on the arm and a policeman's cap. Tristan looked over his shoulder and saw Theo retreating sheepishly towards the balcony.

'You all right down there, Tristan?' the policeman asked, as he offered the boy a hand up.

Jay hurried across as Sergeant Chris Ellington helped Tristan to his feet.

'Hello, Dad,' Jay said, as he broke into an involuntary smile. 'I never knew you were coming today.'

'I didn't say anything because I wasn't sure,' Sergeant Ellington explained, as he held the carrier bag out towards Jay. 'There you go, son. Your nagging and less than subtle hints have finally paid off.'

35. Crammed Like Sardines

Summer got outflanked by more wily passengers as she boarded the commuter train. With the larger express cancelled, she found herself packed so tight that she couldn't even raise her arm to grab the handrail, not that there was anywhere for her to fall amidst so many bodies.

Coco had boarded two doors down, but Summer's view of her was blocked by a wall of men standing around her. Summer felt anonymous, but that was no consolation if the others got identified by their guitars and she ended up alone in London, with no money for a ticket home.

At every stop Summer imagined police with dogs hauling passengers off the train as they searched for them. She imagined handcuffs, cells, sirens, prison vans, interview rooms. All the stuff she'd seen on TV, only with herself at the centre of it.

But she reached London Euston unscathed and the packed train spewed bodies, like a giant lung exhaling. As the first passengers stepped out, Summer gained some breathing space and the realisation of horrific pins and needles in her right leg.

She managed a backwards glance at Coco as the seated passengers shoved impatiently. When she took a step her leg felt like a dead weight. She was last out of the carriage, except for an elderly lady dressed in funeral black.

Coco's afro bobbed twenty metres ahead as Summer gave the old dear a hand down to the platform. Her leg still felt funny, but at least she now had the confidence that she could walk on it without falling flat on her face.

'I've got to get a taxi,' the lady explained. 'Do you know where they are, at all?'

'I've never been to London before,' Summer confessed, as she began to feel nervous about imminent ticket barriers. 'I think I might have lost my ticket.'

'It's all open here,' the lady explained. 'They usually clip them on the train, but with it being so packed the guard had no way to get through.'

This felt like the first good news Summer had heard all day. Passengers streamed past on both sides, but she stuck with the old lady, figuring she made a near-perfect disguise.

Beyond the nose of the train a grey concrete ramp led up to the station's main concourse. As the old dear said, there were no ticket barriers, but there was a phalanx of British Transport Police, dressed in high visibility vests and traditional police helmets.

There was no way to be sure, but it seemed likely that the

officers were there to pick them up. Summer hoped the old lady would make her look like she was travelling with her grandmother, but Coco was dark-skinned and gangly, with big hair and a guitar case. She was surely about to run out of luck.

'It's an old friend's funeral,' the elderly lady said, unprompted. 'We worked together in the curtain department.'

Summer didn't answer, unable to think of anything beyond Coco's bobbing afro. Once Coco reached the top of the ramp the floor levelled off and Summer could no longer pick her out. So she focused on the police helmets, none of which seemed to move. It seemed Coco had made it, but she couldn't be certain.

'Nigh on forty years,' the old lady continued.

'Sorry,' Summer said as she put on a false smile. 'I was a million miles away. That's a long time.'

With Coco apparently getting through, Summer felt more confident.

'You must have sold a lot of curtains between you,' Summer said.

The old dear chuckled appreciatively. 'Oh, I should think so.'

When they passed through the barriers they were still in conversation. Summer looked down, avoiding eye contact with any of the cops. She felt sick, then relieved as she spotted Coco across the busy white-tiled concourse. She was speaking with a student lad. He had giant sideburns and

Coco's guitar hanging off his arm.

'It was nice speaking to you,' Summer said. 'I hope you still make the funeral on time.'

'Lovely to meet you,' the old dear said.

Summer glanced backwards. Michelle and Lucy had got on near the back of the train, so they ought to be somewhere behind her. Then she picked up her pace to catch up with Coco and her new friend.

'I'm in London for a few days,' Coco told him. 'Give me a call tonight and we'll hook up. I'll buy you a beer, seeing as you helped me with my guitar.'

He had bad skin and a stoop. Coco was out of his league and the guy was grinning so hard that Summer felt sorry for him. 'It was great talking to you, Ariel,' he said, as he handed Coco's guitar back. 'Is your shoulder all right now?'

'I'll survive,' Coco said, then she waved as the young lad headed for the escalators going down to the Underground.

Coco spotted Summer, but they didn't speak until they'd gone through a set of automatic doors and out into the warmest day of the year so far.

'Ariel?' Summer said, managing a tense laugh. 'Nice name.'

Coco shrugged. 'When I got talking to him, I was wedged up against the train door with my head craned over. I kept seeing TV aerials on top of houses.'

There were wooden picnic benches stretched out in front of the station and a line of food cabins, with Krispy Kreme and Starbucks in the middle. Summer was about to ask

Coco if she'd seen the Weis when she spotted them sitting together on a tabletop.

The four girls felt like they'd been through a war as they all hugged and smiled.

'I thought I was going to *die* when I walked past all those cops,' Coco gasped.

'How'd you two get out here so fast?' Summer asked.

'We were in the rear carriage,' Lucy explained. 'So we jumped down on the tracks and cut across to the opposite platform.'

'Risky, but it worked,' Michelle grinned.

'We shouldn't stick around here together for too long,' Coco said. 'There's probably CCTV.'

'I've seen taxis with their lights on going up the side of the station,' Lucy said. 'Shall we pick one up along there?'

As Coco and Summer nodded in agreement, Michelle pulled her hand out of her pocket and spoke in a gruff voice. 'My name's Mr Eyeball, can I come too?'

The other girls recoiled as Michelle held the train manager's glass eye between her fingertips and swivelled her hand around as if she was playing with a sock puppet.

'Oh you're *sick*,' Coco said, as she backed away from the table. 'What's the point of stealing her glass eye?'

'She's probably got boxes of 'em,' Michelle giggled, before looking at her hand and speaking in a cutesy voice. 'Don't worry, Mr Eyeball, Mummy loves you lots and lots and lots, whatever those other horrid girls say.'

36. Summer Gets Killed

As a relieved Tristan staggered breathlessly towards Mr Currie and his mum, Jay opened the bag his dad had given him. He saw a leather jacket, but his initial reaction was wary. He'd always assumed that if he got a leather jacket someone would either give him the money, or take him shopping to buy it. He wasn't so sure about something picked out by his dad, whose casual attire revolved around lemon polo necks and grey slip-on shoes.

But he needn't have worried. It was the exact jacket he'd tried on about six weeks earlier when he'd been out with his mum. At the time he'd assumed she was letting him indulge his fantasy as a reward for helping with the monthly frozen-food shop, but there had clearly been phone calls between his parents behind the scenes.

'It's *awesome*,' Jay grinned, as he pulled the jacket up his arms over a hoodie and gave his dad a hug.

It was slightly long in the arms, but that was good because

it meant it would still fit in the autumn when it started getting cold again.

'Thought I'd spoil you,' Jay's dad explained. 'Seeing as I have cause for celebration.'

'You passed your inspector's exam?' Jay said cheerfully. 'Well done!'

By this time they'd strolled across to the rest of Jay's family.

'Hiya, Chris,' Heather said, as she hugged Jay's dad and gave him a kiss. 'Do you think Jay'll stop bloody nagging now?'

'If he doesn't I'll shoot him,' Chris replied.

Len shook Chris' hand, Babatunde was introduced and it was all smiles, except for Theo who felt instinctively nervous around police officers and steered clear. Jay didn't let his emotions show, but he was chuffed with his new jacket and it felt great having his mum and dad together to watch him play.

'Can I try your police hat?' Hank asked, as he looked up pleadingly.

'Just for a minute,' Chris said, as he passed it down.

'Can I try your stun gun?' Adam joked.

Chris laughed. 'It's flat actually. I used it on a ginger tom that keeps shitting in my garden.'

'I wouldn't mind one of those zapper things to keep you boys in line,' Heather laughed.

'I wouldn't mind one to use on Kai,' Jay said. 'Have you ever actually blasted anyone with it?'

Everyone looked disappointed as Chris shook his head. 'I'm mostly behind a desk, these days. Lots of forms and regular hours, just how I like it.'

'You didn't say you were coming,' Heather noted.

'I'm actually on a court day,' Chris explained. 'But the judge adjourned, so I'm free until one. Will you play before then?'

'Should do,' Jay said. 'We're scheduled for 12:30.'

'I can just about manage that,' Chris said. 'But I'll have to dash straight off afterwards. I take it you finally decided on a name?'

'The organisers put us on the spot and Jay came up with Jet for some reason,' Len said.

'I can think of worse names,' Adam said.

Babatunde nodded in agreement. 'We might end up sticking with it, just to save any more punch-ups.'

Chris looked at Jay. 'So you named the band after yourself?'

Jay gave his dad a *What did you tell them for?* expression, before turning nervously to his band mates. Adam took a couple of seconds to figure it out.

'Jay Ellington Thomas,' Adam blurted, as he eyeballed his brother. 'J-E-T, you cheeky little git!'

Babatunde howled with laughter and shook his head. 'Jay, you're a sly dog.'

Jay acted innocent, but couldn't completely stifle his grin. 'It just slipped out,' he said. 'I never even realised it was my initials.'

Adam tutted. 'Yeah, right.'

But Jay was saved from a further roasting because his band mates' eyes caught the four stressed-looking girls arriving through the side doors.

'Easy on the eyes,' Babatunde purred. 'I call dibs on the long-legged one with the afro.'

'I'll have the hot blonde in the black dress,' Adam laughed. 'Jay and Theo can fight over the two Asian birds. Owwww, that hurt!'

'Don't be so *bloody* sexist,' Heather said, as she flicked Adam's ear again. 'You make them sound like cattle.'

'I assume they're the girls that want to use my drums,' Len said, as he watched them talking with Steve Carr.

This got confirmed as Steve led the girls over. Despite Adam and Babatunde's bravado when the girls were across the hall, they both went quiet as the four of them approached.

'This is Industrial Scale Slaughter,' Steve explained.

'Thanks for lending us your drums,' Coco told Len.

'Anything for a beautiful young lady,' Len smiled. 'Judging by the accents you're all from Birmingham.'

'Nearly,' Coco said. 'A few miles down the road in Dudley.'

'Did you have a good journey down?'

The girls looked at one another, all guilty smirks, but they were admitting to nothing with Chris standing three metres away in police uniform.

'We usually have one band setting up one side of stage

while the other plays,' Steve explained. 'But as you're using the same drums, I'll do a quick sound check for both bands. After Jet have played, you'll just have to swap your guitars over and the engineer will adjust the sound levels. You've got a little while to get a drink and sort yourselves out. Any other questions, just come and find me.'

'No worries,' Lucy said.

'We appreciate you helping us out,' Coco added.

As Steve walked away Jay found himself standing half a metre from Summer. He was usually shy around girls, but they were so close that it seemed more awkward to keep silent than to say something.

'How long have you four been playing together?' he asked.

Summer smiled as she turned around. She was a couple of centimetres shorter than Jay. Her hair was a mess and her skin glazed, like she'd been running or something, but she had a sweet face and a great body.

'The other three have been together for nearly two years,' Summer explained. 'I just came in as singer a few weeks back. I really like your new jacket by the way.'

Jay looked baffled. 'How'd you know it's new?'

Summer reached up and flicked a cardboard tab hanging from a zipped pocket on Jay's arm.

'Oh,' Jay said. His face burned bright red as he reached around and ripped it off. 'I would have looked pretty dumb up on stage with that still on.'

'Oh, cute!' Summer said, as Hank stood beside Jay in his police hat. 'You haven't come to arrest me, have you?'

Hank made a pistol with his fingers. 'I'll kill you with my stun gun.'

'I'm Jay, by the way,' Jay said awkwardly, as Hank went *bang*.

Summer took a stumble backwards, acting like she'd been shot. 'I *was* called Summer,' she said. 'Glad I met you before I died.'

37. Rock War Men

Adam and Babatunde found their tongues, before Theo came downstairs and introduced himself to the four girls. Being in bands gave them stuff to talk about and Hank played the role of cute six-year-old for all it was worth, sitting on the girls' laps and scoffing Coco's Starburst.

Erin, Alfie and Salman also came over. Behind them stood a group of adults: Chris, Len, Heather and Mr Currie. The only hold-outs were Tristan and Mrs Jopling, who sat in the lounge area with cups of tea and matching scowls.

Jay loved the sense of being in a big friendly group, wearing his new jacket, talking about music, and above all the way Summer kept smiling and talking to him, even after his older and hunkier brothers had arrived on the scene.

'So what's our competition been like?' Lucy asked, as she looked back at the stage.

The band currently playing was called Frosty Vader. Their

sound was dominated by a Hammond organ and electronic samples of explosions and baahing sheep, while their lead singer danced about dressed in science lab goggles and a T-shirt with pictures of Beaker and Bunsen from *The Muppet Show.*

'The standard's not been *that* great,' Adam said. 'Especially considering this is supposed to be one of the biggest battles in the country.'

'Brontobyte were *shit* hot,' Salman said, before laughing.

'We nailed it,' Erin said proudly.

'You ripped off *my* song and your drummer can't play for shit,' Jay said. But he rued his words because it made him sound mean, and Summer stopped smiling at him.

'Rage Cola?' a woman holding a cooler box asked.

It was the same girl Theo had met earlier in the breakfast queue, but now she was accompanied by a tall bloke in his late twenties. He had olive skin and was dressed trendily in boot-cut jeans and a flowery shirt. He introduced himself as hands poured into the cooler to grab cans.

'I'm Zig Allen,' he began. 'Have you guys seen the *Rock War* leaflets we've been handing out?'

He got an unenthusiastic mixture of nods and headshakes as cans popped open.

'I work for Venus TV,' Zig continued. 'I'm the director and project manager for *Rock War.* We launched our website ten days back, and I'm here to meet with young adults like you, get a taste of this scene and encourage great bands to upload your profiles.'

Jay looked at Zig and felt awkward as he spoke honestly. 'No offence, but those reality shows are all a bit lame.'

Lucy had only just been handed a *Rock War* leaflet, but she nodded in agreement. 'Especially if it's for kids. Channel 3 Kids is all polo shirts, good teeth, let's all jump in the swimming pool! Nobody over the age of five even watches it.'

Adam pointed at Hank. 'Even he's outgrown it.'

Zig shook his head. 'It's not a kids' show. All our sponsorship and most of the production budget for *Rock War* comes from Rage Cola. They're marketing Rage to fourteen- to twenty-four-year-old males. That audience doesn't watch kiddies' TV and they're as cynical about talent shows as you guys are.

'My background is in rock video and environmental documentaries. I wouldn't dream of asking you to sing cheesy Backstreet Boys songs. I don't want your grannies doing a voice-over while we show pictures of your sixth birthday party, or some bald game show host patronising you with stupid jokes. It's gonna be a hardcore, rock music-oriented show.'

'Pay me ten grand and I'm in,' Theo interrupted.

A few people laughed before Zig continued. 'The first part of *Rock War* will go out three days a week during your summer holidays. We're gonna pick the twelve best bands who upload website profiles at ragecola.com. Then we're gonna put you all in a big country house. We'll have some real rock stars there to give you tuition, and stuff like team building exercises, plus a lot of fun stuff like parties and day trips.

'Everyone will have their own camcorder, so you get to make video diaries, which you can put on the website, and we'll use excerpts in the show. I want the whole thing to be edgy and a bit dangerous. So we'll be showing you cooking your own meals in the house, getting off with each other, jamming with your band mates and generally just messing around. If you get in, I reckon it'd be the best summer of your lives.

'At the end of the six weeks, we're going to set up a special *Rock War* tent at the Medway Festival, and you'll all get to play in front of 140,000 people.

'The second phase of the competition starts in September. We'll film you back in your ordinary lives, going to school and rehearsing with your band during the week. Then each Saturday, we'll fly you off to do concerts all around the country. Probably in venues like this. We'll bring in big headline acts too, who some of you will play with and hang out with for the day. And of course, if it's in your manor you can invite all your mates along, too.

'This part of the *Rock War* show will go out on Channel Three on Sunday evening, and either one or two bands will be voted off each week. The winning band gets a major label recording contract, and spends Christmas in the Caribbean recording their first album.'

Zig's spiel had done the trick and the kids all looked pretty knocked out.

'I bet about a million bands upload their profiles though,' Salman said.

'Your chances are better than you'd expect,' Zig told Salman. 'What I'm looking for is quite specific: good bands with three or four members all aged between twelve and seventeen. We've had the website up a while and we've only got about eighty band profiles uploaded, but most of them are absolute jokers.

'I'm not in any position to offer guarantees, but I'd go as far as to say that any band good enough to finish in the top few places at a battle like you're in here today has a *completely* realistic chance of making it on to the show.'

'So how do we enter?' Jay asked.

'Open a profile on the website, upload a demo, maybe a video clip, some pictures, song lyrics and stuff like that. It's just like setting up a Facebook page. If we like what we see, someone from Venus TV will be in touch.'

Lucy and Coco looked at one another. 'It's gotta be worth a shot,' Lucy said.

'Count all of us in,' Adam agreed.

'I'll speak to my mum,' Alfie said.

'You're only eleven,' Jay noted. 'So Brontobyte can't enter.'

Alfie looked at Zig in a state of alarm. 'I'm *almost* twelve.'

'If your birthday's before the summer holidays you should be OK,' Zig replied.

Alfie cracked a relieved grin and flipped Jay off. 'June 24th. In your face, suck breath!'

Zig had sold the kids dreams of *Rock War* so effectively that they were surprised when Steve Carr strode over and distracted them.

'Jet and Industrial Scale Slaughter?' he asked, and waited for nods to confirm it. 'We're running dead on schedule, so I'll need both bands backstage with your equipment and ready for a quick sound level check in just over ten minutes.'

*

As the Pandas of Doom rehearsed together, Dylan was finding his niche. Max had a high opinion of himself, but when it came to song writing he had some justification. Dylan lacked Max's creativity, but his understanding of music and his instrumental skills enabled him to quickly turn Max's overblown ideas into songs you might want to listen to.

This versatility also freed up the other three members, who could all sing. Max had a biting, slightly girlish voice and a lanky, compelling stage presence. Eve had to be coaxed into singing, but when she did it was sweet and every word seemed etched with her chronic shyness. Leo growled and sweated, a working man's blues coming from the fifteen-year-old son of a systems analyst.

Lunch was delivered to the lounge area at quarter past twelve, brought by a butler on an antique serving trolley. It was a big spread: fresh-baked bread, cheeses, half a salmon and a fruit bowl. The lower tray had juices, coffee and cakes.

'In my house you go down to the kitchen and put ham

between two slices of bread,' Leo said, shaking his head in disbelief as the butler headed out.

Dylan felt embarrassed as he grabbed a bread knife and sawed into a round loaf, still warm from the oven. 'Olive and walnut bread,' he explained, as he stuffed a piece into his mouth. 'My favourite.'

'So your dad has a full-time chef?' Leo asked.

'There's always a chef on duty from five in the morning until midnight,' Dylan said. 'If any of you want drinks or snacks, you just pick up any phone and dial 7 and they'll sort you out.'

'This *is* good,' Leo said, scoffing the hot bread as he loaded a plate with everything he could lay porky fingers on. 'If I lived here I'd be *so* fat.'

'You're already fat,' Max noted, as he inspected the cheeseboard.

'Fatter then,' Leo laughed. 'I thought *I* was a spoiled rich kid till I got here.'

'When I first got to Yellowcote, I didn't even know how to use the kettle in the rec room to make tea,' Dylan confessed. 'All you do here is pick up the phone.'

'Sweet tooth,' Eve said, as she went straight for chocolate and orange cake and a dollop of clotted cream.

'So what else have you got here?' Leo asked. 'Swimming pool?'

'We've got pools,' Dylan nodded.

By this time they'd all filled their plates and were moving on to the sofas.

'He said *pools*,' Leo noted. 'With an *s*.'

'There's actually a big projector in our spa area,' Dylan explained. 'You can lie in the hot tub and watch a movie. That'd be a cool thing to do this evening if you like. We've got spare swimming gear and I can speak to the kitchen and get them to make a cinema trolley: popcorn, sweeties, hot dogs, or whatever.'

'Chlorine brings me out in a rash,' Eve said.

'Oh well,' Dylan said, with a shrug. 'The main cinema room has a bigger screen and better sound anyway.'

'La-de-dah,' Max said.

Leo had spotted a Mac in the corner of the lounge. 'Mind if I use that? I assume it's got internet.'

Dylan gave a nod and Leo fired up the Rage Cola website. It was one of those annoying sites where it takes forever to download pretty menus and a fancy 3D interactive Rage Cola can.

You could manipulate the black and gold can with the mouse, making the condensation on the outside dribble in different directions, open the ring pull and pour the contents to the accompaniment of a satisfying fizzing sound, or an eruption if you'd shaken the can up.

'Stop playing with the can, Leo, it's not your penis,' Dylan said. 'Click where it says *Rock War*.'

Leo clicked, bringing up another tedious array of download bars and swirly 3D graphics. The end result was a picture of a Fender Stratocaster guitar and three options along the bottom: *Watch Rock War Trailer*, *View Profiles &*

Vote and *Upload Profile*.

'Upload profile,' Max said.

'I can read, Max,' Leo said irritably.

The next screen had a set of instructions along the side, but a video clip started playing automatically in the main panel. It showed a Dracula-type figure, wearing heavy white make-up, with long hair and purple-tinged sunglasses. His accent was American deep-south.

'I'm Billy-Don, lead guitarist from Fourth Down and Ten, and one of the many experts you'll meet at the *Rock War* summer camp if your band gets picked. I'm about to guide you through the five steps needed to upload your band profile, set your design and background, upload videos and songs and contact your friends to get them voting on the Rage Cola website. Your first job is to fill in the form, and remember: you must have an adult's permission before uploading your personal data. When you've finished, click ENTER and I'll be back to give some tips on how to make your band profile stand out from the pack.'

The video stopped and the screen changed to a lengthy band entry form.

Leo looked back at the band mates surrounding him. 'Shall we go for it?'

'What's to lose?' Dylan asked.

38. Countdown to Oblivion

Jay, Theo, Adam, Babatunde and Len were all backstage with their equipment as Frosty Vader packed up in Zone B. The seventh band was about to start their set in Zone A.

'Show respect for the band playing on the other side of the partition by making as little noise as possible,' Steve Carr warned.

'No problem, mate,' Len said, as Jay headed towards the door leading back on to the dance floor.

'Where you going?' Babatunde asked.

'Quick piss,' Jay said.

'You just went,' Adam said.

'I always go loads when I'm nervous. Don't worry, I'll be thirty seconds.'

Jay felt embarrassed as he left his guitar with Len and dashed across the front of stage past the three judges. The gents' was a foul pit at the end of a long corridor, with no soap, busted taps and missing doors on half the stalls.

After unbuttoning his jeans, Jay peed one tiny squirt, shook off a couple of drips, then glanced at himself in the mirror. He mussed up his hair, which was looking a little too civilised for a wannabe rock star. Then he studied his new jacket.

It looked kind of big and not as cool as he'd hoped. He thought about taking it off, but then his dad might be offended. Also, with the jacket and hoodie on his arms were bulked out and he wondered if he'd be comfortable playing.

But when Jay stepped back and took a deep breath, he knew it wasn't his arms, or his hair or his jacket. It was just nerves, and he needed to get hold of himself and run back to the others in time to set up. He set off down the hallway at a dash, dodging the guitarist from Frosty Vader.

On the way he passed the open side door, which bands were using to bring equipment in and out. He slowed when he eyeballed Summer, standing out on the tarmac looking upset. Part of him wanted to run on and not miss the sound check, but she looked pitiful and he stepped into the sun.

'Are you OK?'

Summer didn't speak, but she had teary eyes and a little pool of sick between her plimsolls.

Jay pulled a bottle of water out of his pocket. 'You want to wash your mouth out?' he asked. 'It's a new bottle.'

Summer broke the seal on the plastic bottle and sloshed out, spitting her mouthful on the tarmac.

'Thanks,' she said.

'Is it nerves?'

Summer nodded. 'Plus my nan was ill this morning, and we had the journey from hell to get here.'

Jay nodded sympathetically. 'I get the *worst* nerves. I've peed six times in the last half-hour.'

Summer bent forwards like she was going to be sick again, but it was just a dry heave. Jay felt awkward, because he was desperate to get back to his band, but it would be rude to abandon Summer. Then he heard a clanking noise and looked behind.

He looked back and saw two blokes in high visibility vests fitting a vehicle clamp to Theo's Nissan. He thought about intervening, but with Summer and the sound check already on his mind it was too much to process.

'I've really got to get back,' Jay said. 'You'll need to sound-check with us. Are you coming?'

'I should never have joined a band,' Summer sniffed. 'It was ridiculous. I was in my year seven musical and all I did then was puke my guts up.'

Jay couldn't think of anything more to say. 'I've got to go in,' he said finally, as he cut through the door into the musty hall. 'Sorry.'

After a couple of steps Summer caught up behind. 'Came all the way down from Dudley,' she said, having to yell because they were near the speaker stacks. 'I can't let the others down after all that's happened today.'

'You'll be fine,' Jay said, as he squeezed Summer's arm. 'We'll make tits of ourselves together.'

Summer smiled and nodded in agreement as they hurried

across the dance floor. Len and Babatunde were already on stage setting up the drums. Jay and Summer doubled their pace as they walked through the stage door. A concerned Lucy came forwards and looked at Summer's grey pallor.

'Are you OK? I looked all over for you.'

'I'll manage,' Summer said quietly. 'It's just nerves.'

'Bloody long thirty seconds,' Adam said, as Jay stepped on to the stage. 'What are you playing at?'

Jay didn't reply because he was distracted by Theo standing in front of him. He wanted to tell Theo that there was a man out back fitting a clamp to his Nissan, but they were due to play in less than five minutes and they'd have no singer if he stormed off to row with parking attendants.

Jay felt guilty as Theo grabbed hold and shook him by the shoulders. 'You got the jitters, little bro?' he said, with a laugh. 'Never worry about what other people think. They're all dickheads anyway.'

Lucy brushed past in the background where she inspected the drums and had a quick conversation with fellow drummer, Babatunde.

The band playing in Zone A had hit the end of their ten-minute allocation and the engineer in the control booth cut off the PA. Their spiky-haired singer threw her microphone stand over, pushed her way between the partition and launched a volley of bad language at Steve Carr.

'Same rules for everyone,' Steve shouted back. 'Now get out of my face, or you're disqualified for unruliness.'

'Nazi!' the girl screamed. 'We only needed fifteen seconds.'

Steve ignored the abuse and got on with his job. 'This is a quick, basic sound check,' Steve shouted. 'Jet first, then Industrial Scale Slaughter. Jet, are your guitars plugged in?'

Jay spun around and was relieved to find that Len had his guitar waiting.

'I've plugged you in and tuned you up,' Len said irritably, as he fed the guitar strap over Jay's head. 'You need to get that head straight, boy.'

'Sorry,' Jay said, as he realised that the clothes thing wasn't entirely nerves and paranoia. The long cuffs on the leather jacket would interfere with his fingers. He dropped his guitar in a state of panic, ripped off his jacket and threw it at Len.

When a band played a real gig, microphone placement, sound checks and setting up could take an hour or more, but with eighteen bands to get through, the process had been stripped to a bare minimum. Steve had each vocalist or instrument play for a couple of seconds and the engineer in the sound booth at the back of the hall twisted a few knobs when he figured the levels were about right.

Jay played a few chords and stopped when Steve Carr gave him a nod, then he looked out from the stage. There were at least a couple of hundred people in the hall. Some bands who'd played early had already left for lunch, but they'd been more than replaced by bands and spectators arriving for the afternoon leg of the battle.

Three judges sat at a long table a couple of metres back from the stage. There was a fat guy with a beard and a skinny woman with witch-like grey hair. The only one Jay had heard of was a younger bloke: a Terror FM DJ called Trent Trondheim who looked bored as he repeatedly stabbed a polystyrene coffee cup with a pencil.

Brontobyte had lined up just behind the judges, all standing with their arms folded. Tristan tried to look mean, but Salman, Alfie and Erin were doing it for laughs, pulling silly faces and trying to put off their rivals.

'You're set,' Steve Carr said, giving a double thumbs-up as he jumped off the back of the stage.

Jay glanced back at Len, who mouthed *Knock 'em dead*. The engineer pulled up the sliders, linking Jet's instruments into the main PA system. Jay's pulse quickened as a buzz of electricity ripped through the mighty stack of loudspeakers beside the stage.

He readied his fingers for the first chord and plucked his bottom string experimentally. The sound ripped out of the loudspeaker beside his head and all the way to the back of the three thousand-capacity hall, through the speakers rigged along the side walls. The power was awesome. It was like being God.

'We're starting with a new song,' Theo shouted, as he grabbed the microphone from its stand. 'My brother Jay wrote it and it's called "Friday Night Chip Shop Fracas".'

Babatunde did four beats on his cymbal to cue the band. Adam started grinding the rhythm on bass guitar and Jay was terrified that he was about to screw up his complicated intro.

He felt like he was thinking too hard, taking in too many things at once and unable to focus. Babatunde had erupted like a volcano. The disc jockey had dropped his cup in astonishment. Tristan had the weirdest expression on his face.

I'm gonna screw this up, I'm gonna screw this up, I'm gonna screw this up.

Jay thought he'd missed his cue, but he looked down and found his fingers playing the song. He'd practised a thousand times and it sounded better than he'd hoped. But it was an odd sensation, like he was looking down at himself from space, with some other guy playing.

Theo made a huge, gut-wrenching roar into the microphone and began spurting the lyrics.

> Chip shop on a Friday night,
> Always gonna be a fight,
> Hope my ma will be all right . . .

Len had been in the music business for more than thirty years and he'd helped to devise the set. Jay's new song took up the first three minutes, followed by 'Christine' without any pause between. Babatunde was the band's most obvious strength, so Len gave him ninety seconds of explosive drum solo while the others took a breather. Most bands finish with their biggest hit, but nobody knew any of Jet's songs yet, so they rounded off with 'Walk This Way'.

The Aerosmith classic had one of the all-time great guitar

riffs. It was Jay's biggest challenge in the nine and a half-minute set and he looked down at his fingers as he nailed every chord change.

Sweat pissed down his face, but he was on fire and stopped playing with eighteen seconds to spare, exactly like they'd done in rehearsal.

'Judges, I know where you live,' Theo shouted menacingly. Before smiling, 'And a big hello to my little brother Hank!'

Jay looked around at Adam, grinning helplessly as claps and whistles came out of the crowd. Adam smiled back. Babatunde had jumped up from his kit and gave Jay a high five. The judges were smiling and nodding with approval. Len had jumped back on stage and he slapped Jay and Adam on the back.

Jet had played a blinder.

39. Is ISS Better?

Jay, Adam and Babatunde rushed off the back of the stage past the four members of Industrial Scale Slaughter coming the other way. Theo leaped a metre and a half from the front of the stage, before scooping Hank off the floor and throwing his little brother high into the air.

'You said my name!' Hank shrieked excitably. Theo didn't usually have much time for younger siblings, so it was a big moment for Hank.

As Theo strode towards the back of the hall, Babatunde led Jay and Adam out of the stage side door. Erin was all smiles.

'Congratulations! You guys were really good.'

'You're not so bad yourself,' Babatunde said, though it wasn't clear that he was referring to Brontobyte's music.

Up on stage the girls were having a mini-row because Michelle had left tuning her guitar until the last second.

'Sorry about that,' Summer told the crowd meekly, as

Michelle grabbed her vocal mic and yapped like a dog. 'We're Industrial Scale Slaughter and this song is called "Dark".'

Jay spun around to watch his rivals. He didn't recognise the song, so he guessed it was one of their own. They sounded sharp, but there was nothing to write home about until Summer's mouth opened.

The lyrics were bland, but Summer's voice put a shiver down Jay's back. When the first verse ended she looked straight at Jay with a nervous smile.

Jay got the biggest rush. Summer was older, she was stunning and she lived a hundred and fifty miles away. Three things that made her impossible to have, but he'd never wanted anything so badly in his life and for an instant it didn't seem impossible at all.

This perfect moment ended as Theo gave Jay a friendly thump on the back before lifting him off the ground and giving him a painfully tight hug.

'You rocked that, you skinny sack of shite!' Theo roared.

As Jay's feet touched back down he saw his mum smiling at the edge of the dance floor. It was good seeing her happy, but then he remembered what he'd seen just before going on stage.

'They've clamped your car,' Jay shouted over the music, as he pointed at the sunlight through the side door.

'What?' Theo roared.

Jay moved his head closer to Theo's ear. 'Your Nissan. You parked on the zigzags by the fire escape.'

As Theo swore and ran off, Jay thought about going after

him, but he didn't want to be around when Theo went mental, so he headed towards his mum at the back of the dance floor.

She kissed him on the cheek. 'You're not bad with that guitar,' she smiled. 'I'm proud of you.'

'Is my dad around?' Jay asked, as he peered left and right.

Heather shook her head. 'He dashed off right after your set, but he said you blew him away and he's gonna try and come back later to watch the results.'

*

Bright sunlight hit Theo's face as he stepped outside. It was a beautiful spring day, with the smell from Camden Market food stalls around the corner and light glinting off the nearby canal. But Theo's eyes fixed on the tatty yellow clamp fitted to the front wheel of his Nissan, and the penalty notice on the windscreen.

> This vehicle was illegally parked on private property.
> Release Fee £125.
> Contact Stavros Parking Enforcement.
> Cash, Visa, MasterCard, Amex accepted, no cheques.

'Shit,' Theo yelled, then got into an even worse mood as he realised he was standing in puke.

Nobody likes getting clamped, especially by some dodgy-sounding private clamping firm that bordered on an extortion racket, but Theo had extra problems. He had no credit card, he certainly didn't have £125 in cash and even though the car was stolen he couldn't just abandon it. He'd been using the Nissan for five months, so the interior contained more than enough fingerprints to violate his parole and earn him a one-way ticket back to young offenders.

On the upside, Theo had stolen quite a few cars in his time. He knew a man who chopped stolen cars up for parts and he'd have something in his lock-up that would cut through a couple of chains.

He pulled out his phone, dialled, and was surprised by a woman's voice coming down the line.

'Hey, it's Theo. Is Stuart around?'

The girl sounded like she was stoned off her head. 'Not just now,' she said, before giggling.

'Well, can you get him?'

The pause lasted so long that Theo started thinking the call had disconnected.

'Nah,' the girl said finally.

Theo sighed. 'Listen, this is *important*. I need to talk to Stuart *urgently*. I need him to get down to the Old Beaumont in Camden with his acetylene cutting torch.'

'It'll take a while,' the girl laughed. 'I've got his mobile now. I'm his little sister. Do you remember me?'

Theo had been to Stuart's house a couple of times, and he pictured who he was talking to: early twenties, frizzy hair, nice body, but staring eyes and a weird face. Her name was either Karen or Kerry.

'So has he got a new number?' Theo asked. 'I've *got* to speak to him. Sooner the better.'

'He can call out, but you can't call him.'

Theo was getting more and more frustrated with the cryptic answers, but there was only one place he knew where you could call out, but not receive.

'Did Stuart get nicked?'

'Yeah, I told you that already,' the girl insisted. 'Cops raided the lock-up. Found a brand-new Lexus in three hundred pieces. Stuart and Carl are both on remand, man.'

Theo couldn't believe his bad luck.

'Have you got any spliff, Theo?' the girl asked. 'You wanna come round here for a smoke?'

'Maybe some other time,' Theo said bitterly. 'I've gotta go.'

As he hung up, a kid from another band walked by with a guitar case. 'Your set was great, dude,' he said.

'Cheers,' Theo said limply.

With no money and no gear to cut the clamp Theo was screwed. It was a small car park and he was blocking a fire exit. They'd probably tow the car in a few hours and once they did that, it would be extremely hard to get back because apart from a set of keys he had no proof of ownership.

He had no driver's licence, no insurance documentation or vehicle registration document. Eventually the clamping company would contact the police, who'd realise the car was stolen, dust for fingerprints and pay a visit to Thomas' Fish Bar to arrest him.

Theo only had one option: to destroy the evidence by torching his beloved Nissan.

40. Theo's Wild Ride

Summer felt her cheeks burn, ignited by two hundred sets of eyes and pressure to perform from three band mates behind her. But as she sang the opening lines of 'Dark', she shut her eyes and imagined herself back in the pit, swigging Sprite between verses, tapping bare feet and nothing but a brick wall to look at.

Then Michelle threw her concentration, moving to the front of the stage and playing her bass while balancing on the edge, teasing the crowd. No sane musician would wreck a short set by jumping off. But with Michelle, who knew?

Summer couldn't get back to the happy place and doubts hit like a slug in the gut. She wanted to be home playing Scrabble with her nan, or buried under a duvet. Anywhere but here.

'Yeeh-haar!' Michelle wailed.

Michelle didn't have a microphone, but Summer heard and it made her fluff the first line of the second verse. After that Summer sang all the right words, but nothing felt right.

When Dark ended, Summer looked across at Michelle and shouted with uncharacteristic force. 'How can I concentrate with you jigging about right in front of me?'

Michelle turned and scowled. Summer took a step back, half expecting a guitar wrapped around the head.

Fortunately Lucy backed her up. 'You know she's in a state, Michelle.'

The second song was 'Bears, Bikes, Bats and Sex'. Usually Michelle just sang random notes or the odd line in certain songs – countering Summer's vocal power with a thinner, high-pitched tone – but now Michelle joined Summer at the microphone, singing every word and doing a spastic, hip-swinging dance with her guitar.

It was impossible to say why, but it sounded OK. Summer even laughed as she copied Michelle's crazy bum wiggle and her voice soared with new-found confidence. It hadn't been the perfect start, but they had four minutes left to pull their set back from the brink.

*

Theo tried to make himself inconspicuous as he got in the driver's seat of the big Nissan. He'd stolen a few cars in his time, but the five months he'd had the Nissan was a record and the thought of burning her out because of a stupid wheel clamp did his head in.

There was a bunch of stuff he didn't want to lose hidden amongst the mess. He found a scrunched-up Tesco carrier bag and began stuffing in CDs, a spare mobile, packets of half-eaten sweets, a denim waistcoat and a bra with hearts on that reminded him of happier times. He opened the glove box and took out the swanky satnav he'd bought for thirty-five pounds in the White Horse, along with a giant pub-sized bottle of Smirnoff vodka that his aunt Rachel hadn't missed yet.

Theo unscrewed the bottle cap and slugged a couple of mouthfuls for courage. Then he fully reclined the driver's seat, crawled into the back and began splashing the clear liquid over the rear seats and into the boot. He kept going until there was two and a half litres of highly flammable vodka soaked into the seats and carpet.

He threw down the bottle and sat back up. Nostalgia hit as he put his hands on the familiar steering wheel, looked through the front windscreen and remembered good times: driving fast, scaring the crap out of pedestrians on crossings, drinking with the lads, the girl in the heart knickers and accidentally reversing through Morrisons' plate-glass window.

'Gonna miss you, old girl,' Theo said fondly.

He was crying, and not just from the eye-watering aroma of evaporating vodka. But as Theo went for his lighter he saw the opportunity for a final short-but-glorious trip.

With the four-wheel drive, Theo reckoned the clamped Nissan was good for twenty metres across the car park and that was the distance between the front of his Nissan and the rear of Mrs Jopling's orange Porsche Cayenne. It was parked tantalisingly close to the edge of the Grand Union Canal with Tristan's drums visible through the rear window.

'Call my mum a slag, eh Tristan?' Theo told himself, as he cracked an evil smile.

Theo worried that the alcohol fumes might ignite when he started the engine. He grabbed the bag with all his stuff inside and opened the door so he could easily jump out before turning the ignition.

There was no fireball as the engine clattered to life and after a quick glance to make sure nobody was around, Theo squeezed the gas pedal. The metal clamp shuddered as the car moved forward, but it wasn't enough to keep the car still and the big 4x4 gained speed.

Steering was a nightmare. The clamp caused all sorts of flickering lights and *bing-bong* warnings from the dashboard and its weight overloaded the power steering.

The sound of the steel grating on tarmac was deafening, and sparks spewed out several metres. After catching the rear right-hand side of an Opel van, Theo braced for impact. He locked his arms rigid against the steering wheel as his front headlight shattered against the Cayenne's rear bumper.

Full contact violently jolted Theo's head. The front of his beloved Nissan crumpled, but it had pulled off its final task. Mrs Jopling's big Porsche shot forward. Alarms sounded in the van and Porsche as Theo floored his brake.

The Porsche teetered on the canal's edge for a couple of seconds, as if deducing whether the water was too cold. It finally tilted over as Theo grabbed a lighter and a ball of newspaper and stepped out of the Nissan for the last time.

Theo only meant to knock Mrs Jopling's car in the water,

but the canal was about fifteen metres wide and the water level quite low. This had obscured everything but the funnel of the boat tied up on the embankment.

As Theo set light to the newspaper and threw it inside the Nissan, the Porsche crashed nose first into the bow of a narrow-boat. The alcohol erupted violently into pale blue flames. Heat blasted Theo's back as he sprinted away, and a huge black shadow loomed behind him.

The weight of the Porsche pushed the bow of the narrow-boat down, which in turn lifted the back end high out of the water. It was like *Titanic* in miniature, as plastic chairs, buoys and potted plants slid down the narrow-boat's steeply angled roof and splashed into the water.

Theo kept low as he jogged out of the car park, then slowed down and tried his best to look innocent as he cut on to the high street.

Industrial Scale Slaughter were playing loudly inside the hall, so only an elderly dog walker on the footpath across the canal witnessed the extraordinary scene of a floating Porsche, a burning Nissan and a huge wave as the boat crashed back into the water.

Man and dog raced up a steep grass embankment as a metre of water surged towards them. The stricken boat settled momentarily, but it had flooded through the front. The last of three mooring ropes ripped apart as it dived nose first to the bottom of the canal.

The high embankment meant that only fifteen centimetres of water swelled up over the edge towards the Old Beaumont.

It gushed across the car park, spreading out and growing shallower, but it was still several centimetres high when it reached the venue's side entrance.

Most of the water drained down the hallway leading to the toilets, but enough surged on to turn a third of the dance floor into a shallow puddle.

Steve Carr led the charge outside to see what was going on.

The torrent had briefly floated some of the cars parked nearest the canal, washing them back several metres and causing scratches and minor damage. But the Nissan was high off the ground and its interior burned ferociously.

Jay had taken Hank to the toilet and messed with his hair in a cracked mirror as an ankle-deep wash surged across the tiles towards him. The water had collected years of filth from the Old Beaumont's floors and it was grey with dirt, ring-pulls and cigarette ends.

He thought about jumping up on to the sinks to save himself, but he was more concerned about Hank, who'd just finished peeing.

'What's happening?' Hank bawled, looking alarmed as his brother scooped him off the tiles.

Jay's Converse flooded with icy water and the bottom of his jeans got soaked as he splashed up the slope towards the main hall, with Hank's arms around his neck.

By this time most of the crowd inside the Old Beaumont wanted to know what was happening and a dozen bodies jostled in the doorway.

Jay put Hank down on the tarmac and looked around. He'd beaten the rest of his family out into the sunlight, but not Mrs Jopling. She'd run up to the canal side, getting as near as she dared to the burning Nissan, and gave an horrific scream as her beloved Porsche bobbed in the canal.

41. Hard-Working Girls

The four members of Industrial Scale Slaughter were under bright spotlights and the glare made it tough to see anything more than ten metres beyond the stage. When their fourth and final song ended, they got no cheers or applause, just the main house lights coming up and the sight of people either heading out the side to see what was going on, or through the main exit to grab lunch.

Even the judges were looking to see where the sudden flood had come from and Michelle was pissed off. She unplugged her guitar and made a precarious leap from the stage. She splashed down in a centimetre of canal water and violently swung her instrument overhead. It crashed against the judges' desk, shattering a glass water jug and soaking their written notes.

'Do you know how much crap we went through to get here?' Michelle screamed. 'The least you shitbags can do is have the decency to look at us.'

The judges backed off in fright, as Michelle's guitar hit the floor. Up on stage Summer felt drained. They hadn't played their best and Michelle trashing the judges' table seemed to cut any chance of sympathy votes.

'Not our day, is it?' Lucy sighed, burying her head as Coco shook hers. 'What's going on out there? Looks like the canal flooded or something.'

With the PA switched off and the side doors open, the girls could hear the commotion outside. Down on the dance floor, Summer was surprised to see the handsome judge trying to reason with Michelle.

'I love that you've got your own sound,' the judge told her. 'Most teen bands spend too much time trying to be someone else.'

Then he approached the edge of the stage and looked up at Summer. 'And you're the best young singer I've heard in a while. You're a bit young now, but take my card and call me in a couple of years. I might be able to help you, if the whole industry hasn't gone down the pan by then.'

Summer reached down and took the business card: *Connor Cook, A&R Executive, KMG Records*.

'Thanks,' she said, feeling slightly better about herself.

Then the judge turned away and asked the other judges where they were going for lunch.

*

Black smoke poured from the dying Nissan as plastic and rubber fumes choked the air. There were about forty people standing about as a pair of fire engines turned into the car park. Mrs Jopling was at the centre of it all, putting on a show.

'I know who did this!' she screamed, as she pointed at Big Len and Heather. 'It was one of that lot. Theo most likely.'

Jay stood a few metres from his mum, with Hank tugging on his arm and begging to get lifted up so that he could see better.

BMWs drew up and a pair of cops emerged from each one. The fire crew had wheeled their hose across the car park. Their chief yelled at the crowd, herding people back as his men blanketed the smouldering Nissan in white foam.

Len and Heather were in the retreating crowd coming towards Jay. When Heather spotted Jay she stormed over and pointed at the burning Nissan.

'Is that your brother's car?' Heather demanded, in an angry whisper, as Len lifted Hank on to his shoulders.

'How should I know?' Jay asked, emphasising his point with a dramatic shrug. 'Theo's never home. Who knows what *your* son gets up to?'

'You'd better not be lying to me, Jayden,' Heather growled. 'Tell me the truth. Have you seen Theo running around in that car?'

Heather could make Jay's life miserable, but getting grounded, having his pocket money cut or even breaking up the band was *nothing* compared to what Theo might do if he grassed him up.

'Mum, I swear, OK?' Jay said. 'I have *no* idea whether that's Theo's car or not.'

'This isn't over,' Heather warned, with an ominous finger wag. But she had to halt the interrogation because a policewoman was approaching.

While Heather had been grilling Jay, the freshly arrived police officers had spoken to Mrs Jopling, who'd angrily repeated her suspicions about Theo.

'Heather Richardson? I understand that you have a son called Theo,' the policewoman began. 'Do you know where he is right now?'

Heather was furious, but that didn't mean she wouldn't defend her boys from the cops. She spoke with the posh voice that she usually used on the telephone.

'I haven't seen Theo since he came off stage with his band.'

'Well, do you have his mobile number?' the officer asked. 'We'd really like to speak with him and it's in everyone's best interests to clear this up speedily.'

'Oh, you know kids,' Heather said, as she smiled at Jay and made a false laugh. 'I've got eight of them and I can never keep track. They're always switching phones and getting new numbers.'

Jay tried not to smile at this blatant lie: his mum was like a bloodhound. She knew all her kids' mobile numbers by heart and you could guarantee a call if you missed a curfew by more than a couple of minutes.

The policewoman's lips went all thin and Jay could tell that she didn't believe a word his mum had said.

'Well, let me know if you do *happen* to hear from him,'

the policewoman said accusingly. 'There's an expensive car and a boat wrecked. It's not a problem that will just go away.'

As the policewoman walked off, Steve Carr was cutting between the crowd with a pair of police officers in tow. He stood a couple of metres from Jay and Heather as he pointed up to a CCTV camera mounted on the wall of the club.

'There's a wide-angle lens on that which covers the whole car park,' Steve told the cops. 'The recorder's in my office backstage and I'd suggest we go and watch the tape.'

42. Chip Shop Slut

Jay looked up at the camera with a sense of doom, then across at his mum.

'I know where the office is,' he told her quietly. 'It's right where Steve had us waiting before we played. If they get that tape, Theo's buggered.'

Her eyes opened wide. 'So you *do* know it's his car?'

Jay smiled nervously and covered his slip-up. 'I don't *know*, but who else is gonna pull a stunt like that? The boat and the car's gotta be a hundred grand's worth of damage. Theo's already on parole and if they get that recording they'll lock him up and throw away the key. I might be able to get the tape if you distract the cops.'

Heather thought for a couple of seconds. Jay was a good boy. She didn't want him getting into trouble, but seeing Theo locked up again would break her heart. She gave Jay an uncertain look.

'Try and get in there,' she said reluctantly. 'But don't take *any* stupid risks.'

As Jay cut back inside the Old Beaumont, Heather eyed Mrs Jopling, who stood near the fire engine giving details of her stricken car to a police officer. She pushed through the crowd, charged towards Mrs Jopling and belted her with her giant mum-sized handbag.

'You nasty old cow!' Heather shouted, as Mrs Jopling's butt hit the wet tarmac. 'Take it all back! My Theo ain't done nothing.'

A policeman lunged towards Heather and tried to restrain her. Heather knew she'd done enough to get arrested for assault, but she'd been in court enough times – on her own account and with family members – to know she was unlikely to get any more than a caution, or a small fine, for belting Mrs Jopling with a handbag.

She'd land herself in much more serious trouble if someone got injured, so she had to make the biggest, rowdiest scene that she could, without actually doing any damage. To this end, Heather ducked under the policeman's arms, dived on top of Mrs Jopling and clamped her arms tightly around her waist.

'Chip shop slut,' Mrs Jopling shouted, as her artificial nails clawed deep into Heather's neck.

'I need back-up!' the policeman shouted, as he looked warily at the tangle of flailing arms and messy hair in front of him.

Tristan wasn't so cautious. He waded in to protect his

mum, grabbing a handful of Heather's hair and snapping her head backwards.

Adam was in the crowd with Babatunde. He couldn't stand by while Tristan attacked his mum, so he grabbed Tristan by the ankles, punched him in the ribs and started dragging him towards the canal.

As Jay had hoped, the policewoman and the two cops who'd been looking up at the CCTV camera rushed towards the punch-up, but it was one of the firemen who grabbed his mum under the arms.

Mrs Jopling kicked upwards, hitting Heather in the belly with the heel of her boot. The pain gave Heather a hit of anger. To the fireman's surprise, she broke loose and – giving up her no damage strategy – stamped on Mrs Jopling's hand.

As Mrs Jopling rolled around screaming, Adam grabbed Tristan by his collar and belt, picked him up and set off towards the canal. Tristan twisted and spat, but Adam was too strong for him.

'Don't throw me in,' Tristan begged. 'I can't swim.'

At the same time, Erin was running towards them. 'Adam, let him go! He could drown.'

Theo probably would have thrown Tristan in no matter what, but Adam wasn't a psycho. He changed direction and dumped Tristan on the bonnet of a parked Mondeo. This made a good thump and left a dent in the metal, but Tristan wasn't hurt.

'Count yourself lucky,' Adam barked, then a hand

grabbed his arm and a huge black fireman tugged him backwards.

'Pack it in, eh boys?' the fireman ordered, as he stood between Tristan and Adam. 'You're gonna land yourselves in serious grief with all these cops about.'

As soon as Tristan felt safe he slid down off the car and gave Adam the finger. 'I swim great by the way. I just got my Gold Challenge award.'

Adam looked appropriately riled and glowered at Tristan. 'You'd better steer a wide berth when school starts again,' he warned. 'Me and Theo might just have to see how well your head swims in the toilets.'

'You won't lay a hand on him,' Erin said fiercely, as she sidled up to Tristan.

Five metres away, Heather and Mrs Jopling had now been separated by a mixture of police and fire officers, but they continued to scream abuse at each other. Len stood off to one side, comforting Hank, who was sobbing helplessly.

One of the police officers was a sergeant. He looked stressed as junior colleagues looked to him for instructions.

'Nick the women and the two sons,' the sergeant shouted. 'Sharon, order up a van and get back-up. We need to secure the area and start taking witness statements. We need forensics and photos of the damage to the cars. I want this *whole* car park cordoned off. Phil, get inside with Mr Carr and go to his office. If that camera's running, it'll clear this right up.'

*

Jay's two oldest brothers, Dan and Theo, were always in trouble with the cops, Adam's record wasn't unblemished, his aunt's pub was notorious for its trade in stolen property and even his mum had been done for handling stolen goods. But despite the heavy criminal background, the biggest thing Jay had ever stolen was a Parker pen from another kid's pencil-case when he was in year four.

He'd been nervous before going up on stage to perform, but he now realised it had been a good kind of nervous, like electricity going through his body. This was bad nervous. Nausea and dread, with a tightness in his chest as if Kai had just thumped him.

The main hall was mostly empty. Some of the afternoon bands were hanging around and there were quite a few people up back in the lounge area, unravelling packed lunches, or queuing up for burgers or bacon sarnies at the food counter.

Jay put his hood up, and pulled the drawstring tight, hoping that it made him harder to recognise as he darted in front of the stage. There were only two people on the dance floor area: a lonely figure watching over the Terror FM merchandise stand and a janitor.

Judging by the cleaning equipment on hand, it was far from the first time that the Old Beaumont had been flooded by the adjacent canal. The janitor was using a two-metre-wide V-shaped mop to scoop water from the dance floor, while a petrol-powered fire pump had been wheeled out from under the stage. It made a thunderous racket as it sucked the filthy water out of the bathrooms and back to the canal via a fat outlet pipe.

Jay was prepared to be challenged: he'd just say he'd left his jacket backstage. But nobody took any notice as he cut through the stage side door beside the loudspeaker stack. He felt all clammy and the hood over his ears made his nervous breathing seem really loud.

The top half of the office door was frosted glass. It had *Marty Schott Venue Manager* painted on the glass, but the name had been scribbled out and *Steve Carr* written above it with a spirit marker.

Jay didn't want any fingerprints giving him away, so he pulled his cuff down over his hand as he turned the silver doorknob. He jiggled it back and forth. The glass shuddered, but the door was locked.

With no idea how long his mum's distraction tactics would delay the cops, Jay felt a new sense of urgency as he inspected the keyhole in the centre of the metal doorknob. Theo probably would have been able to bust it open in five seconds, but Jay didn't have a clue. He either had to give up, or smash the glass.

With luck, the noise of the pump would disguise the smashing glass, but this was a serious step. If someone walked in now he could just say he was looking for his jacket, and whether they believed him or not they couldn't prove otherwise.

Once he smashed the glass, there was no way to deny

what he was up to. And it wasn't just that he was breaking in. He was breaking in, secure in the knowledge that Steve Carr and the cops would be here at any moment.

43. Top Notch Thai

Jay thought about his mum's words: *Don't take any stupid risks.*

Smashing the glass was a stupid risk by almost any definition, but his family always being in trouble had taught Jay one thing about the law: if you're under sixteen, you'll only get a police caution for a first minor offence. And a kid smashing a window was about as minor as it got.

So he was balancing a stiff talking-to from a police officer and the cost of replacing the window, against a long sentence for Theo, a broken heart for his mum and the loss of his band's lead singer.

It seemed like a no-brainer, but Jay was crapping it and also disappointed in himself. He'd always thought he was a better person than a yob like Kai, but here he was breaking and entering, and causing criminal damage.

Jay looked around trying to find something he could use to break the glass and spotted a fire extinguisher next to the four steps leading up to the stage. As he grabbed hold, he looked out across the stage. His view of the dance floor was limited, but Jay reckoned he'd have seen bobbing heads if Steve Carr and the cops were coming.

Scared of flying glass, Jay shut his eyes as he pushed the end of the fire extinguisher through the pane. The noise was about ten times louder than he'd imagined and he was utterly convinced that either the cops or the janitor were about to burst through the stage door and grab him.

But nobody came as he used the bottom of the extinguisher to bash out the jagged shards stuck in the bottom of the window frame. Then he put the extinguisher down, pulled his cuff back over his hand and reached through the broken glass to grab the doorknob on the other side.

It was a precarious business, because big chunks of glass still hung from the top and sides of the broken pane. Jay gripped the knob and for two horrible seconds it seemed it wasn't going to open. His cuff made it hard to grip the smooth metal, but he took one final squeeze and finally mustered enough force to shift the bolt.

More glass rained down as the lightweight door swung open. Jay snagged his hoodie as he pulled his hand out through the door and cringed as he imagined veins in his arm getting sliced.

His soggy black Converse crunched on the broken glass as he stepped into the office. It was a large space, with two desks and a musty air, despite the big sash window at the far side of the room being wide open.

Jay spotted a television monitor and a pair of aged VHS

surveillance recorders standing on a trolley between a water-cooler and a battered photocopier. As he crouched down in front of them, he flew up in shock as something clattered behind him.

Jay thought it was over as he spun around, but all he saw was a pair of budgies in a cage, standing atop a heavy-duty safe. He managed a relieved smile as he hurried back towards the recorders.

There was no way of knowing which one recorded the signal from the car park camera so he pressed both eject buttons with his cuff-covered hand. As the two recorders whirred and spat out tapes, Jay heard Steve Carr coming through the stage door. It sounded like he was speaking to a police officer.

Jay could almost feel handcuffs on his wrists as he grabbed the two videocassettes and buried them in the pocket of his hoodie. He was too weedy to barge past two grown men, but he was on the ground floor so the window offered him a chance.

Getting to the window involved crawling over Steve's cluttered desk and Jay got a huge shock when he looked out. All he could see was the canal lapping a metre below, though when he stuck his head right out he saw a ledge about fifteen centimetres deep just above the waterline.

The ledge sloped slightly downwards and looked far from safe. But while Jay didn't fancy a dunk in cold, filthy canal water, he'd earned his Gold Challenge award on the same day as Tristan, so it wasn't like he was going to drown.

'Damn!' Steve roared, putting his hands on his head as he stepped on the broken glass in the doorway.

'Don't disturb anything,' the police officer warned. 'It could be evidence.'

This remark saved Jay's bacon, because Steve looked down to see where he was stepping. If he'd looked straight ahead he would have seen Jay's trailing leg swing out on to the ledge.

'Looks like he's long gone,' the policeman said, grunting with frustration as the person he was looking for shuffled along the ledge less than three metres away.

Jay pressed his back to the wall and struggled to keep upright as he looked around. The canal was about fifteen metres wide. Large blobs of the foam used to extinguish the burning Nissan cruised on a gentle current, like mini icebergs.

To Jay's right, the ledge stretched about twenty-five metres along the side of the Old Beaumont, but he'd have to cross back in front of the window to get there and even if he could make it without falling in, he'd emerge into the crowded car park.

The left initially looked more promising. About twenty metres away the canal widened out and changed direction. There was a footpath where the Old Beaumont's brick walls retreated by several metres, but also a big hitch: a gap of several metres between the end of the ledge and the start of the footpath.

Jay realised he'd have to swim and thought about his

belongings. His phone was in his jeans, along with his wallet and under-sixteen travel pass. Then there was his watch. He'd forgotten to take it off in the shower a few times and it had survived, but would it withstand full submersion in the canal?

As he considered all this the policeman's head popped out of the window. Jay pressed his arms flat against the wall and turned away, hoping that the back of his purple hoodie was less visible than his face.

'He might have swum across, but I doubt it,' the officer told Steve. 'I've dealt with Theo Richardson before. He's no Einstein. Frankly, I'm surprised he was smart enough to come back for the tape. But, I'd bet my right nut that we'll pick up DNA, or a footprint that matches his boots.'

Footprints.

Jay's jaw gaped. He'd carefully covered his hands with the cuff of his hoodie, but he hadn't considered footprints. His sodden shoes had probably left a trail all the way across the dance floor, through to the office and even showing his escape route across Steve's desk top.

His Converse high tops were completely wrecked and the worn sole would leave marks as distinctive as any fingerprint. And he'd snagged his hoodie on the glass in the door and probably left behind a few fibres from that. He'd have to dump all his clothes when he got home.

If he got home.

The longer Jay stuck around, the greater the risk that

someone would come strolling along the opposite embankment and spot him. He had to move. He didn't want to make a big splash and alert the people inside the office, but his precarious position on the ledge made it almost impossible to enter the water delicately.

Jay began by bending his knees. As his hoodie scraped down the brick wall he looked into the water and saw a huge furry body swimming by, a few centimetres below the surface. He thought it was weird for a cat to be swimming in a canal, until he saw the long pink-hued tail and realised it was a giant rat.

This completely freaked him out. He remembered learning about the plague being spread by rats in history class. And if rats lived in the canal, didn't that mean they pissed and shat in the water? The thought was so gross that he considered waiting it out. If Steve and the policeman left he might be able to sneak back through the office.

But Jay's left trainer skidded as he pushed up to straighten his knees. His body tilted sideways and his right leg plunged into the water, closely followed by the rest of his body. Momentum carried him under. For a couple of seconds the freezing water shocked him stiff, but his natural buoyancy brought him back to the surface.

Jay shuddered and gasped as his head broke the surface. He felt heavy with all his clothes on. A few drops of water had sneaked between his lips and it had a vile, gritty taste. There was also an oily film on the water's surface, either oil from the sunken canal boat or some chemical from the fire-suppressing foam. Whatever the cause, his eyes felt like they were on fire.

He forced them open and looked about, disorientated. Jay hadn't selected a route before falling in and what with the sick taste and burning eyes he picked the quickest way out, kicking back against the canal's wall and launching himself at the opposite embankment.

Jay swam powerfully, crossing the water in barely twenty seconds. By the time he got there a little white cabin cruiser had appeared around the bend and was coming his way at a speed way over the canal's ten mile an hour limit.

Upper body strength wasn't Jay's greatest virtue and he had a struggle trying to grip the slippery canalside kerbstones and pull his body half a metre up and out of the water.

As the cabin cruiser drifted past, Jay stumbled breathlessly across the canalside path and up an overgrown embankment, shivering, dripping and fighting to see through stinging eyes.

He looked a sight as he straddled a low wall and looked around. Camden Lock Market was a big tourist draw that sprawled over a huge area. Most of the market opened seven days a week, but Jay found himself in one of its remotest outposts where the stalls only opened on weekends.

He was standing on cobbles and surrounded by dilapidated wooden stalls and a huge graffiti-strewn concrete slab left behind by a bankrupt property developer. It was a depressing spot, but Jay realised that he'd lucked out: it was the perfect place to remain inconspicuous while he sorted himself out.

He jogged twenty metres and shivered as he crouched

down in the gap between trailers containing Shane's Pancake Shack and Top Notch Thai. He heard voices in the distance and spotted a little gang of pre-teens using the slab for skateboard practice.

Jay pulled out his phone. If it worked he'd be able to text Len or his mum and get them to pick him up, but predictably the water had killed it.

He'd stand out a mile if he hit the street dripping water, so he slipped off his hoodie. The videotapes were still wedged in the pocket and he pulled them out before balling up the soaked garment and wringing out as much water as he could. He peeled his T-shirt and let the sun warm his bare back as he wrung that too.

After another glance to make sure nobody was around, Jay put the T-shirt back on and hurriedly squeezed water from his socks and jeans, while trying not to imagine how embarrassing it would be if someone came by and saw him sitting there in his boxers like some kind of sex fiend.

A police siren made him jolt as he dragged the wet jeans back up his legs, but it was miles away. He wondered about his mum as he stuffed his socks in his pocket and pulled his squelching Converse over bare feet. She'd bought him a good five minutes to grab the tape, but at what cost?

After fixing a lace, Jay studied himself. His clothes were still clearly wet if you looked at them, but he was no longer dripping conspicuously. He thought about asking one of the little skateboarders if he could use their phone to call Len, but he imagined the scene of a group of ten- and eleven-year-olds being approached by someone his size. There was no way they'd risk handing over a phone and it was probably better if he didn't draw attention to himself.

Home was a good forty-minute walk. He could grab a bus if he crossed the bridge over the canal and walked back to the high street, but he decided to walk part of the way and pick up the bus in a side street where there was never a crowd at the stop.

Once he got on board, he'd go upstairs and hide at the back. If he didn't have to wait too long at the stop, he'd be home in less than twenty minutes.

44. Hindustan Ambassador

After stuffing their faces and uploading a rudimentary profile on the *Rock War* website, the Pandas of Doom rehearsed for two more hours before finally getting sick of it. Dylan let his three band mates pick out guest rooms and gave them time to shower, unpack, chill out or whatever else they wanted to do.

He surfed the web and went on Facebook for a while, before heading back to see how his guests were settling in. The house had everything you could ask for, but Dylan had grown apart from all the village kids after three years boarding at Yellowcote and his remote home sometimes felt like a luxurious prison during school holidays.

Leo had become a mate over the past few weeks, and although Max and Eve were oddballs it still felt pretty good having friends to stay. Dylan hummed cheerfully as he walked along a covered glass walkway towards the guest rooms, which were all in a modern annexe fifty metres from the main house.

His dad often had parties. People helicoptered in from all over the country and the guest suites would regularly accommodate chamber orchestras, or other musicians who were there to record a film score.

One end of the annexe had a modern glass atrium, linked to the walkway. Inside this space were thousands of tropical plants, set around a steaming circular pool. Leo lay at the pool's centre, on a floating chair. The tray in the arm-rest contained a non-alcoholic cocktail and a bowl filled with fried chicken wings, most of which he'd already eaten.

'See you've settled in,' Dylan said, his voice echoing across the pool.

'Your dad came over here to use the gym,' Leo explained, as he paddled the chair towards Jay with his hands. 'He told me your kitchen makes awesome wings and he wasn't wrong. I had a good old chat with him. Seems pretty normal considering some of the stories I've heard about Terraplane.'

Dylan shifted awkwardly. 'When my dad's in the right mood he can be the nicest bloke in the world. But if he's had a few beers, or snorted too much coke, he's perfectly capable of being a complete arsehole.'

'Like how?' Leo asked.

Dylan laughed. 'Sending me to Yellowcote's a *great* example. I liked it here in the village, but my dad got it in his head that he wanted me going to some snobby school and nothing I said would change anything.'

'Yeah,' Leo said, as he stretched out into a yawn and looked around at the tropical plants. 'You've had a hard life.'

'If you're gonna get sarcastic I'll turn the wave machine on and flip your fat butt off that chair.'

Leo looked excited. 'Waves?'

Dylan pointed at a control panel on the wall by the main entrance. 'It's all up there. Anyway, I've charged up my dad's big Nikon. I was thinking the four of us could quad bike up to that spot I was telling you about and take some quality pictures to upload to our *Rock War* profile. After the weather we've had today we should get a really good sunset. I'll take a video camera as well, just in case.'

'What if we want pictures of all four of us?' Leo asked.

'I'll bring a tripod. We'll need to get moving soon though, because I'll have to make sure the quads are fuelled up and show you three how to use them.'

Leo rolled off his chair, before plunging into the waist-height water and wading towards the pool's edge.

'What about my chicken bones?' he asked.

'Leave 'em on the edge. The cleaning crew deals with them.'

'Cleaning *crew*,' Leo laughed. 'Can I move in permanently?'

Dylan nodded. 'I think there's a vacancy for a minimum-wage toilet scrubber.'

As Leo grabbed a plump towel from a rack beside the pool and started drying off, Dylan headed out into a sky-lit hallway.

'I'll go find Max and Eve.'

There were guest rooms off either side of the hallway. To make the annexe less hotel-like, Dylan's stepmum had furnished every room in a radically different style. Dylan's band mates were the only guests, so he'd let them pick rooms to suit their personality.

Max's room was called The Lair. It was done out to resemble a movie villain's den, with lots of chrome and black leather. There was a moodily lit piranha tank and a bank of six screens on which you could plot world domination, or watch Sky Sports.

After knocking and telling Max that they'd have to leave in twenty minutes to catch the sunset, Dylan moved three doors down to Eve's choice, Little India. This room was part maharajah's palace, with elaborate carvings up the walls and huge sculpted wooden elephants, and partly Indian ghetto, with Bollywood movie posters and a bed made from a battered Hindustan Ambassador car.

After knocking twice and getting no answer, Dylan opened the door and leaned in cautiously. He wasn't comfortable around girls and his pulse quickened as he saw Eve asleep on the bed.

She wore the T-shirt she'd had on earlier, but it had ridden up, so that her back was visible all the way up to her bra strap and shoulder blades. She'd also stripped her jeans and trainers, leaving one sock and striped low-rise knickers over her bottom half.

Dylan had rated Eve six out of ten when he'd discussed

the matter with Leo, but his only sexual experience was snogging a chubby Rustigan girl at an inter-school social, so any girl sleeping with most of her body on display got him pretty excited.

'Eve,' Dylan said loudly. 'You've got to wake up if we're gonna get these pictures taken.'

She didn't stir, so he moved towards the bed. The room was light and he could see the top half of her butt crack.

'Eve, I'm sorry,' he repeated nervously.

This time Eve stirred, but as her body moved there was a strange rustle of a plastic bag. Dylan had been too focused on Eve's flesh to notice the white bin-liner lying on the white bed-linen. As Eve rolled on to her side the bag came with her, glued to her belly by smears of clotted blood.

'*Please* don't tell Max,' Eve begged. 'He'll completely freak out.'

Dylan had no clue what he was looking at. 'Tell him what?'

Eve spoke with hurt in her voice, rather than the usual dull monotone. 'I'm the stereotype. The emo chick who enjoys cutting herself.'

As she peeled away the plastic – which Dylan now realised had been there to protect the bedclothes – he noticed a little clamshell sunglasses case lodged between the pillows. He felt sick when he realised that it was a complete self-harming kit, with Stanley blades, scalpel, sticking-plaster and a small bottle of liquid disinfectant.

'Please don't tell Max, OK? He'll freak out. He'll ruin this trip and I'll get all kinds of shit from my parents.'

'I . . .' Dylan began, but he was totally dumbstruck. He'd heard about people cutting themselves, but wished he could run off to the internet for a couple of minutes and come back when he had some clue how to handle the situation.

'Max is a loser, I won't tell him anything,' Dylan said, after what felt like the longest silence of his life. 'But you're covered in blood!'

Dylan sat on the corner of the bed as Eve tried to explain. 'I play hockey at Rustigan, you know that, right?'

'Sure.'

'So suppose I'm in the changing room after a match. Whether we've won, or lost, it doesn't matter which. But all the other girls are *so* into it. *The referee was against us, this girl is a bitch, oh my god it's so exciting we're third in the league.* And they're all squealing and throwing their bras up in the air.'

Dylan tried not to get distracted by the thought of a room filled with girls throwing bras around.

'I never feel like that,' Eve said. 'Sometimes I pretend, but I never really care about stuff. In fact, when I said I was an emo that's bull, because I'm the complete opposite of emotional. I'm just numb.'

'But why cut yourself?' Dylan asked.

'The pain is really intense. It's the only thing that makes me feel alive.'

'You should speak to someone about it.'

Eve sighed as she rested a slightly bloodied hand on Dylan's leg.

'I cut my belly now because everyone checks my wrists,' she explained. 'They caught me when I was twelve and it was *huge*. Parents went berserk. I had a psychiatrist and a hypnotist and a counsellor. Apparently I have a psychopathic personality disorder with some narcissistic tendencies. Which is just a fancy way of saying that I don't give a shit.'

Dylan almost laughed.

'You're quite similar to me, in a way,' Eve said.

Dylan looked surprised. 'In what way?'

'You're a loner. You've only really known Leo and Max for a few weeks, but you haven't got any other good mates. At least not that I've seen.'

'There's Ed,' Dylan said vaguely. 'But he's hardly a soul mate. There just aren't many kids like me at Yellowcote. They're either massive sports jocks, or music geeks.'

'You *like* music though.'

Dylan shrugged. 'I like music. But the kids there don't create music, or even listen to it. It's all like, *Oh Sebastian, I've got to practise for my grade seven flute exam next week. Oh Angus, you're so inferior, I'm already on level ten.* Like, how can you turn music into grades and exams? It's the most depressing idea in the world.'

'I know girls *exactly* like that at Rustigan,' Eve said, as she reached into the sunglasses case and pulled out a clean scalpel blade. 'I think you're depressed,' she said, with a mischievous raised eyebrow. 'You want a go with this?'

Eve's humour was black, but Dylan liked it. She made him feel comfortable, which he wouldn't have believed when he knocked on the door a few minutes earlier.

She'd had her hand on his leg for more than a minute and so Dylan reached across and touched her shoulder.

'Sorry,' Dylan said, as his arm retreated. 'Cheesy move.'

'I've never had a boyfriend,' Eve said, as she moved her face closer to Dylan's.

Dylan could smell Eve's breath. It was warm and smelled slightly nasty, but the intimacy of it turned him on. And maybe Eve was a crazy belly slasher. Maybe she was only a six out of ten, but she was lying next to him, on a bed, in her underwear, with a hand on his leg. And now she was up close he liked the freckles on her nose and her dark brown eyes were kind of awesome.

'You're cool,' Dylan said softly.

And then they kissed.

45. Jay the Hero

Jay went in the shower, ran the hottest water he could stand and scoured with a flannel, because the thought of the filthy canal water made him feel gross. He scrubbed inside and behind his ears, between each toe and finger, shampooed all his hairy bits and gargled and spat three shots of Listerine. Finally he spent ages running clear water down his face to wash out his eyes, but they still stung as he hopped across the hallway with a towel around his waist.

His phone and watch stood on damp newspaper, along with the soggy contents of his wallet.

'I'll sort you out,' Theo said admiringly, as he squatted on Jay's bunk. 'New phone and whatever else you need. I never knew you gave a shit about me.'

Jay always felt awkward when he was undressed around Adam or Theo. They made him feel like the puny *before* picture in an advert for body-building equipment.

'I was more worried about Mum to be honest,' Jay said. 'I

don't think she could handle it if you went back in young offenders again.'

'She's a tough old bird,' Theo said.

His dismissive tone irritated Jay. Their mum *was* tough, but Theo never seemed to grasp how badly she got hurt when one of her kids messed up. There was no point saying anything though, because Theo would just lose his temper.

'Where's the videotapes?' Theo asked, as Jay squirted himself with a can of Lynx.

'I killed them,' Jay explained. 'Broke the cases open, unspooled the tape and dumped it in used oil from the fryers downstairs. Then I took them, along with my hoodie and trainers, and dumped them in the communal bins over on the far side of the flats.'

'Perfect,' Theo nodded as he looked at the soggy newspaper and Jay's stuff. 'You must be out for two or three hundred quid's worth of gear. Take a look online. Tell me what phone and watch you like and I'll sort it for you.'

Jay shook his head, before pulling on his Ramones T-shirt. 'I don't want you nicking stuff on my behalf. There's old phones floating around the house that I can use and I'll ask Auntie Rachel to keep an eye out for anything decent that crops up in the pub.'

Theo spoke firmly. 'If the cops had got that tape, I'd have gone down for two or three years. So for the next two years, every fit bird, every boxing match, every night of drunken recklessness will all be down to you. So I'm gonna pay you back whether you like it or not.'

To emphasise his point, Theo stood and gently shoved Jay up against the wall. He was all smiles but Jay was still intimidated.

'What's it gonna be?' Theo asked. 'And if you say *nothing*, or *forget about it* I'm giving you a slap.'

'I dunno,' Jay shrugged, as he moved to his wardrobe and grabbed a clean pair of jeans. 'The band is the most important thing in my life. Keep coming to rehearsals, stay out of trouble and try not to upset Mum too much.'

Theo covered his head with his hands and groaned with frustration. 'I don't mean *promises*,' he said. 'All my life it's been *promise to behave, promise not to steal another car, sign a behaviour contract.* I've never kept any of them, so there's no point, is there?'

Jay thought as he opened the underwear drawer he shared with Kai. 'You can let me call the band Jet. I mean, we'll have to vote, but if you support me it shouldn't be hard.'

'Done,' Theo nodded. 'But that's a tiny thing.'

Jay looked into the drawer and saw that Kai had shoved his muddy school football shorts in there, instead of putting them in the laundry.

'He's totally disgusting,' Jay complained, as he dumped Kai's shorts on to the carpet. And then everything clicked into place. 'You know what would make my life easier?'

'What?' Theo asked.

'Have a word with Kai. Ask him to stop pushing me around and generally being a dickhead.'

Theo thought for about two seconds before laughing

noisily. 'Now you're talking!' Then he shouted, 'Kai!'

Jay had imagined Theo taking Kai aside for a little talk, but Theo didn't do subtle.

'Kai, you chunk of crap,' Theo shouted as he ran downstairs towards the living room. 'Answer when I talk to you or I'll crack your head open.'

It was rare for any of Jay's family to get the flat to themselves, so while everyone else had been at the Old Beaumont, or next door being looked after by Auntie Rachel, Kai had spent the morning sprawled out in the living room using the PlayStation.

'What bit you on the arse?' Kai asked, as he rolled on to his side, narrowly avoiding the plate of pizza crusts that remained from his lunch.

'You're in deep shit, Kai,' Theo shouted, pounding his fist into his palm. 'That's what's up.'

Jay stood in the doorway, looking on gleefully as Theo grabbed Kai off the sofa and slugged him in the guts.

'I never did nothing,' Kai said, covering his face with his arms and squirming as Theo menaced him with both fists.

'You see this boy?' Theo said, pointing at Jay. 'From now on, you don't diss him. You don't touch him. You don't leave your stinking clothes lying around. In fact, you'd better not even look at him funny, because I'll smash you so hard you'll be picking your teeth out of the carpet.'

Jay would have felt guilty if he'd inflicted Theo on anyone human, but Kai had been on his case for years and payback felt good.

'What's your problem?' Kai said angrily. 'We go boxing together, man. Why side with the scrawny geek over me?'

Theo's answer was a hard slap in the face. Then he wrenched Kai's arm up tight behind his back and dragged him up in front of Jay.

'Jay showed a lot of class today,' Theo said. 'That's all you need to know.'

'Please,' Kai begged, as his knees buckled and tears welled in his eyes.

Theo cranked up the pain and spoke to Jay. 'Any special requests? Feel free to take a shot, bust his nose or whatever.'

'Just make sure he leaves me alone.'

A tear streaked down Kai's face as Theo whispered in his ear. 'When I let go, you're gonna get on down your knees and say something to Jay, and I'd better like what I hear.'

Kai groaned as Theo let his arm go, then hesitated for a couple of seconds as the door at the top of the stairs opened. He'd hoped for Len or his mum, but it was only Adam, back from the police station.

'What's going on?' Adam asked, though it became obvious as Kai went down on his knees in front of Jay.

'I'll stay away from you,' Kai said sourly. 'Cross my heart and hope to die.'

'And you're sorry,' Theo said.

Kai glanced angrily back at Theo, but did what he was told when he saw Theo's fists ready to knock him into next week.

'Yeah, I'm sorry,' Kai said.

Theo gave Kai a gentle kick up the bum. 'On your feet.'

Kai was red with humiliation and holding back tears as he got up. He raced upstairs and slammed the door of his room. Jay looked up nervously, half expecting to hear Kai trashing his stuff or something, but it stayed quiet.

'Nice one, Theo,' Adam grinned. 'It's always good to see you putting your taste for psychotic violence to good use.'

Theo looked pityingly at Jay. 'You should come to boxing or something, though. I'd show you the ropes. There's some unsavoury characters at the club, but none of them would mess with you if I'm around.'

Jay shrugged, smiled and felt a little awkward. It was good seeing Kai get owned, but he hated being weedy and Theo's suggestion that he should try making a man of himself put a dent in his ego.

Theo spoke to Adam. 'So what happened at the cop shop?'

'Me and Tristan are sorted,' Adam explained. 'I might have to pay for the dent Tristan's fat arse made in the Ford and it looks like we'll both get a police caution.'

'What about Mum?' Jay asked.

'Mrs Jopling called in some big-shot lawyer, then she went completely psycho. They've had to sedate her. Len's waiting there, but he's not heard anything about Mum apart from the fact that she's down in the cells.'

Adam looked at Theo. 'So did the cops speak to you?'

'Nah,' Theo replied. 'They've got no proof. Mrs Jopling told them it was me, but she never saw anything.'

'Your Nissan was totally burned out inside,' Adam said. 'The back end is all black where the fuel tank blew up, but they might pick up something on the bonnet.'

'What does a fingerprint on the *outside* of a car prove?' Theo asked, shrugging casually. 'I'll just say I leaned on the car when I went out for a smoke. The only way they'll get me is if someone grasses me up and says that they saw me going around in the Nissan.'

'Have you got any enemies?' Jay asked.

'A few hundred,' Theo laughed.

'There's a boat and a car wrecked,' Adam noted. 'A Porsche floating in a canal is the kind of thing that might get in the news, so I'd bet the police will put more effort into the investigation than they would with some routine car theft.'

Theo flicked his worries away with his right hand. 'I'm not torturing myself over it. If I get nicked, I get nicked. Half the people in prison are caught because of some random thing they never even thought of. Young offenders is *nothing*.'

Jay suddenly sounded less confident. 'What do you mean by *random things?*'

Theo smiled. 'Getting nervous, little man?'

'I didn't leave fingerprints in the office,' Jay said. 'I dumped the shoes. So there's no evidence, is there?'

'Sometimes no evidence is enough,' Theo said cryptically.

'Eh?'

'What shoe size are you?'

'Five,' Jay answered.

'OK,' Theo nodded. 'Now suppose someone eyeballed you swimming across the canal. And they've got a description of what you're wearing.'

Jay looked alarmed. 'A boat went by just after I climbed out. They might have seen me.'

'That's not good,' Theo teased. 'Now imagine that the person who witnessed you swimming across reports it to the cops. You stood up on stage in those clothes in front of two hundred witnesses. And the police have got soggy size five Converse trainer prints all over the floor. What's the first thing the cops will ask you?'

'They'll ask to see my Converse trainers,' Jay said. 'But I threw them out, so they can't prove anything.'

'Exactly,' Theo agreed. 'And how suspicious is it that you came home and threw away all your clothes? You'll look as guilty as hell.'

'I'm screwed!' Jay gulped, clutching his head and feeling like he was about to throw up. 'I never thought of it like that.'

'Cops'll get you that way *every* time,' Theo explained. 'They're not stupid. They eat kids like you for breakfast.'

'It's my first offence though,' Jay squirmed. 'So I wouldn't be in that much trouble, would I? Probably just a caution.'

Theo sucked air noisily between his teeth. 'Stealing videotapes and breaking a window would only get you a caution. But they could claim that you were involved in the whole thing: accessory to destruction of car and boat, tampering with evidence, conspiracy, theft.'

Jay looked warily at his big brothers. 'Please tell me you're winding me up somehow?'

Adam laughed. 'On the bright side, if you and Theo go down, me and Kai will have bedrooms to ourselves.'

Jay felt pure desperation. 'I thought I'd got away with it. If I go to young offenders, man! Oh god! I'd get murdered in a place like that.'

'Yeah,' Theo laughed. 'I'd take up my offer of some boxing tips if I were you. Once the thugs sense you're weak they'll beat you every chance they get. And if you snitch they'll slash you up.'

Adam nodded. 'Tell him that story about that little skinny kid who got his arms and legs broken by his cell mate.'

'He wasn't that much of a weed,' Theo said. 'Not compared to Jay, anyway.'

'Shut up,' Jay said, completely freaking out, hands shaking. 'I can't handle this.'

Adam snickered as Theo hummed the funeral march.

'Dun, dun, dun-nuh.'

Jay scowled at Adam. 'How can you laugh? I thought we were mates.'

As Jay imagined himself locked up in a cell with some crazy psycho, Theo put his hands on Jay's shoulders.

'Just messing with your head,' Theo confessed. 'If the worst happens, I'll cover your back.'

Jay wiped his eye and gasped. 'Seriously?'

'If they get enough evidence to nail me for the cars and the boat, I'll just tell the cops that I took the surveillance tapes as well,' Theo explained. 'They won't fuss over some shoe prints if I make a confession.'

Adam pointed at Jay and howled with laughter. 'That was cool though, you were bricking yourself.'

'I *hate* you guys,' Jay said, as he broke into a relieved smile.

Adam gave Jay a friendly shove. 'What's the point having a little brother if you can't put the shits up him once in a while?'

'Quarter past three,' Theo noted, as he looked at his watch. 'We'd better get moving if we want to get back to the Old Beaumont in time for the results.'

46. And the Winner

Summer, Lucy, Coco and Michelle bought lunch from a Mexican food stall and ate by the canal, a few hundred metres from the Old Beaumont. They were wiped out after their crazy morning and spent a full hour sitting in the sun with their legs dangling over the water.

Even Michelle managed to sit still, though she spent a lot of time with her iPhone. She managed to find out that cheaper but slower trains ran to Birmingham from Marylebone station. As well as saving money, the alternate route meant they wouldn't risk bumping into someone they'd whacked with a guitar earlier in the day.

She also visited the Rage Cola website and set up a profile for Industrial Scale Slaughter. But it was slow typing without a keyboard, so they agreed to add more details and upload pictures and music clips over the following days.

Before returning to the Old Beaumont, the girls took a quick tour of Camden Market. Lucy bought a fat leather belt and Coco got some handmade soaps for her mum. Summer needed all of her charm to persuade a stall holder to sell a £6 floppy black hat for the £2.33 that she had left in her purse.

Back at the venue they found that most of the car park had been emptied. The burned-out Nissan was on the back of a police tow truck and a yellow crane had been driven in to pull Mrs Jopling's Porsche out of the drink.

It was way after three p.m., but there were still six bands to play, because there had been delays in pumping out the bathrooms, plus with the car park blocked off parents were having to play chicken with traffic wardens, or carry equipment from vehicles parked in side streets anywhere up to a mile away.

The girls had been slightly perturbed playing after Jet's cracking performance, but the standard of the afternoon groups gave them more confidence. Some were good, some OK and at least one group sounded like it had been formed the night before.

By four the hall was fuller than it had been all day, as groups from the morning came back to hear the results. Jay, Adam and Theo came in together, though there was a bit of a row with the doorman because Jay's re-entry ticket had turned to soggy pulp in the canal.

The brothers steered clear of Erin, Alfie and Tristan, who were hanging out with Salman and his grown-up brother, Nabhan. They found Babatunde sitting on the stairs, deep in conversation with Mr Currie.

'You boys did great,' Mr Currie told them. 'Based on what I've heard so far, you're well in with a chance of some prize money.'

Jay spotted Summer a few metres away and headed her way.

'Nice hat,' he told her. 'Sorry about the drama during your act.'

'Thanks,' she said. 'Polo?'

Jay smiled and popped the circular mint into his mouth as Babatunde, Adam and Theo joined the fray.

'It's the Birmingham beauties,' Theo said.

It sounded creepy to Jay, but the girls all laughed. Jay was jealous of how comfortable Theo seemed to be around girls. He tried to think of something to say, but before long Summer got talking to Adam, while Babatunde and Theo spoke with Lucy and Coco. This left Michelle, who'd stuffed a whole pack of orange Bubblicious in her mouth, but still couldn't blow anything bigger than a ping-pong ball.

'Hey, son,' Chris said.

Jay smiled at his dad, who'd changed into a vaguely embarrassing get-up of trainers and navy Puma tracksuit. He also held a kit bag with the handle of a badminton racket poking out the end.

'Met Police league round robin match tonight,' Chris explained, as Theo eyed him suspiciously. 'Looks like they're running a bit behind here, but I'm free until seven.'

Michelle interrupted rudely. 'Weren't you dressed as a pig earlier?' she said, before making an *oink-oink* noise.

Theo and Adam laughed, but Jay had seen enough rows for one day, so he just tutted and led his dad a couple of metres back towards the stairs. 'Ignore that one, she's nuts,' he whispered. 'Do you know when Mum'll get out?'

'Shouldn't be long. I spoke to a couple of the guys. Even if it comes to court she'll get a fine at worst. Theo's the one who should be worried. He's put a few noses out of joint at the station. If they don't get him on today's caper, it's only a matter of time before something else catches up with him.'

'I hope not,' Jay said, as the spotlights swung across the stage and the last band got ready to play. 'Theo's not a great singer, but he makes a bloody awesome front man for Jet.'

*

It was quarter past five when the house lights went up. As the last band packed up their equipment, Steve Carr conferred with the three judges and spent a couple of minutes adding scores on a calculator, before handing the final results to Terror FM DJ, Trent Trondheim.

The crowd grew tense as the goateed DJ tried climbing up the front of the stage, only to make a tit of himself and take a longer route through the side door and up the steps.

'It's been a weird day,' Trent began in a gravelly voice, as members of eighteen bands, plus parents, mates, siblings and a photographer from the local paper, looked on. 'Strange things have happened. Cars have ended up in places they shouldn't have. Fortunately not mine.'

A laugh ripped across the room. As Jay looked around he saw the *Rock War* producer Zig Allen filming proceedings with a little Panasonic camcorder. He made a mental note to start working on a profile for Jet when he got home.

'We actually have a tie for third place,' Trent said. 'The prize will be shared between two bands, who each scored forty-five out of a possible sixty points. Now put your hands together for Frosty Vader and the Scabies Squad.'

As the crowd clapped, two bands approached the judges' table where Steve Carr handed out envelopes of vouchers and silver trophies shaped like electric guitars.

'In second place with forty-eight points, a great little rock band that kept playing under very difficult circumstances. The only thing is, we might have to knock the cost of a new water jug off their prize money . . .'

Michelle, Coco, Summer and Lucy started jumping about and screaming as soon as they heard the word *jug*.

'Well done,' Jay said, but he felt gutted because the rest of his band was in there with the girls, jumping around and getting hugged, while he was a few metres back with his dad.

'The spilled water meant I spent my lunch break wandering around Camden Lock looking like I'd pissed my pants,' Trent continued. 'But I've just about forgiven our runners-up: Industrial Scaaaaaaaale Slaughterrrrrrrrrrr!'

As the girls rushed forward to collect the trophies and vouchers, Jay looked over at Salman, Alfie and Tristan. With one prize left it was win or bust for both bands, but he was convinced that Brontobyte hadn't outscored Industrial Scale Slaughter and Frosty Vader. If Brontobyte had won it would be a travesty.

Trent gave a dramatic pause and lowered his voice even further. 'This is the big moment,' he said.

Tense laughter rippled across the audience.

'Terror FM run these competitions all across the country,' Trent announced, clearly getting a kick out of keeping his audience on tenterhooks. 'It's been my privilege to judge more than a dozen of them. Our winners today recorded the highest score I've ever seen. With a *whopping* fifty-eight points out of sixty, our top cash prize, a live interview and air play on my Terror FM show goes to . . .'

Jay's heart thudded as Trent made another dramatic pause. Jet had been good. But were they fifty-eight points good? Jay hadn't seen all the afternoon bands and for all he knew there was one that had blown everyone else off the stage.

'. . . a band who I'm told didn't even have a name when they arrived here this morning . . .'

Jay's mouth dropped open. Now it had to be. *Had* to be.

'. . . but it might just be a name you'll hear an awful lot more in the future . . .'

Jay looked around and saw Len, Hank and his slightly battered mum running into the hall behind him.

'The winner of Rock the Lock 2014 is Jet!'

In the next exciting episode . . .

Jet are red-hot favourites to be selected for *Rock War*. But will their lead singer be spending summer at rock school, or behind bars?

Are Brontobyte good enough to be picked by Zig Allen? Will Alfie get pubes? And what the hell does Erin see in Tristan?

Will Dylan and Eve find true love, or is it just a fling? If the Pandas get picked for *Rock War*, will the press discover his true identity? And will Max get the smack in the chops he so richly deserves?

Plus, could a shocking CCTV recording tear Industrial Scale Slaughter apart? And how many times will Summer throw up when she has to sing live in front of five million television viewers?

Read on for an exclusive first chapter of the next Rock War book, *Boot Camp!*

1. FORBIDDEN FAT

July 2014
Camden, North London

The chip shop closed at one-thirty on Saturday mornings. By daybreak, the oil in the deep-fat fryers had a solid white crust, but still retained enough heat to gently warm Jay Thomas's outstretched palm.

In younger days, Jay had been fascinated by the way bubbling oil cooled to solid white fat, delving into the warm crust with a finger before making a half-baked attempt to smooth out the evidence. The oil beneath the white crust stayed hot and he'd have been yelled at for going near it.

Jay got yanked out of Memory Lane by a thump on the floor above. He shared the flat over the chip shop with his mum, stepdad and six siblings. The place was rarely quiet, but he'd learned to tune out noise, like his little siblings chasing around, or brother Kai cursing at FIFA 2014.

But the floor-shaking crash of a case packed with studio

lamps wasn't familiar, and nor was the shouting that followed it.

'Get the leads first, Damien!' a cameraman yelled. 'Then I can start wiring up while you're carrying all this gear in.'

Jay heard Damien grunt, then the twenty-something runner bolted downstairs and out the rear door to one of three vans the TV crew had parked in the courtyard out the back. Jay caught a glance, as Damien and a pretty runner called Lorrie exchanged words.

I already told you there's no leads in this van . . .

Well if they're not here we must have left them when we picked up the gear at ProMedia . . .

John's gonna blow his stack if . . .

As Damien headed up to break the bad news to his boss, Jay felt a nervous ache in his belly. His heart was thumping, he'd barely slept and his mum had given him a couple of Imodium to settle a rebellious stomach.

Getting picked for *Rock War* was the most exciting thing that had ever happened to Jay, but right now a chunk of him craved simpler days, driving his Lego trucks between chip-shop tables and standing up with salt stuck to his knees.

'Are you Jay?' a woman shouted.

Jay spotted her squinting through the letterbox opening, halfway up the shop's metal grille.

Someone else yelled from a top-floor window, 'Can we have some quiet on set, *pleeeease*? We're trying to shoot an interview.'

Rather than shout back at the woman, Jay made a 'go around' gesture and headed out the rear door into warm air and breaking sun. It was Friday rush hour on the main road out front and a truckload of rubble rumbled by as the woman offered a slender hand attached to a wrist festooned with fluorescent wristbands.

'I'm Angie, director camera-unit B. Can you spare us ten for an interview?'

Jay ran a hand through his scruffy hair and shrugged. 'I kinda look like shit, and I'm still in my night shorts.'

'No worries,' Angie said, as Jay picked up an Aussie accent. 'The just-out-of-bed vibe is exactly what we're going for in this segment. It's the first day of summer holidays. You're heading off to *Rock War* boot camp. You're excited and a bit overawed, which is exactly what we want to capture on camera.'

Jay liked hearing that he was *supposed* to be excited and overawed. He didn't exactly agree to be interviewed, but Angie's arm guided him towards the pub next door anyway.

The White Horse pub and the adjoining chip shop had been owned by Jay's family for more than fifty years. The pub was run by Jay's auntie, Rachel. She lived over the pub, with her four daughters, a granddaughter and a few hangers-on. As Jay followed Angie through the White Horse's swinging saloon doors, he was surprised to see black sheeting taped over all the windows. Lights and cameras were set up to film interviews, with the pub's dartboard as a backdrop.

'I've captured one from next door,' Angie said, smiling triumphantly at her crew as she led Jay inside.

The crew comprised a camerawoman, a sound man and a runner, plus Angie the director. Jay's cousin Erin stood at the bar, looking fit in tight denim shorts and a lime vest. She was tanned and athletic, and Jay felt really awkward. He usually only wore shorts in bed and was self-conscious about being skinny, hating the idea of his bare legs getting on TV.

'Do you think I could nip back and get some jeans?' Jay asked, as the runner swooped with a make-up kit and started dabbing foundation on his forehead.

'It's just so you don't look greasy under the lights,' the guy explained.

Nobody answered Jay's question about the jeans and he was too intimidated by all the fussing to ask again.

Two minutes later, he was on a bar stool in front of the dartboard, with a wireless microphone taped under his shirt, two cameras aimed his way and his cousin Erin on another stool next to him.

'All set?' Angie asked, as the cameraman let her take a look at his framing. Then she turned towards the two teenagers and tried to sound soothing. 'Try and relax, I'm going to ask a few questions about your bands. If you fluff your answer or say something you don't like, just start the answer again and we'll patch things up in the edit suite . . . Camera? Sound? OK, Bob . . . ? Action!'

Angie put on the glasses around her neck, grabbed a

question sheet from a tabletop and stepped close to Jay and Erin.

'I'll start you off gently,' she began. 'I want you both to say your name, your age, the name of your band and what your role in the band is. OK?'

The two teenagers both nodded as Angie pointed at Jay.

Jay froze. It felt like he was seeing a hundred things at once: heat from the lights, sandbags holding the equipment stands down, two dozen cables sprawling over cigarette-burned carpet. Millions of people would see him this way for the first time – with slim white legs and hand-me-down Superdry shorts.

'Loosen up around your shoulders,' Angie said soothingly. 'Imagine it's just you and me, over a nice cup of coffee.'

'Err . . .' Jay began, feeling like all the moisture had been sucked from his mouth. 'My name is Jay Thomas. I'm thirteen years old and I'm the lead guitarist with Jet . . . Was that OK?'

Angie gave Jay a double thumbs-up. 'You're a natural,' she lied, before pointing at Erin.

'I'm Erin,' she said, looking coy as she flicked hair off her face. 'I'm thirteen years old and I sing vocals and play guitar for Brontobyte.'

'And how do you two know each other?'

'We're cousins,' Erin said, smiling again. 'We're only two months apart in age and we live next door to each other. So when we were little, we were like that.'

Erin held up her hands and placed one on top of the

other, before continuing. 'In all my earliest memories, Jay is with me. Just rolling around the floor, playing tag. Wrestling and stuff.'

'Cute,' Angie said. 'But if you're so close, how did you end up playing in different bands?'

Erin shrugged and smiled. 'We're still mates, but I don't think we've been like, *mega* close, since . . .'

Jay spoke. 'Probably year four or five at school. We started getting more into our own mates. And boys and girls are into different stuff.'

'Sounds about right,' Erin agreed.

Jay drew some relief from the fact that his cousin sounded as nervous as he felt.

'As I understand, Jay, you used to be a member of Brontobyte,' Angie said. 'Can you tell me a little bit about that?'

'I guess,' Jay said warily, as he turned slightly on the bar stool. The camera operator silently gestured for him to move back to face the lens. 'I started Brontobyte with two of my mates, Tristan and Salman, plus Tristan's little brother Alfie. We played together for a couple of years, but there were a lot of musical differences and in the end I walked away.'

Erin scoffed. 'That's not *exactly* how I heard it!'

Jay turned towards her accusingly. 'Well, I left, didn't I?'

Erin seized the opportunity. 'Jay gave his bandmates an ultimatum,' she explained. 'Either they replace Tristan as drummer, or he walks. Jay lost the vote.'

Jay scowled at Erin, angry that she'd chosen to dig up his humiliation. On the other hand, Angie looked pleased. She'd clearly been going for this angle all along.

'It was hardly a fair vote,' Jay explained. 'Tristan voted for himself, and Alfie knew he'd get his arse kicked if he voted against his big brother.'

Erin smirked. 'If you say so, cuz.'

'You weren't there,' Jay spat. 'And you would take Tristan's side now because the idiot's your boyfriend.'

There was a lull. Jay *was* angry, but he didn't want to fall out with Erin, or look petty in front of the camera. He shrugged and gave Erin a smile to indicate that he wasn't taking this too seriously.

Erin understood Jay's gesture, raising her hands and giving a false laugh. 'You say Tristan's an idiot, but wasn't he was your best friend for like, seven years, or something?'

Erin's question stumped Jay, so he changed tack. 'I happen to take my music seriously. Whatever you think of Tristan as a person, he can't play drums to save his life.'

Jay realised that *I happen to take my music seriously* sounded pompous, and cringed.

'In case you haven't noticed, Jay*den*, your lead singer ain't exactly about to sell out the Sydney Opera House. And Tristan's drumming wasn't so bad that it stopped the judges from picking us for *Rock War*.'

'Who needs a great singer?' Jay said, needled but keeping up the smile for the cameras. 'Were Kurt Cobain or Elvis great singers? Is Bob Dylan a great singer? It's stage presence that counts. And as for the real reason Brontobyte got into *Rock War* . . .'

Now Erin's face flashed with proper anger. 'What?'

Jay shrugged, and put a hand over his face, as if to indicate that he didn't want to say it on air.

'No,' Erin said, leaning forwards and placing one hand on a hip. 'Brontobyte got into *Rock War* because what?'

'Fine, let's air *all* our dirty linen in public,' Jay spat. 'Jet got into *Rock War* because we won Rock the Lock and put a great three-track demo online. Brontobyte only got in because of your rivalry with us. Having two bands that hate each other makes for good TV.'

'Listen to yourself,' Erin sneered. 'You're just jealous because your band kicked you out and me and Trissie got together.'

Jay ignored his cousin and kept going. 'You're a novelty act. Brontobyte is like the old granny contestant. The one who keeps falling on her arse on that ballroom dancing show, or the four-eyed kid who can't juggle on *Starmaker*.'

Erin didn't reply straight away, and Jay felt anxious as her eyes drilled him.

'You're so full of it!' Erin snapped, as she aimed a slap at his cheek.

Jay ducked the slap, but there was no avoiding a powerful two-handed shove that sent him sprawling sideways off his stool.

'Chicken-necked geek!' Erin shouted, knocking a studio light flying as she stormed out of shot.

Jay spent a couple of seconds reeling on grungy pub carpet, before using the stool as a prop to get up. Once he was vertical and had straightened out his T-shirt, he realised that the camera was still running.

Angie lunged with an off-the-cuff question.

'Jay, Brontobyte and Jet are going to be spending the next six weeks in close proximity at the *Rock War* boot camp. With all this tension between the two groups, how do you think that's going to pan out?'

Jay realised he'd been manipulated by Angie's questions and decided not to give her anything more to fuel the fire.

'It'll be peachy,' he growled. 'Fine and bloody dandy.'

JAY, SUMMER, DYLAN and their bands are headed for boot camp at Rock War manor. It's going to be six weeks of mates, music and non-stop partying as they prepare for stardom.

But the rock-star life of music festivals and glitzy premieres isn't all it's cracked up to be. Can the bands hold it together long enough to make it through the last stage of the competition, or will there be meltdown?

THEY'VE GOT EVERYTHING TO PLAY FOR.

Hodder
Children's
Books

ROCKWAR.COM

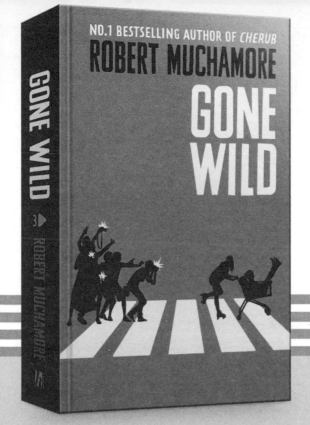

Rock War is the most-watched reality show on British telly, and it's only halfway through. JAY, SUMMER, DYLAN and their bands have all made it past the tough boot camp stage, and now the last six will fight it out until the season's finale, live on Christmas Eve.

But it's not all about the music. Summer was hit by a motorbike at the end of boot camp. Jay's brother Theo can't keep out of trouble – or out of handcuffs. And Dylan, the outsider, is investigating corruption within the workings of the competition itself.

THEY'VE GOT EVERYTHING TO PLAY FOR ...

Hodder
Children's
Books

Also available
as an ebook

ROCKWAR.COM

THE RECRUIT
Robert Muchamore

A terrorist doesn't let strangers in her flat because they might be undercover police or intelligence agents, but her children bring their mates home and they run all over the place. The terrorist doesn't know that one of these kids has bugged every room in her house, made copies of all her computer files and stolen her address book. The kid works for CHERUB.

CHERUB agents are aged between ten and seventeen. They live in the real world, slipping under adult radar and getting information that sends criminals and terrorists to jail.

THE ESCAPE

Robert Muchamore

Hitler's army is advancing towards Paris, and amidst the chaos, two British children are being hunted by German agents. British spy Charles Henderson tries to reach them first, but he can only do it with the help of a twelve-year-old French orphan.

The British secret service is about to discover that kids working undercover will help to win the war.

Book 1 – OUT NOW

www.hendersonsboys.com

Hodder Children's Books